ALSO BY SAM LEE JACKSON

<u>The Jackson Blackhawk Series</u>
The Girl at the Deep End of the Lake
The Librarian, Her Daughter and the Man Who Lost His Head.
The Bag Lady, the Boat Bum and the West Side King
They Called Her Indigo
The Darker Hours – A Detective Boyce Mystery

And

Shonto's Kid

The Girl at the Deep End of the Lake

The Girl At the Deep End of the Lake

SAM LEE JACKSON

PIPING ROCK PUBLICATIONS

Copyright © 2016 SAM LEE JACKSON.
All rights reserved. No part of this book may be reproduced, stored, or transmitted by any means—whether auditory, graphic, mechanical, or electronic—without written permission of both publisher and author, except in the case of brief excerpts used in critical articles and reviews. Unauthorized reproduction of any part of this work is illegal and is punishable by law. For permission requests, write to the publisher, addressed "Attention: Permissions Coordinator," at the address below.

Piping Rock Publications
3608 E Taro Lane. Phoenix AZ 85050
www.samleejackson.com

ISBN: (sc) 978-0-9998526-2-0
ISBN: (e) 978-0-9998526-3-7
Library of Congress Control Number: 2019909753

Because of the dynamic nature of the Internet, any web addresses or links contained in this book may have changed since publication and may no longer be valid. The views expressed in this work are solely those of the author and do not necessarily reflect the views of the publisher, and the publisher hereby disclaims any responsibility for them.

To Carol, my better angel and the brightest light in my sky, who knows why, or should.

Chapter One

"Should I shoot her in the head?"

"Hell, no," the other voice said. "Somebody will hear it."

It was the middle of the night and the voices were coming from below me on the end of the pier. I was trying to sleep on top of the old houseboat I was living on, Pier C, Slip 32 at Pleasant Harbor Marina on Lake Pleasant, north of Phoenix. It was warm inside and I didn't want to spend the money on the gasoline it would take to run the air. I had slept in a lot worse places. Uncomfortable, sandy, dirty, buggy places in faraway lands while waiting for the target to show.

Instinctively I reached for my prosthetic foot when the second voice said, "Just throw the bitch in, she'll sink like a rock."

I could hear the rustle of plastic sheeting as I rolled over. I had my foot in my hand when I looked over the edge. The end of the pier was dimly lit, but I could make out the two of them. One was a big Mexican looking guy, the other was smaller with a wife-beater tee shirt and tats all up and down his arms and across his neck. They had hoisted what looked like a long wrapped package to their shoulders, then slid it silently off the end. For a second it floated and they watched until it began to sink, then they turned and trotted back down the pier. The package was just under the surface when I saw it move and I went over the side.

The Lowrance HDS-5 depth finder mounted in the cockpit had told me that the water was eighty feet deep at my mooring, so I kicked hard when I hit the water, knowing that if the package was weighted it could get away from me. My fingertips brushed it, but now it was straight up and down and sinking fast. I felt the panic of failure rising in my throat and I kicked with all I had, stretching my hands out into the darkness and there it was and I touched it, then it was gone. Then there it was again, and I got a finger hooked into a fold of plastic, and this gave me a handhold, and I brought it to my chest. It was definitely a someone, but they weren't moving now. I kicked for the surface. It seemed to take a year.

We finally broke the surface and I struggled to hold the head end of the package up out of the water as I kicked for the end of the pier. I grabbed a slimy algae-covered support rod and pulled us up against the flotation barrels. Now what? There were no ladders and the water-heavy package was hard enough to keep up out of the water, let alone lift it up on the deck. While I considered this, a backlit head drifted over the edge and looked down on me. With a start I thought it was one of the two guys. I was gathering myself to pull the package under the pier when a woman's voice floated down.

"Are you all right, Mr. Jackson?"

"Can you get a hold, and hold on till I can get up?"

An arm came down and the woman grabbed a handful of plastic.

"Got it?"

"It's heavy," she said.

"Hold on," I said and released the package. I grasped the top of the deck and pulled myself up, pushing with my good foot. I scrabbled up on the deck and the woman said, "Hurry, I can't hold it much longer."

I knelt down beside her on my knees and grabbed the package with both hands. With a shoulder- popping effort, I pulled it up out of the water. The water poured out of it, and with each gallon it got lighter. I laid the body out on the deck and began ripping the plastic away from the face. As I pulled the plastic away, the woman gasped. "My God, she's just a child."

I stripped the plastic off and pushed it aside. It was indeed a girl child. She looked to be about twelve years old and she wasn't breathing. She wore the tiniest of cutoff jean shorts and a halter top. She had red high-heeled shoes. I rolled her onto her stomach, then lifted her so she bent in the middle. I tried to jostle the water from her lungs. Now she was light as a feather compared with the waterlogged package in the lake. I felt for a pulse and didn't find one. I placed her onto her back and began chest compressions. My old training kicked in. The same rhythm as the Bee Gee's *Staying Alive*. Compress, compress, compress, compress, stayin' alive, stayin' alive, stayin' alive, stayin' alive. Careful not to crack the sternum. If necessary then maybe, but try not to.

A gallon of lake water erupted from the depths of her stomach and lungs and she began to cough so hard she couldn't catch her breath. The woman reached across and wiped the wet hair from her face. I lifted her arm and jerked on her, and she took a long gurgling breath. She began to pant and groan and her eyes were half closed and unfocused. I looked at her arm and saw fresh needle tracks.

"She's stoned," I said.

The woman said, "Bring her down to my place," and I looked at her for the first time. Nice looking woman.

"You know my name," I said.

"The marina people told me who you were."

"Where's your place?"

"I'm on the Moneypenny, the 80-foot Stardust just down there," she said pointing.

I stood up. "Hold on while I go up and get my foot."

She looked at my stump and said, "I'm sorry. I didn't even notice."

"The marina people didn't tell you?"

"You weren't the only full-time resident they named for me and I'm really not that nosy."

"Be right back," I said.

I monkeyed up the aft ladder and found my foot and put it on. Back on the deck, the girl was still unconscious but breathing with a ragged regularity. I scooped her up and followed the woman back down the pier. Her houseboat was about ten down and a serious upgrade from mine. She stepped on board ahead of me and opened the sliding glass door. The lights were on, but subdued in the lounge.

"Bring her back," she said, leading me past the galley and down a narrowed hallway. She opened the door to the first stateroom and said, "We can put her in here."

The stateroom was small, just large enough to hold a queen sized bed and a small dresser. I gently laid the girl on the bed. "She's going to soil your bedspread."

"It will wash."

I started to loosen the girl's shoes when the woman laid her hand on my forearm. "I can take it from here. There are towels in the bath under the sink."

I found the towels and brought two back after using one on myself. She took them without looking at me and began rubbing the girl down. "There's a bar beside the couch. Fix yourself a drink."

The bar was beside a long leather couch that faced a large screen television. The TV was on, the sound on mute. Images of an old black and white movie danced across the screen. There was an empty cocktail glass on the coffee table. A maroon afghan was puddled on the floor as if it had been hastily discarded. Also on the coffee table were some magazines, all addressed to Mrs. Romy Bavaro or Mr. and Mrs. Frank Bavaro.

The bar held several decanters. I lifted the top of one and sniffed it. Smelled like scotch. I poured some in a glass. The ice bucket was empty. I took a small sip and smiled. It was a good scotch. I knew a girl in Rangoon that kept all her booze in decanters so she could buy the cheap stuff and no one knew what brand it was. Swirling the liquid in the glass, I stepped out on the bow and looked down the pier toward the light over the supposedly secure gate that was hanging open. No one in sight, no one out of their boats wondering what the commotion was about. No two bad guys. Nothing but the gentle creak of a boat pulling at its mooring, the soothing lap of small waves and a kiss of a breeze. Not a bad night for dying, I thought. Not for old empty, tired men or even some burned-out younger men with little to live for. Young men with insomnia, night sweats and demons. But not for the girl. Just too young. Druggy or no, she didn't deserve to be somebody's throwaway. I wanted a cigarette. I hadn't smoked in years.

When I stepped back in, the woman was backing out of the stateroom and taking great care to quietly shut the door. I moved to one of the swivel chairs that bracketed the television. I draped the towel on it to keep it dry. She picked up the used glass from the coffee table and moved into the galley. She put the glass in the sink. She got a new glass and came back in. She moved to the bar and took the lid from the ice bucket.

"I'm sorry," she said. "I can get you some ice." She started to move to the galley.

"Don't bother," I said. "Neat's fine."

"I'm going to get me some," she said.

"I'm okay."

She rattled around in the top of her oversized refrigerator, then came back to the bar and poured what looked like vodka over the ice. She took a seat on the couch, setting the glass down without taking a drink. She smoothed her hair back and leaned back with a sigh. She crossed her legs and I enjoyed that. I took another drink and watched her. Slim and fit looking, her hair done professionally. Early thirties, no rings. Her eyes moved around the room, then finally lit on me.

"Why would those men do that?"

I shrugged, "There are a thousand reasons why one human will kill another."

She picked up her drink and looked at it, but still didn't drink. "You sound very jaded."

I shrugged again, the king of articulation.

Again, she looked everywhere but at me. She finally took the tiniest of sips from her glass. I waited.

"The poor little thing. She seems to be sleeping okay." She set her drink down again. "I think she should stay here tonight. Let her sleep." She nodded to herself, "Better off here than putting her through a trip to the emergency room where they'll just want her to sleep."

Finally, after the silence had gone a while, I asked, "Do you know the girl?"

She stared at me, "God, no. Why would you say something like that?"

"What haven't you done?"

"What haven't I done? What do you mean, what haven't I done?"

"You haven't called the police, Mrs. Bavaro," I said, draining my glass.

Chapter Two

"Romy Grandberry," she said, draining her drink. "Mr. Bavaro and I are no longer together."

"Of the New England Grandberrys," I said.

Her eyes were surprised. "How did you know that?"

I laughed. "I didn't. I was joking. Just sounds like a name in an old Katherine Hepburn movie about old money."

"My father was Angus Grandberry," she said.

"The industrialist?"

"And when I was very small he was the son of one of the largest bootleggers on the east coast and when Daddy was older he became the ambassador to France." Her smile was wan. I couldn't tell if it was poor little rich girl or the fact it was three in the morning.

"My father was a car mechanic," I said.

I watched her struggle with what she would have to tell me. "But he was a very good car mechanic," I continued.

"I'm sure he was." Finally she looked directly at me. "You don't know who Frank Bavaro is?"

"I don't get out much."

"You don't watch the news?"

"The news makes me tired. I like music and I read a lot. I also slay the top water bass and grill a mean steak. Oh, and I can shake a near perfect martini, do a one handed pushup and hold my breath for almost four minutes."

She smiled and finished her drink. "That sounds very impressive. Frank is a very successful man. An attorney, with very powerful clients, two of whom are brothers. Pedro and Luis Flores, they head the largest cartel in the Americas. Of course that can't be traced to him, but every FBI agent in the U.S. knows who Frank Bavaro is. I guess I was his socialite trophy wife. Arm candy to impress all of those he called snobs but wanted very much to be like. If I did call the police and they found out who owned this boat, that little girl in there would stand no chance of coming out of this. Not without her picture being smashed all over the newspapers."

"Why did you get involved?"

"I couldn't sleep and I was standing on the bow getting the night air when the two men ran by. I was in the shadows so they didn't see me. Then I heard you go into the water and I just felt something was wrong."

"I'm glad you did."

"Well, now I'm not so sure."

"I can move her to my place."

She shook her head, "No, let her sleep." We sat in silence a long moment. Then we looked at each other. I had lots of questions, but they were for the girl.

"Okay," I said, standing. "We'll look at it in the morning

and see where we are. She okay now? Breathing okay?"

"She's fine now."

"Thanks for the drink. And thanks for the help. I would have had to drag her to the back of my boat and get her up the ladder. I don't know that she would have survived."

She stood. "My Dad always said that we were put here for a purpose," she said, placing her glass on the coffee table. "It's just that we may not know what that purpose will be. Maybe this was mine. Goodnight…"

"Just Jackson."

"Jackson."

I walked back down the pier to my boat knowing she was watching. I worked hard at a natural gait. No limp.

Chapter Three

For the previous ten years my body had been taught to exist on minimal sleep, so when the sunrise crept around the blackout curtains in the master stateroom I came awake. I was getting older. There was a time that as soon as my eyes opened I could leap into action. Now I had to clear the fuzz out.

By the time I had come back aboard and stripped out of my wet shorts and tee shirt, the temperature had dropped enough so that I just unfastened my utility foot, placed it beside the bed and stretched out. I had pushed everything from my mind and had fallen asleep immediately.

I ate a bowl of Greek yogurt and granola and drank a large glass of orange juice. By then, the coffee had percolated and I poured some in my big mug. I added Sweet and Low and Half n' Half and stirred it with the same spoon I had rinsed off and laid aside yesterday morning. I took the mug out onto the stern and sat in one of the webbed chairs and looked at the morning. It was late October and the weather was just becoming why someone would choose to live in

Phoenix. Between June and October the weather forecaster here had the easiest of jobs. Show up in front of the camera, still with sleep hair and in pajamas, proclaim the day would be hot and sunny, then go back to bed.

The water was still and glassy. If I were a water skier this is when I would be out. Occasionally a small ring would appear on the surface as a fish came and kissed the top. A hundred yards out a big one ripped up out of the water, turned and made a huge splash. The underbelly flashed yellow and I knew it for one of the large carp that camped near the marina. I thought of the little girl, wrapped in plastic, slowly gliding toward the bottom. There to rest until the bluegill and turtles worked their way through the plastic wrapping to feast on the rotting flesh inside. And finally the body would be free of the weights that held it and the gasses would slowly float whatever was left to be washed up on the shore months later as food for the crawfish.

An early morning fisherman went ripping by in the distance, and once again I marveled at the fact that fishermen with their slim sparkly boats and huge motors always felt the fish were somewhere down the lake instead of where they put the boat in. I took the cup back in and rinsed it out and padded down the hallway to the master stateroom. I put on a pair of swimming trunks and a swimming foot and slowly lowered myself down the aft ladder. The water felt cold against my skin, but I knew that in a few minutes the water would feel warmer than the air. I struck out with long even strokes toward the buoy marker that was a hundred and fifty yards away. I had a small twinge in my shoulder from lifting the dead weight of girl up out of the water. After my first lap it was loose and barely noticeable. I usually swam three laps at dawn before the traffic in the marina would make it impossible. At the end of the third lap, I was hanging onto the aft ladder waiting for my heart to normalize. The gold leaf lettering was fading and peeling. It announced to any passing craft that this old tired scow was called the *Tiger Lily*. A realtor had suggested I purchase it after she had suppressed a smile when I told her how much I had to spend on a permanent place. It was forty years old and fifty-two feet with a fourteen foot beam. The master stateroom was roomy enough for a king-sized bed and a closet. It had an oversized shower in the head, a small guest stateroom, a galley and enough room in the lounge to be decorated in rummage sale chic. I could hook into the electric on the pier and paid a small rental for the mooring. Once a month, or whenever I took her out, I would visit the bilge pumping station known as the honey pot and empty her out. I had been here for a while now and she was all I needed.

By seven-thirty I had taken a long, time-killing shower and was tired of waiting. I pulled on a black tee shirt and a pair of jeans and started down the pier to the Moneypenny. The marina was coming to life and a line of boats was at the ramp waiting for their turn. I reached the Moneypenney just as Romy was pulling the curtains aside. She unlocked the sliding door and opened it.

"Good morning," I said. "I thought I'd check on your guest."

Romy smiled, "Come on in. I just checked her, she's still sleeping." I followed her inside. She was wearing one of those beige chic blouses that has a half collar that rose halfway up her neck. She had on faded pink shorts and I admired her slim rear and long tan legs as she led me to the galley.

"I have coffee on," she said over her shoulder.

"Thanks," I said, climbing up on one of the four stools that sat along the teakwood counter that separated the galley area from the lounge.

"Cream and sugar?"

"Sure, thanks."

I watched her fix the coffees with a minimum of effort and movement. She placed mine in front of me and moved around the counter and took the stool one removed from mine. She suppressed a yawn, covering it with the back of her hand.

"Short night," I said.

She nodded, taking a small sip of the coffee, then blowing across the top to cool it. Holding her cup, she looked across at me. "What about you?"

"What about me?"

"Last night you asked me why I didn't call the police and I was so busy explaining why I didn't that it wasn't until after you left that I thought *what about you*. Why didn't *you* call the police?"

"Fair enough," I said, sipping the coffee. I shrugged. "I guess I'm not much of a police guy. I try to handle my own problems."

"That's not much of an explanation."

"Well, how about this. When I was a kid I read every book I could on King Arthur and his knights. I want to be a Lancelot, or a Gawain, riding around saving damsels and righting wrongs. Chasing windmills with a swayback horse and tarnished armor."

She was smiling at me, "Still not much of an explanation."

"There's an old Chinese saying that if you save someone's life, you owe him yours for the rest of your life. I didn't want to turn her over to strangers."

She laughed, "We are strangers."

"No I'm the rusty knight that pulled her out of the water, and you are the queen of sanctuary. That makes us family."

"Sir Jackson, saver of damsels."

"Has a nice ring, don't you think."

She laughed again and I liked the sound of it. She finished her coffee.

"Besides, Miss Romy, you gave me enough of a reason not to call the police."

"Would you like a refill?" she said, sliding off her stool.

I stood up. "No, I've had some earlier. I'm coffee'd up. I thought I'd run into town and pick her up some clothes. What size do you think she wears?"

She set her refilled cup on the counter and coolly studied me, "Why would you do that?"

My turn to study her. I could sense a small cool flavor of suspicion. "Well to be honest, I'm reading you as the kind of person that is going to be willing to help her out, which means she may be here until she figures out what she's going to do. Maybe she's the one that will call the police. At any rate, she's going to need some clothes other than what she had on last night."

"I would say a size zero in women's or a large in a child's."

"I'm just thinking a pair of jeans and shorts and some tees and underwear and flip-flops. Basics."

"Get some small Tampax. She's on her period. That won't embarrass you will it?"

"When I was a boy I used to spray paint them red and pretend they were sticks of dynamite."

She guffawed. "Oh my God, boys!"

"At any rate I think I can handle it." She followed me out to the bow, still chuckling.

I stepped onto the pier, "I'll be back in a while, if it's okay."

"That's fine," she said cocking her head, studying me again.

When I reached the end of the pier and opened the gate, I looked back and she was still there watching me. I gave her a small wave and she waved back, then turned and went back inside.

Chapter Four

I think I'd rather be at the dentist than go shopping. Wearing my articulated foot, I pulled the dust cover from my '06 Mustang GT, wadded it up and stuck it in the trunk, then drove out to the highway across east to I-17 and took it south to Happy Valley Road. I knew of a huge shopping complex there. Another glass and concrete monstrosity in the middle of waterless desert lands. The droppings of a giant dragon of commerce and corporate profits and greed, with enough taxes and lobby to cause usually honest council members to look the other way. I pulled into the vast and filled parking lot and parked farther away than I needed to. I locked the car out of habit and walked across the expanse of asphalt. It was already hot and a million acres of city created an inversion that kept the city from ever cooling. I went into one of the huge superstores past the octogenarian greeter and walked around until I found a clerk about the same size as the girl. From then on it was easy. I was back at the marina before noon.

When I stepped onto the bow of the Moneypenny, the

curtains were closed. I had two full bags of stuff and I set one down and was about to rap on the glass when Romy peered out at me. A moment later, the curtains pulled back and she unlocked and opened the door. As I stepped inside, I caught a movement down the hallway.

"She's up," Romy said. "Let me get her. She's a little skittish."

I set the bags by the couch, then sat down trying to look as non- threatening as possible.

I could hear Romy's voice. Speaking softly to the girl then, she came out of the guest stateroom with the girl behind. Romy came into the living room, but the girl stopped by the galley counter, her large brown eyes darting from me to the outside and back again. Her hair was long and stringy, still damp from a shower. Her skin was pale, almost translucent. There were dark smudges under her eyes. She was trembling. She reminded me of a dog I had once that would quiver at the sound of thunder.

Romy looked at the girl. "This is Jackson. He is the one that pulled you out of the water."

The solemn eyes took me in.

"What is your name?" I asked.

"This is Lucinda," Romy said.

"Pleased to meet you, Lucinda," I said.

"I don't remember any of that," she said. "You got a cigarette?" Her voice was soft and young with a slight accent I couldn't identify.

"No, I'm sorry I don't." I looked at Romy and she shook her head. "What do you remember?"

"You with the cops?"

I shook my head.

"Why should I tell you anything?"

"Maybe I can help."

"What the fuck are you, a social worker?"

"That's some mouth for a little girl."

"I ain't a little girl. I can take care of myself."

"Like last night," I said. "Why don't you tell us what happened. I think you can tell we are just trying to help."

She shrugged, "It don't matter, does it?"

"I don't know. Until I know who did this and why they did it. Then maybe it will matter." I watched her. "Tell you what, tell us why a fourteen or fifteen year old girl was stoned on whatever you stuck in your arm and was wrapped up in plastic and dumped in the lake by two gangbangers and I'll get you some cigarettes."

"I'm sixteen," she said.

"You look twelve," Romy said.

"Roland likes me to look young. Did you see them? The ones you say threw me in the water. What did they look like? I don't think I believe you."

"Roland your pimp?"

"He's not a pimp. He takes care of me."

"Like last night?"

"I don't remember last night. Can you get me the cigarettes?" then she leaned over and threw up on the floor. Romy jumped up and hustled her into the bathroom. I found some dishtowels in a drawer in the galley and started cleaning up the mess. Not much to clean up. Nothing in her stomach but lakewater.

Romy came back out into the lounge. "She's lying down again. God, I feel like I'm the one that needs a cigarette."

"You smoke?"

"Not for years."

"Still time to call someone."

She moved to the couch and sat on the edge, elbows on knees and hands clasped together. "No, I told you about that."

"Maybe we could get her in a shelter?"

She shook her head, "No, she's fine here. I was getting bored sitting around this big old boat anyway."

I stood there watching her. She looked up and I could see the resolve in her eyes. I picked up the sacks I had brought in and moved to the galley counter. I emptied the contents on the countertop and she came over to stand beside me. She sorted through the clothes and held each one up as only a woman can do. She made little noises of approval. She looked at me with a smile.

"How in the world would a man your age know what to pick for a teenager?"

I laughed, "Simple really. I found a clerk that was a teenage girl the same size and had her pick it out."

She opened a drawer and pulled out a pair of scissors and started snipping the tags off. She stopped at a pair of blue jean cutoffs. "Yes," she said. "I can see a teenage girl picking these, but there is just not enough material here. Way too much skin showing."

"Do you have children, teenagers?"

Her turn to laugh. "No, we don't have kids. I don't think

either one of us are real kid kind of people."

"You seem to be a nurturer."

She looked at me and I noticed the gold flecks in her brown eyes. "I told you, I'm just a little bored." She bundled up the clothes in her arms, "Let me take these to the back. There's nothing us girls like better than trying on new clothes. Why don't you come back for dinner tonight? I'll let you fix that marvelous martini you were bragging about."

"Sounds good. I'll bring cigarettes to bribe her with."

She chuckled, "I don't know why but that sounds awful. Around six okay?"

"Sure."

Chapter Five

I made my way back to the Tiger Lily, my articulated foot working perfectly. I hadn't had this one for long, and marveled at how the technology had improved over the last few years. I changed into a worn, soft, old tee shirt and a pair of worn swimming trunks. I turned on the Sony receiver, found the streaming Sinatra channel on the radio, and moved the dials until it was pushing through the Bose speakers. I had grown up listening to my father's music and still liked it. I pulled the Shakespeare rod out of the locker and rigged it with a piece of shad I had in the freezer, hooked a dropshot ten feet above the hook and dropped the weight and bait over the stern. I placed that handle in the holder I had mounted beside the ladder. It would hold any fish up to fifty pounds without coming out. I clipped a bell on the rod, went in, drank a glass of tomato juice and unstrapped my foot. I stretched out on the oversized yellow couch.

It seemed like I had just blinked when I awoke to the bell tinkling. I swung my legs over and hopped to the stern. The tip of the rod was bouncing, and I pulled the rod clear and unclipped the bell, at the same time setting the hook. I could feel the weight and the movement on the line and felt the same rush I always felt. I leaned back against the rail so I wouldn't have to put my stub down and I reeled carefully, holding the tip as far from the side as I could. I didn't want the fish to go under the boat and snap the line. After a moment I could feel the movement of the fish to be slow and sluggish and I knew I didn't have a bass or even a channel cat. Sure enough it finally rolled to the surface to reveal the ugly mud-sucking snout of a carp. I grabbed the world's largest dip net. I leaned against the corner and finally got the creature in. He had to go eight to ten pounds. I know some people consider these a delicacy, but I don't. I got him untangled, unhooked and let him back over the side. Have a good life down there, sucking up whatever you suck up. One fish's mud is another fish's candy.

 I put the rod back in the locker and made my way back to my foot and looked at it, then decided to shower before my dinner engagement. Forty minutes later, foot in place, I was at the marina store paying the young teenaged clerk for a pack of cigarettes. He gave me my change, the pack and a book of matches with the Paradise Harbor logo on it. Again, I marveled at the cost of these damned things. I had smoked enough of them in my youth and my first two tours but had finally decided that watching my uncle die, shrunk down to under a hundred pounds and coughing his life out should be enough warning and I quit cold turkey. It wasn't that hard. Not as hard as the training I had gone through. You just say" done" then you do it.

I didn't know what brand the girl would like, so I picked the girly looking ones. Turned out to be a mistake.

The drapes to the lounge on the Moneypenny were open, but I didn't see anyone inside when a voice came from above.

"We're up here."

I looked up and Romy was peering down at me.

"You can take the stairs on the port side."

I lifted the bottle of wine I had brought and the pack of cigarettes, "Geeks bearing gifts," I said.

"Geeks?"

"A joke," I said. "Helen of Troy. Greeks."

She looked at me seriously, then said, "You might leave the little package down there for right now."

I waved the cigarettes and she nodded. I set them on the small round table that was on the bow and found my way to the spiral, wrought iron staircase that was halfway down the outside walkway. It wound its way to the top. Fancy, fancy.

The top of the boat was set up like a lounge deck outfitted with round tables and cushioned chairs and loungers. At the bow there was an above-deck cockpit with two captain's chairs. There was a portable bar on wheels to the side.

Romy was seated at a table, a drink with a lime in it in front of her. The girl was on a lounge chair wearing one of her new pairs of shorts and a shirt she had pulled up and knotted above her navel. She wore a floppy maroon hat and an oversized pair of sunglasses that had to be Romy's. She was reading a fashion magazine.

"Fix yourself a drink," Romy said. "Maybe one of those

fabulous martinis you were bragging about."

"No brag, just fact, ma'am," I said moving to the bar. "How about you?"

"Sure."

"I want one," the girl said.

"Not on my watch," Romy said.

The girl looked at her over the top of the sunglasses. "I'm a lot older than you think I am."

"You said you were sixteen," I said pouring the Gray Goose into the shaker.

"That's just a number."

"That's what we are working with," I said. I looked into the cooler attached to the bar. Romy lived well. "How about a Coke or an Orange?"

"You got Dr. Pepper?"

"There should be some," Romy said. I dug around in the ice and fished one out. I popped the top on the opener that was attached to the side and handed it to the girl. She took it without a word.

"You're welcome," I said.

"I ain't Martha Stewart," she said her accent softly slurring the S.

"Your momma taught you better."

"My mother taught me shit."

I looked at Romy and she imperceptibly shrugged her shoulders. I finished the martinis and carried them over to Romy. I placed hers in front of her and took the seat where I could face them both. She sipped her drink.

"Very good."

"Thank you," I said. I sipped mine and damn she was right. It was good. Probably the quality of the vodka but I'm going to take the credit.

I had a very small and slim little camera that I have used from time to time and I pulled it from my pocket. I took a picture of Lucinda and her head snapped around.

"What are you doing?" she glowered.

"Please take your hat and glasses off."

"Why should I?"

"He just wants your picture, dear," Romy said.

"Why," she said again.

"I need something to hang on my wall so I can have wonderful dreams at night."

"Screw you."

I looked at her for a moment. Defiant and sullen and probably scared to death.

"How about because I jumped in the lake in the middle of the night and saved your ungrateful ass."

Chapter Six

The girl stared at me a moment, then took the hat and glasses off. I took several pictures, getting up and moving around to get different angles. I sat again and took a sip and said, "Thanks."

We sat in silence for a while, then I said, "You ready to tell us what this is all about?"

She was taking small sips of the Dr. Pepper and staring out over the lake. I glanced at Romy.

"We are just trying to help you," Romy said.

Tears sprang to the girl's eyes. We sat in silence for a while longer. Sometimes it's not what you say, it's what you don't say. She took the silence for much longer than I would have thought, then she said, "I ran away from home," wiping her eyes. "Well, I didn't really run away, I walked away. Nobody noticed anyway."

"Where did you run to?"

"I went to the mall. I met Roland on Facebook and we met at the mall and I didn't have to go back."

"You met just Roland?"

"No, he has a lot of friends."

"What are their names?"

She looked at me and the suspicion was back, "Why?"

"If we are to help you, we need information. We don't know what's important or not. We'll just ask questions and maybe something will come together that will help us help you."

She was quiet a moment. "There was Emily, she's nice, and Juanita and Roberto, who was a complete jerk, and the one they called Dog and there was Petey and I don't know, there were a bunch."

"But Roland was in charge?"

She nodded.

"What does Roland look like?"

"He's good looking. Got a lot of tats."

"What kind?"

She shrugged, "I don't know. All kinds. Got a cool looking eagle."

"A lot of other girls there?"

"Yeah, I guess so."

"How did Roland get on your Facebook?"

"I don't know. He was just there one day."

"How old is Roland?"

"I don't know, older but really cool, you know."

"Does he have a last name?"

She thought a minute. "I guess so, but I don't think I ever heard it."

"Why would someone want to dump you in the lake?" Romy asked.

She lowered her head and rubbed a forearm across her eyes. "I don't know. I did everything they asked."

I finished my martini and looked at the empty glass. One martini is never enough. I fished out the olives and popped them into my mouth, then stood to fix another. I looked at Romy but she shook her head, holding up the glass, showing it only half empty. Or half full. As I fixed mine, I asked, "Just what was it they asked you to do?"

Lucinda brought her knees up and hunched forward, hugging them. Her shoulders were boney and thin. She shrugged.

"Whatever," she said.

"What did you eat dear, where did you sleep?" Romy asked.

She looked up, almost proud now. "They have a whole warehouse. We all just stayed there."

"How many people?" I asked.

She shrugged, "I don't know, maybe twenty or thirty."

"What's the name of the gang?"

She looked at me, defiant again, "Who said it was a gang?"

"Was Roland the leader of the gang?"

"Everyone did what he said."

"And he protected you?"

"He said I was his favorite. He said I was his good luck charm."

"Are they MS13?"

She seemed surprised. "How do you know about MS13?"

"Were they MS13?"

She shook her head. "They called themselves the Seventh Avenue Playboy Diablos, but some had MS13 tats."

"Roland have MS13 tats?"

"Nah."

"So why would the Seventh Avenue Playboy Diablos dump you in the lake?"

She shook her head violently.

"They didn't do it?" Romy asked.

She shook her head again.

"Then who did?"

I could sense she was withdrawing.

"Why don't you tell us what you remember?"

She was silent for a long moment. I didn't think she would reply when she said, "We just spent the day hanging out, doing a little blow, playing the new Locust Invaders game someone had brought. Suddenly Petey came and got me and said Roland wanted me to go with him." She shrugged, "I just thought it was for another date."

"Date?" Romy asked.

"Nobody gets a free ride," she said defiantly. "Sometimes I'd go on dates Roland set up. Sometimes I'd get a hundred, two hundred bucks."

"Did you go on a date, last night?"

"No. It was kinda weird, Roland had Petey and Dog take me uptown, down by where the Diamondbacks play. They had me stand out on the corner. It was getting dark so I was supposed stand under a street light. I thought it was so the John could see me but nobody ever came and finally Petey and Dog took me back."

"What happened then?"

"Nothing. Roland was really pissed about something so I just stayed out of his way. Then later he came and made me shoot up. Said he wanted to party."

"Shoot up with what?"

She shrugged again. She seemed to do a lot of that. "I don't know. I don't like it. I don't like needles."

"But Roland wanted you too?"

She nodded.

"What happened then?"

"I don't remember. I guess I got really fucked up. Next thing I remember is waking up here on this boat."

"Who are your parents?" Romy asked.

She shook her head violently, "No. No parents."

"They must be worried sick," Romy said.

"I'm not going back," she snarled.

Romy looked at me and I shrugged. "What is your last name?" I asked.

She shook her head.

I held up the camera. "You've been going on dates then you might have a rap sheet. I can take your picture downtown and show it to the police and maybe they can tell me who you are."

She shook her head again. "I have never been arrested."

"How long have you been with the Diablos?"

She was looking away, across the water.

"A year? Two years?"

"I don't know. Since early summer I guess." She turned and looked at me accusingly, "You said you would get me cigarettes."

I looked at Romy and she was looking back, nothing showing on her face. I nodded.

"Yes, I did. They are on the bow, on the round glass table. I didn't know what kind you liked."

Lucinda bolted from her chair and went down the spiral staircase, two steps at a time.

Romy was watching me. I shrugged, "I made a promise."

"And you always keep your promises?"

"Better if you do than not."

"Lot of people don't care."

"Yeah, I know."

"So what makes you different?"

Chapter Seven

I got up and walked over to the bow and looked down. Lucinda was on a chaise lounge holding the open pack, a cigarette in her lips.

"These don't light themselves," she said looking up at me.

I reached into my pocket and found the book of matches I had picked up at the marina store. I tossed them down and she deftly caught them and lit the cigarette. "Don't take that inside," I said.

"These suck," she said, holding up the cigarette package.

"Don't smoke them," I said.

She gave me the finger.

"Articulate," I said and went back to Romy. She was watching me. I sat down and took a sip of my drink.

"What makes you different?" Romy repeated.

I could smell the cigarette smoke. I took a drink. "My parents split when I was seven. I learned that I could count on me, but not necessarily on other people."

"Sorry to hear that," she said.

"Nothing for you to be sorry about. It's just that I found if I did what I said I was going to do, it was easier for me to count on me." I looked out across the lake, "It's going to be a beautiful sunset. Would you like to take a sunset cruise?"

She laughed, "The Moneypenny is way too big to take out on a short cruise. Two or three days maybe."

I smiled and nodded. "No, I wasn't thinking that. I've got a 20 foot Grumman sport deck runabout, wet docked over on the small boat pier. I keep it gassed up and ready. I could walk over and be back here in twenty minutes."

"That sounds lovely," she beamed. She stood up, smoothing out the back of her shorts. "I had steaks laid out, but why don't I make some sandwiches instead? We could have a picnic on your boat. Are sandwiches okay with you?"

"Better than what I'd be making."

I followed her down the staircase. I had to go to the Tiger Lily to get the keys. "How about a sunset boat ride?" I asked Lucinda as I stepped off the Moneypenny.

She just looked at me as she lit a new cigarette off the last one. I sure know how to charm them.

It was a little longer than twenty minutes. When I pulled the green canvas cover off the boat I called *Swoop*, I found the Arizona dust had still worked its way onto the bench seats. I wet a towel I kept on board and wiped everything down. Ladies like things clean.

I had named the boat Swoop in honor of my high school buddy, Rich. We were minority kids in a mostly black school and we both had our share of trouble at home. He had said one day that sometimes he just wanted to get up and swoop out of that place. Just "cut and run" as he put it. Rich died in Iraq. Same kind of thing that got him got my foot. When I bought the boat off the lot I knew her name.

The girls were waiting on the bow when I rumbled up. I had rigged a six-foot aluminum pole with a line attached to the end and also attached to the starboard side of the boat so that I could reach out and snag an anchor cleat on another boat or the dock if I was by myself. I put the 120 horse Johnson outboard on idle and pulled up next to the Moneypenny. I flipped a mooring fender over to absorb the bumping of the two boats. Romy helped Lucinda into the boat, then handed down a wicker basket and a small Coleman cooler and two jackets. Then she stepped in herself. Lucinda was sporting that teenaged bored look that they master around age fourteen.

Romy pushed off and I put her in gear. We chugged along in the no-wake zone until we reached the no-wake buoys, then I gently brought her up to speed. I'm of the opinion that it's not good to jump an engine into high gear when it's been sitting for a length of time. Let her warm up. I put her nose directly at the setting sun and soon we were cruising along at a respectable forty miles per hour. Forty on the water feels fast, especially if your boat only draws a foot of water. On plane, half of it was out of the water. Swoop was made of aluminum so the weight of the motor was the only thing keeping her from flying.

Lucinda had moved to the bow and had her face into the wind, her hair trailing behind. I couldn't see her face but I sensed she was enjoying it. I found a cove on the western side and swung about. I flicked on the depth finder and saw we were in twenty feet of water. I swung the anchor over the water and hit the release. When it hit bottom, I released a couple feet of slack so a breeze wouldn't lift it up. The sun was hovering above the crest of the mountain, so both girls put on their jackets. Romy opened the cooler and offered me a Stella Artois. She offered the girl a Dr. Pepper but the girl shook her head. Romy unwrapped sandwiches and passed them around. The girl ate the center out of hers and threw the rest in the water. Romy tore off small pieces of hers and ate each piece with great care. I devoured mine. It was delicious.

We all sat quietly, two of us concentrating on the food, the girl staring across the water at the distant marina. She shook out a cigarette.

"Wait till we're moving before you light that," I said.

"Why?"

"Because I don't want to smell it."

She sullenly stuck the cigarette in her lips but didn't light it. It was quiet on the lake with the only moving boats off in the distance where we couldn't hear them. The sun was setting behind the mountains that rose up on the western shore of the lake and the sky was turning saffron and magenta. Phoenix is famous for its Arizona sunsets but something tells me it is as much the dust and pollution as being the old west. After a while the shadow of the mountain reached us and I pulled the anchor, started the motor and slowly pulled us back into the sunshine. I cut the motor. Lucinda had her hand trailing in the water.

"The water's cold. Do you swim in this every morning?"

"Every morning I can."

"You're tougher than me," Romy said.

"I think you're nuts," the girl said. I sat in the gently rocking boat and watched the girl and waited for it. I wasn't disappointed.

"I'm cold, I want to go back."

I looked at Romy and again she gave her imperceptible shrug. I finished the beer and put the empty back in the cooler.

"It was still a good idea," Romy said.

"I'm glad you thought so," I said, starting the motor.

It was dusk by the time I had dropped the girls off and returned Swoop to her slip. I covered her with the fitted canvas cover and walked back around to the Tiger Lily. Once aboard, I didn't turn any lights on. I pulled out my old comfortable pea jacket and fixed a rock glass of scotch. I went out on the stern and sat and sipped the scotch and watched the last of the light leave the lake.

The next morning the girl was gone.

Chapter Eight

I had finished my swim, fixed a small breakfast and was working up a sweat in the topside cockpit. I was replacing a moldy piece of teakwood with another piece I had shaped and sanded. A movement down the pier caught my eye and I turned to watch Romy coming toward me. She was wearing a sleeveless red blouse and a pair of faded blue shorts. She wore a scarf on her head and sported an oversized pair of sunglasses. Anyone else would have been incognito but it was unmistakably Romy.

I moved to the front where she could see me.

"The girl's gone," she said, peering up at me. Even with the sunglasses she shielded her eyes from the sun with her hand.

"Gone gone, or just taking a walk?"

"One of the kids at the store saw her on the payphone in the bar. Next time she looked, she was gone. I walked up to the parking lot but I couldn't find her anywhere."

The store was a small general store where I had bought the cigarettes. It was attached to the restaurant and bar that accompanied the gas pumps and ski-doo rentals and all the other commercial endeavors that took advantage of the lake. On weekends it was packed and I'd enjoyed it more than once myself. The store was usually manned by high school kids. There was a frequent turnover.

"Maybe she called her parents?" she added.

I turned and wiped my face and hands with a shop towel then went down the aft ladder way. I stepped off onto the dock. "Not likely," I said. "Not the way she was acting toward them yesterday. No, she probably called that Roland guy."

"After what he did?"

"She doesn't believe it. He's cool. She's his favorite."

"Favorite whore, maybe. He's just using her. If she did call him, what's to stop him from finishing the job this time?"

"The question is, why did he dump her in the lake in the first place? The way she was talking she seemed pretty docile. Hang out, do some blow, turn a trick. Sounded like a money maker." I shook my head, "No, I don't get it."

She seemed close to tears, "So what do we do. Just forget about her?"

"What do you want to do?"

"Find her. Get her back to her parents." She took off the glasses and looked at me, her eyes large and deep. "We have to find her."

I looked off over the lake a moment. "How about your husband. You said he's connected. You think he could get a line on this Roland?"

She made a sound that could have been a laugh. "You don't know what you are saying. Frank is the hookup for multi-billion dollar drug dealers. Not street thugs. His clientele carry rolls of thousand dollar bills in their pants pocket. They don't cook bath salts and stick needles in their toes. And I told you, he's my husband in name only. Frank is a Catholic and the Pope won't let him consider a divorce."

The breeze was coming up and the Tiger Lily was gently nudging the dock. I looked out across the lake. There was an armada of sailboats, the sails looking like giant white wings. The breeze blew her hair across her face and she brushed it back.

"What makes you think I can do something?"

"I don't know," she said. "Maybe it's because you went into the lake in the middle of the night without hesitation. Maybe it's because you are the only one here. Maybe it's because I've been the helpless little rich woman my whole life and I don't have a clue as to what to do."

I looked at her looking at me, a twinge of anger in her eyes, then I turned and looked across the lake. It seemed like a long shot. Even if I managed to find the girl, what then? Maybe she didn't want to be found. In fact, I'd bet on it. Since I had moved onto the boat, the lake was the only thing I knew. Or wanted to know. I had been determined to drop out of the world. The moment I lost the foot I was out and alone. All the skills I had honed in the previous years were worthless in the world. Find the girl? I wasn't sure where to even start.

But I had to admit I had been getting a little bored lately.

"The two foes of human happiness are pain and boredom," I said finally.

"What?"

"Schopenhauer."

"What?"

I shook my head, "Okay, let me see what I can do," I said. "I can go downtown and check to see if she was lying about never having been arrested and I can check missing persons. Maybe her parents are more concerned than she thinks."

She handed me a slip of paper. "This is my phone number." She had her cell phone in her hand. "Give me yours so we can stay in touch."

"I don't have one."

"You don't have a phone number?"

"I don't have a phone, but I'll stop and get one. I'll call you with the number once it's connected."

"You actually don't have a phone? Everyone has a phone."

"I don't usually have anyone to call. Besides, Lucinda didn't have a phone."

"You bet your ass she did," Romy laughed. "Every teenager has a phone. She just didn't have it on her when you pulled her out. It's probably at the bottom of the lake."

"Okay, I'll do what I can, but you know it's a long shot."

"I know."

An hour later I was back at the Walmart where I had bought the girl's clothes. A young man who looked to be about twelve finally realized that I didn't want the latest super phone and the two year unlimited calling and texting plan. After the kid showed me that even the simple ones could be used like a camera, I walked out with a simple phone and a phone card with five hundred minutes on it. I drove to the far end of the parking lot and parked the GT in some shade. I rolled the windows down. There was enough breeze for it to be pleasant. I called Romy and got her voicemail. One of those generic voicemails that just repeats the number back to you. I read my new number off the card the kid had given me and at the same time memorized it. I sat for a few minutes thinking, then I dialed another memorized number that I hadn't called for over a year. After a long pause and some clicking noises I could finally hear it ringing. It was picked up on the third ring.

"Hello," said the soft grandmotherly voice.

"Hello, Martha," I said. "It's Jackson."

"Oh my, oh my," she exclaimed. "Jackson. I'm so glad you called. It has been a long time. Are you alright?"

"Right as rain," I said. "How are you and the family?"

"Everyone is real good. The grandkids are in high school and everyone is just fine. The boys are on the football team and Jennifer is the treasurer of her class."

"Sophomore, right?"

"Oh heavens, she's a junior now."

"Time gets by doesn't it?"

"It sure does. Now I know you didn't call to chit chat, let me get him for you."

"It was nice talking with you, Martha."

"Wonderful to hear from you. He'll be excited." I could

hear her set the phone down and heard faint voices in the background. Finally I could hear the phone being picked up.

"Well, young man, it's been a while," said that familiar gruff baritone.

"Yes sir, almost a year." I could feel myself almost coming to attention. "How are you, Colonel?"

"Retired and pissed off about it. Forty-five years and they replace me with some snotnose out of West Point."

I laughed. "You and I both know it took more than that to replace you,"

"How are you and your foot getting along?"

"Me and my lack of foot are just fine. They are doing amazing things with prosthetics now days."

"Yes, I see that when I visit the hospital. Are you still living on that boat?"

"Yes sir, still the boat bum."

"What can I help you with?" he said, always to the point.

"Sir, I'm working on something and I was hoping I could enlist your help."

"What can I do for you number ten? I hope it's something dark and juicy."

I laughed, "Juicy enough, sir."

I recounted the events of the past two days, keeping it simple and factual just like the reports I had given him when we were both active.

"So no idea why the girl was dumped?"

"No sir."

"And no idea where she went off to?"

"My gut says back to the gang where she is comfortable."

"Yes, me too. Well, it seems we need to get a lead on this fella Roland. Hold on a moment."

"Sir, one more thing."

"Yes?"

"Can you see what you can find on a Frank Bavaro. He's an attorney that fronts the Hermanos cartel."

"Frank Bavaro? Don't know him but the Hermanos are bad, bad people. Okay, hold on."

He set the phone down and was gone for several minutes, to the point where I started counting the minutes and subtracting them from my five hundred. At six he came back on the line.

"Still with me?"

"Yes, sir."

"Here's a place to start. There's a fella that works in the violent gangs section Phoenix PD, name of Sergeant Mike Mendoza. Ex-Marine. Records show he served under Jerry Anderson, you remember Jerry? One star in Intel Com group."

"No sir, I don't think I worked with him."

"Well, doesn't matter. Mendoza probably knows your Roland or how to find him. Also, there's a halfway house on Fillmore called Safehouse that is ran by Father Jorge Correa. The good Father has the pulse of the south end."

I had fumbled a pen out of the glove box and was writing these names on the box the phone had come in.

"As for Frank Bavaro, I'm going to need more time. I find he is a partner in a law firm, Phelps, Gutierrez and Tamoso, but other than that he's a blank slate. At least on the surface. I'll call you back on that, and, by the way, you know number two is in Phoenix."

I stopped writing. "Blackhawk, here?"

"Yes, he owns a club on Durango Street close to 19th Avenue."

"How long has he been in Phoenix?"

"You had been sent stateside when the unit was disbanded. About a year ago."

"Why didn't you let me know?"

He laughed, "Hell son, you are both professionals. If you wanted to find each other, you would've."

"I had to call you to get a line on a gangbanger."

I could feel him smiling through the phone. "That's because it was easy. If I wasn't here you would have still got there."

"What's the name of Blackhawk's club?"

"El Patron. They do all that Spanish dancing there."

"Blackhawk's not Hispanic, I don't even think he was Indian till he got the code name."

"Probably not, but small stuff like that never stopped him before."

"Thanks for your help, Colonel."

"Anytime, and if you are in Missouri, Martha would be disappointed if you didn't stay with us. So number ten...."

"Yes, sir."

"When you see number two, give him my best." Then in typical Colonel fashion, the conversation was finished and the phone disconnected.

"Yes, sir," I said to the dead phone. Blackhawk in

Phoenix. I sat and thought about that for a few moments. "Damn," I said. I started the Mustang and jockeyed my way out of the shopping center, went through a maddening round-a-bout, merged into southbound I-17, and pointed its nose toward 19th Avenue and Durango.

Chapter Nine

Interstate 17 runs south from Flagstaff to what is known as the Durango curve, just on the north end of the south belly of Phoenix. The oldest freeway in Phoenix is known as the Black Canyon Highway, and as you travel south the city gets older in front of your eyes. Bracketed by old strip centers and older buildings, the tired asphalt is traveled by enough old vintage vehicles and rusty beaters to remind you that you aren't around the Mercedes set in Scottsdale. Traveling the Black Canyon you pretty much feel you are taking your life in your hands. The speed limit was a suggestion not followed by most.

After a couple of false starts, I found the El Patron on a corner north of the Salt River. It was identified by a sign located on a tall steel pole that touted live entertainment. It was a large two-story rectangular building surrounded on three sides by a vast parking lot. If Blackhawk filled this lot he had a very popular place indeed.

There were a half dozen cars parked close to the front, including a very sleek, black Jaguar that had to be

Blackhawk's. I parked the Mustang on the end and walked to the entrance. The door opened easily. It revealed a large foyer with a greeter's podium and bench seats on the wall. The room was empty. I stepped in and let the door shut behind me. It was very dark and I waited for my eyes to adjust. Once my eyes were good, I could see a hallway leading away to my left. I followed it. It was an extra-wide hallway and halfway down there was an open double door to my left. I peered in and saw what appeared to be a small cocktail lounge with tables surrounding a small round dance floor. There was a small bandstand in the corner and about fifteen feet of mahogany bar along the side: a bar in a bar. A few steps further was a similar door on the right. Here was a mirror image of the first room: a bar within a bar beside a bar. Another twenty feet down was another set of large double doors. The place smelled of stale beer and humanity but there was no cigarette odor. Except for the cigarette thing it smelled like every bar I had ever been in, no matter what part of the world.

I pushed on one of the big double doors and it slid open easily. Beyond it was a huge room. The room had a large square bar in the middle. Each side of the square held at least fifteen stools. Against the walls were tables and chairs, leaving the space between them and the bar as a dance floor. The floor gleamed with polish. The ceiling was very high. At the second story level there was a balcony around three sides. A flight of stairs led to the fourth side where there was a door at the top. A much larger bandstand covered one corner of the room. It was filled with sound equipment, mic stands, drums and monitors and such.

Behind the bar a man was washing glasses. A bigger man sat at the bar with what appeared to be a cup of coffee. He was reading a newspaper. He had little reading glasses perched on his nose. His hair was long, past his shoulders, and dark and sleek. He had what was almost a Fu Manchu mustache. He wore jeans, boots and a black tee shirt. His arms were muscled and covered with tattoos.

He turned and looked at me. I walked toward him.

"We're closed. Happy hour starts at five."

I reached the bar and slid up on a stool.

"You hard of hearing?"

"Is the owner here?"

"If you had looked you would've seen a no soliciting sign out front."

I smiled my best smile, which usually makes girls faint but didn't seem to affect this guy. "Would you please tell your boss that an old friend of his is here?"

"Why should I do that?"

"Because if you don't he will be pissed, and if you do he will be happy. How about we make him happy."

The guy looked at me for a long moment. It wasn't one of those hard-ass tough guy looks that macho men try to scare people with. It was just appraisal. The guy exuded confidence and my guess was he could handle himself pretty well.

I held his eye and tried not to quiver. Finally, he set the paper down, laying his glasses on top.

"Name?"

"Jackson."

With that he looked at me another long minute before he slid off the stool. He went around the bar and up the stairs. He disappeared behind the door at the top.

The guy washing the glasses didn't even look up. Dedication.

A minute later the door opened and the guy stepped out. "Come on up," he said, his voice reverberating.

I went up the stairs and he held the door for me. I stepped into a hallway with another door in front of me. The big guy opened this door and I stepped into what appeared to be a waiting room. Two chairs and a couch with end tables with fake plants and magazines. There was yet another door across and the guy opened it and waved me through.

This room was much larger. Blackhawk was sitting behind a massive desk, one elbow on the desk and his right hand resting on an open drawer. He shut the drawer.

"Sig Sauer?" I said.

He nodded, smiling, "Always. Good enough for the Secret Service, good enough for me."

The big guy had followed me into the room and stood to the side of the door with his back to the wall.

Blackhawk nodded toward him, "This is Nacho, my segundo."

"Nacho, like with chilies and cheese?" I said, smiling.

"Nacho, like, if you aren't nice, Nacho will break your legs," Nacho said without expression.

Blackhawk stood and walked around the desk. We looked at each other for a long moment, then we hugged each other. You are not to ever get emotional but I almost was.

"This is my friend, Jackson." Blackhawk said to Nacho. "Anything he wants."

Nacho nodded, "So you are Jackson. Where's your fucking cape?"

"Only on formal occasions."

"I'll be downstairs," he said to Blackhawk. He turned and went back out the door, shutting it behind him.

I looked at Blackhawk. His hair was long, as long as Nacho's. Last time I saw him it was a crew cut. Butch Marine. Other than that he looked the same. About an inch taller than me, about the same weight. He never was a big weightlifter looking guy but he was inordinately strong and he was very quick. He was the most dangerous man I had ever known. Back in the day, two hundred yards away, too far to help, I had glassed him taking out four guys hand to hand, thinking they had him cold.

He looked fit. He gestured to one of the two high backed chairs that bracketed the front of his desk.

"Can I get you a drink?"

I sat down, "Too early for me."

"Good for you," he said. "Lot of us that are out either live in the bottle or eat their gun. How did you find me?"

"The colonel."

"Really? How is he?"

"Don't you know?"

Blackhawk laughed, "Martha talks to you, you think he's on a farm someplace. Tending the garden. He ain't retired.

He's just out. Like you and me. Doing it for God, money and country. Not just God and country."

"He told me to tell number two howdy."

He laughed.

We all had known there were many teams of ten. Our team was known as Strike Force Black Mamba. Number two on the team was B for Blackhawk. I was number ten. J for Jackson. We never knew anyone's real names. They didn't matter. A for Adam. B for Blackhawk. C for Charlie. D for Dakota. Men and women, each one had been through the toughest training the military had to offer, Seals, Rangers whatever, it didn't matter. The ones that couldn't handle it, and it was usually a mental strength thing, rang the bell three times and were done. The rest of us morons kept pushing, too stubborn to quit. Then one day you graduated, and it was the greatest day of your life and you celebrated with your brothers and you got drunk and if lucky you got laid, and then you waited for your orders.

And you waited. And you watched the others called up and pack their shit and leave, and you waited.

Then you received a strange order. You were to bring nothing. They put you on a plane, and when you landed it was night and there was an escort, and they took you to a government building and guys in suits took you through a series of detectors and you sat in a nondescript green room for two hours. The only thing in the room was a camera high in a corner staring straight at you. Then they took you into the colonel's office. A colonel you had never seen before. The colonel smiled and shook your hand, and in his deep baritone told you that out of all the soldiers that had successfully completed the training, you had been selected for a special team. Then later, you found out that they had discharged you so that you were no longer military. Plausible deniability. If something went wrong, you were just some hapless civilian at the wrong place at the wrong time. After this meeting the training really began. I mean real intense covert skills.

One thing I found we all had in common was that none of us had family.

"It's been a while," Blackhawk said. His eyes still carried that bemused look that was always with him. Like he knew the joke no one else knew.

"Last time was when you were handing my boot up to the gunny in the chopper."

He laughed, "Your foot still in it. They ever put it back on?"

"Naw, I got a new one."

"I didn't see a limp."

"Science," I said. "So I guess my question is why you are here?"

"Here? Like in Phoenix?"

"Here as in out of the unit. Far as I can tell, you have all your appendages."

He looked at me, serious now. "They broke us up after you were gone. Offered to replace you with a newbie, but enough of us said no, so they offered the chance to muster out or transfer. I mustered."

"Loyalty to me? Democracy? I never saw that shit."

He smiled, "Not so much as self-preservation. You got a team that works well and your life depends on each other. Echo, Charlie, Fabian and Dakota voted with me and the colonel honored it and said adios. I hear the new guy doesn't give the option. Just bad luck that the IED was where it was. You didn't have to jump there."

"Did you see the girl with the pail of water?"

"Yeah, I saw her."

"I had to jump then."

Blackhawk looked at the wall a while, then back at me. "Yeah, you had to go. Bad luck all around."

"Yeah, bad luck."

Now, I kind of wished I'd accepted the drink. "So now I read and fish and fish and read. I'm pretty bored. Not much use for our set of skills out here."

"Get a bar," he said.

I smiled, "I just did."

"Yeah, so, where are you staying?"

I told him about the boat. Then I told him about the girl.

Chapter Ten

"So, you tilting at windmills now?"

I shrugged, "Chinese law. You save someone's life, you owe them yours. This guy Roland ring any bells? Or the Seventh Avenue Playboy Diablos?"

Blackhawk shook his head. "Get some bangers in here once in a while. Nacho keeps the trouble at a minimum. Not usually the guys start the trouble. Usually the women. Get one guy started at another. Women start doing tequila shots, get drunk, try to make out with the bartenders, scares the good business away so Nacho don't let it get going. No, I don't know any Roland. Let's ask Nacho."

I followed him down the stairs. Nacho was sitting in the same seat but was now watching a basketball game on the television. The dishwasher was gone. We sat on either side of him.

"Tell him," Blackhawk said to me. Nacho reached for the remote and turned the volume down. I told him the same as I told Blackhawk.

"Seventh Avenue Playboy Diablos?" He shook his head.

"I think I've heard of them, low grade punks. Hang out in a condemned warehouse. Cook some bath salts, do some Molly, methamphetamines, cook it, sell it, smoke it."

"They MS13?"

He laughed, "Shit no. MS13 would eat them up."

"The girl said some wore MS13 tats."

"Trying to be bad. Not even in the same league."

"You know of a cop name of Mendoza, Mike Mendoza, or a guy runs a half-way house, a Father Correa?"

"Know'm both," Nacho said. "Mendoza put me away for a couple years. Good guy. The Father takes in girls. Usually with babies. Got nowhere to go."

I laughed, "Mendoza put you away and he's a good guy?"

"I was the bad guy. He did the right thing. Straight shooter, keeps his word."

I looked at Blackhawk and he gave me that inscrutable bemused look. "Nacho was a bad man, now he's pussy cat."

"A regular pussy cat," I said.

"Meow," Nacho said.

Chapter Eleven

We took Nacho's Jeep Cherokee downtown because Blackhawk's Jag and my Mustang were too small in the back for a big man. Nacho drove and wove through the city streets like he did it every day. Maybe he did. He found the parking lot to the police headquarters and got lucky that a truck was pulling out as we were pulling in. We got out of the Jeep and Nacho pulled a Glock 19 from the back of his belt and slid it under the front seat.

"Got a metal detector in the lobby," he said by way of explanation. Blackhawk unstrapped a .38 Smith and Wesson that was elcroid to his ankle. I slid the spring loaded knife with the four-inch blade and pocket clip from my front pocket and slid it next to Blackhawk's weapon under the back seat.

"Traveling light?" Blackhawk said.

"Ain't much danger of a carp attacking me."

We followed Nacho across the lot and up the steps. Sure enough, inside the massive glass doors we were met by a security station set up like a mini airport. I set the alarm off and had to take my belt off.

Once through, Nacho started down the long hallway toward some large opaque glass double doors. We followed. "Where you get that shit kicker belt?" Blackhawk grinned.

"At the shit kicker store. They didn't have a pimp store at that particular mall."

"Too bad," he said softly as Nacho opened the glass door and ushered us in.

There was a uniform behind a long counter. Nacho walked up to him and said, "We'd like to speak with Mendoza."

"Lots of Mendozas," he said, his eyes shifting from Nacho, to Blackhawk, then to me. If we worried him, he sure didn't show it.

"Sergeant Mendoza, gangs," Nacho said.

The officer studied him for a long moment, his eyes going to our hands and our belts. "It's Lieutenant now. What is this about?"

Nacho looked at me.

"There's a young girl missing," I said.

The uniform was looking at me now, his eyes completely non-committal. "Like he said," he said nodding at Nacho, "the Lieutenant is in Gangs. You'll want Missing Persons."

"I believe it is the gangs that have her."

"The Lieutenant is probably busy, I can get you a detective."

Nacho leaned forward, "Would you please tell Lieutenant Mendoza that Ignacio Pombo is in the lobby and would like a word."

The officer studied him a moment, then turned and picked up a phone.

"Pombo?" Blackhawk said.

Nacho looked at him, "What is your real name? Senor Blackhawk Eaglefeather Yellow Tail Pussy Catcher Jones?"

Blackhawk just laughed.

"Pombo is a real, upstanding, honorable name," I said. "Even if it did come from a Disney cartoon character."

"Fuck you, Super Boy."

The officer turned back. "Have a seat, he'll be down."

There were straight backed chairs lining the wall. We sat. Blackhawk and I had learned the hard art of waiting a long time ago. We sat motionless. After a while Nacho began fidgeting. He stood then sat back down.

"I don't like this place," he said. "Bad memories." Blackhawk and I just looked at each other. It was another twenty minutes before a door opened down the hall. There was an exit sign above it and I surmised it was a stairwell. A man stepped out and Nacho stood again. I could tell from Nacho that this was Mendoza. The best way I can describe the man is with the word *compact*. All the parts fit together perfectly. He wasn't tall, but he exuded physical power. The suit he wore was immaculate, the tie all the way to the top. His salt and pepper hair was cut so close his scalp gleamed through. His shoes were black and buffed. They must have rubber soles. He made no noise as he walked toward us. His jacket was unbuttoned and the way it rode, I could tell he was heeled and it was on his right hip.

Blackhawk and I came to our feet. He stopped three paces from us, looking at Nacho. I knew he had taken me and Blackhawk in with a glance. He didn't offer a hand.

"Nacho, long time."

"I've been out three years now."

"I haven't heard your name, so you must be staying clean."

"I'm a tax paying, responsible citizen."

"Good to hear. How can I help?"

Nacho indicated me, "This is Jackson. He's looking for a girl."

He turned to me. No wasted words, no wasted movement.

"Tell me," he said.

I told him the story the same as I had told the Colonel, Blackhawk and Nacho. I was getting good at it. When I finished, he gave no reaction. He turned to Blackhawk, "And you, sir?"

"I work with Nacho and I am a friend of Mr. Jackson's."

Mendoza nodded, "I see." He turned to the uniformed officer behind the counter. "Have Detective Boyce meet us in my office."

"Yes, sir," the officer replied.

"Follow me, gentlemen," Mendoza said and turned on his heel.

We followed him.

Chapter Twelve

Mendoza went up three stories of stairs at a rapid pace with no apparent effort. On the third floor, he held the door for us. We stepped into a large room filled with desks, phones and cops. Some of the cops were talking with civilians. Or maybe they were civilians just for now. Mendoza led us across the large room and held open the door to his office. None of the cops gave us a glance. The back of the office had a window that opened to the outside; the rest was surrounded by plexiglass. The better to see you with, Grandma.

The room had a desk facing front, two file cabinets on one wall and two chairs facing the desk. There was a coffee pot on one of the file cabinets. It was still a third full but the on light was off. As he came in behind us, he snagged a chair from an empty desk and brought it in. He moved around the desk and sat, indicating with a small gesture for us to join him.

As soon as we sat, the door opened and Detective Boyce joined us. Detective Boyce was about five seven, a hundred and thirty pounds, and had long dark hair to her shoulders.

She too was compact, moving easily inside her own skin. She didn't appear to be wearing much in the way of make-up. She moved to the side of the door and leaned against the plexiglass, arms folded across her chest.

Mendoza looked at me. "Let's go through this all again for the sake of Detective Boyce."

Blackhawk and I nodded at her; Nacho said, "Ma'am."

I took out my camera and turned it on. I found the pictures I'd taken of the girl and handed it across to the Lieutenant. He took it and moved it from picture to picture, studying each one thoroughly.

"I live on a houseboat at Pleasant Harbor, I said.

"Where's that?" Boyce asked.

"Lake Pleasant."

She nodded.

"Two nights ago I was sleeping up top when two guys dumped the girl, wrapped in plastic, off the end of the dock."

"What did they look like?" Mendoza asked without looking up from the camera.

I described them. "But it was night and there is a low watt light at the end of the pier," I said.

"Then what?"

"It looked like a long plastic package, but when it hit the water it moved and I knew it was a person. So I went in and got lucky."

"Lucky?"

"They had weighted the girl down and she was dropping fast."

Mendoza was studying me now. He handed the camera to Detective Boyce. "Sounds like it was the girl that got lucky."

"That too," I nodded.

Detective Boyce went through the pictures. She looked at Mendoza and shook her head.

"So the girl was alive."

"After CPR."

"But she's missing."

"A woman on one of the other boats helped me. After the girl spit up half the lake and could talk, she insisted we not call the police. All we got is that her name is Lucinda, she is sixteen and was on the streets staying with what she said was the 7th Ave Diablo Playboys. Headed up by a guy named Roland. She was hooking for him. She stayed the rest of the night and all the next day with the woman on the woman's boat, and then this morning she was gone."

"Who is the good Samaritan?"

"I'd not met her before. She said her name was Grandberry."

"Name of her boat."

"I didn't notice."

"Name of your boat?"

"The Tiger Lily."

I could see Blackhawk shake his head out of the corner of my eye.

Mendoza smiled, "Really?"

I nodded, "Yeah, really."

"That make you Peter Pan?" asked Detective Boyce.

Nacho snorted.

"Just a lost boy," I said, looking at her.

Detective Boyce said, "I'll take this," indicating the camera, "and download the pictures, get us some hard copies."

"Can I have one?" I asked.

"Sure, I'll make several." She opened the door and shut it quietly behind her.

"So, you think the Diablos dumped her, then came later and got her?" Mendoza asked.

"She couldn't believe her best friends could do such a thing. I think she called them from the marina store and then they came and got her. I can't say for certain that the two that dumped her were Diablos."

"Back to the lion's den?"

"That's why I'm here. You know the Diablos?"

"Small time. Meth cookers, crackheads mostly. Petty stuff. Hang out in an old warehouse on Lower Buckeye. We roust them once in a while just to let them know we're watching. Small time stuff. Some of the girls are hooking but I've not seen this one."

He looked at me, leaning back in his chair. "You know this is probably a fool's errand. We get a thousand runaways a year. Most of them end up on drugs and hooking. Most of them don't want to be saved. They just want the next hit." He picked up his phone. "I'll put a black and white in there. See what they find." He punched some numbers then spoke into the phone. When he hung it up he said, "What makes this one so special?"

"She was dumped off my pier," I said.

A moment later Detective Boyce came back in with a folder. She took an 8 x 10 head shot of Lucinda and handed it to me. "I'll check with Missing Persons. Do you have their numbers?" she asked Mendoza.

"Just his," he said, indicating me. He looked at Nacho, "Nacho?"

"You can reach Nacho and me at the El Patron, where we work," Blackhawk spoke up.

"Durango?"

Blackhawk nodded.

"What's your name?" Mendoza asked.

"Blackhawk."

Mendoza didn't look surprised, "Of course," he said.

Blackhawk smiled. Nacho was smiling.

Detective Boyce had another photo in her hand which she handed to me. It was a Hispanic male thirty-plus years old. He was caught in the photo slouched back against a wall. He held a cigarette up close to his face and smoke was coming from his mouth like he had just taken a drag. His slick dark hair was combed straight back and went to his shoulders. He wore a white tee shirt and his neck and arms were covered with tattoos. His right bicep had a very striking tattoo of an eagle. I couldn't make out any MS13.

"Roland?" I asked.

She nodded.

"This mine?"

She nodded again.

Mendoza said, "Well, Mr. Jackson, Detective Boyce will

be in touch if we find anything." He stood. The meeting was over. "Nice to see you again, Nacho. Especially without handcuffs involved." He put his hand out and we took turns shaking it. Detective Boyce didn't offer. She was watching Blackhawk. We filed out.

Down at the Jeep, Blackhawk said, "Well, Kemo Sabe, what now?"

I looked at Nacho. "You think you could find this warehouse?"

"Sure," he said. "It'll be the one on Lower Buckeye with the jackwad crackheads sitting out front."

We found it not because of the jackwad crackheads but because a black and white was sitting out front with the lights flashing.

"Ain't gonna be no one home," Nacho said. He pointed up. "Always got a lookout up there. Any black and white pulls onto this street, they clear out."

"Drive around," I said. "I want to get a look at this place."

Nacho pulled past the black and white and took the next corner.

"What you thinking?" Blackhawk asked.

"I think the girl has to be here. Where else is she going to be? I say we go in hard and see for ourselves."

"When?"

"They spooked now," Nacho said. "Wait a while. Wait for them to get…you know?"

"Complacent," Blackhawk said.

"Yeah, that," Nacho said.

Blackhawk nodded. "You ready for that firewater yet?" he asked me.

"Yeah," I said craning my neck to see the back of the building, as Nacho made another turn. Looked like a warehouse.

"Good," Blackhawk said. "Hey, I've got a question."

"What's that?"

"What you gonna do with her when you get her?"

Chapter Thirteen

It was after ten and we were sitting at the bar in the main room of El Patron. Blackhawk was treating me to a tequila tasting, and I was currently sipping on Arta, a silver agave tequila. Very smooth and very deadly.

The place was jammed, and Blackhawk, Nacho and the bartender from earlier whose name I learned was Jimmy were working the bar. The band had started and the dark-eyed girls were immediately on the dance floor, starting with each other, knowing it would be a few drinks before the men would join them. Earlier I had wandered down to the two other rooms and each was only about half full. One had a long, tall skinny guy doing Waylon Jennings and the other had some kids thrashing their guitars like they had been bad and needed punishment. El Patron was the first joint I had been in that had a suit-your-musical-mood venue.

I was enjoying the lively music in the main room. The band of men in broad sombreros and fancy suits all alike were on the stage. One had a guitar the size of Madagascar. The singer was a striking young woman with flowing black hair and bright skirts, and she held all the single men in the room in the palm of her hand. Probably the married men too, but they dared not show it. They watched her, knowing the wives were watching them. The place had a good vibe, all familiar and comfortable.

Then I noticed the singer watching the back of the room. The men against the wall had all turned their heads.

A phalanx of young men, white and black, had come through the double doors. Jeans, sleeveless ASU football jerseys cut off at the midriff. The really big guys had some bellies but the skinny guys were rocks. The white guys had mostly close-cropped hair. The blacks had long, braided hair. College jocks. My side of the bar was mostly empty so they sat down along it, laughing a little more loudly than necessary.

It was a very large young man that sat next to me. His tee shirt bulged with his pectoral muscles. There were prominent veins along his biceps. Weightlifter and did a lot of it. He had to be fifty pounds and two inches on me. He exuded the self-confident swagger of a man that gets whatever he wants. Even with the tequila in me I could smell the whiskey on him. He put money out on the bar. Nacho came down and gave me a look, then politely took his order. Shot and a beer. Nacho asked him for his I.D. This irritated him, but he struggled it out of his jeans and Nacho made a point of looking it over.

Nacho looked at me again, then turned to fill the order. I noticed that Blackhawk and the other bartender were checking every I.D. Satisfied, they started setting beers on the bar. Nacho brought Big Bubba his drinks and he downed his shot and half the beer and let out a long protracted belch. He turned and studied the dancing women. He must have sensed me looking at him. He turned and gave me the long hard stare that made most men pee themselves. I tried to hold on.

"What you looking at?" he said.

"Nothing much," I said.

Not sure what to say to that, he glared at me some more, then turned and went back to studying the women. Now some of the men had joined them, and the band had the dancers really moving. I finished my tequila and set the shot glass on the bar. Blackhawk looked at me and I shook my head. I had a long drive back to the boat.

I slid off the stool and headed for the men's room. I was impressed. It was spotless. I finished, washed my hands and came back out. The music had stopped. All the jocks were bunched behind Bubba and the dancers were grouped across from them. Between them was Nacho. He was talking to Bubba.

"You boys can sit at the bar and have your drinks. You will leave the ladies alone, or you can get the hell out of here."

Bubba was doing his best to save face, but it was obvious to me he wanted no part of Nacho. After a protracted moment, one of the other jocks said, "Fuck it Bobby, bitches ain't worth it." Bobby stood and stared at Nacho long enough to prove he wasn't afraid. The others slowly began to sit down. Finally, as the last man standing, saving face,

Bobby turned and sat down. Nacho signaled the band and the music began again. I stepped up to my stool and laid a five on the bar. Blackhawk wasn't charging me but I wanted Jimmy to get a tip.

Bobby turned and looked at me. I smiled.

"What the fuck you think is so funny?"

"Saturday Night Live," I said. "Or Jack Benny, or even Robin Williams. I also think Jimmy Fallon is hilarious."

"What are you, some kinda smart ass?"

"Might be, but I've never met a smart ass," I said. "Usually they are just plain asses. However, I have met quite a few dumb asses. Met another one tonight."

"You little shit," he said and reached for me. I brought my opened hand up inside of his and moved his hand to the side. He reached for me again and I moved his hand again.

Showing off his extensive vocabulary he said "You little fuck," and came off his stool and I hit him in the throat with a hard, eight-inch punch straight from the shoulder with my body braced against the bar. He fell back, coughing. He shook his head like a big bear, trying to get his breath. I waited until he straightened up, then I hit him in the top of the ear and temple with the shot glass. He went down like a felled tree.

I put my back to the bar and one of his buddies with long braided, greasy hair started for me, but Blackhawk reached across the bar and grabbed a handful of his hair and slammed his head on the mahogany top. He went to his knees beside his bleeding big buddy. Nacho had materialized behind the rest of them with a ball bat in his hands.

Blackhawk held up his hand, palm out.

"No more."

The band had stopped in midnote and the dancers and those against the wall were all standing, watching. The girl singer had a broad smile.

"Your drinks are on me," Blackhawk said. "And now you will leave."

The big guy was trying to sit up. The blood was running out of his ear and onto his shirt, the other one was on his hands and knees, his head moving back and forth like a spavined bull. The other jocks gathered round and helped them up, which took some doing. En masse they moved to the door. As they filed out Bobby turned and yelled hoarsely, "This ain't over!"

The girl singer said into the microphone, "Oh yes, I think it is," and began to applaud. The women dancers began to applaud and then the whole room was applauding.

Blackhawk was smiling at me.

I handed him the shot glass.

"I think I liked that last one the best," I said.

Chapter Fourteen

It was midnight by the time I stepped on the boat. I turned off the alarm. I had rigged a little laser that tracked across the gangway from the pier to the boat. The light was hidden from view but if the laser had been interrupted by someone coming on board a small LED attached to the lip of the bow would light. The LED was situated so that you had to look for it to see it. The light was green. Once on board, I activated the pressure switch to the gangway from the pier onto the boat. If someone stepped on the gangway a soft gong sound would ring in my stateroom.

I stripped down and took a quick shower and brushed my teeth to get the stale taste of tequila out of it. I slid under the covers of the oversized bed and willed my mind to empty itself. I fell asleep almost immediately. I awoke almost the next minute. The soft gong was still ringing in my ears. Someone was stepping aboard.

I swung out of bed my hand grasping the Ruger LCP .380 I keep attached to a magnetic plate behind my bed stand. I slipped on a pair of swim trunks and stuck my stub into a boot I keep next to the bed. It has Velcro straps and I use it for quick use on the boat. I could hear light tapping on the glass door at the bow. I had the curtains pulled and whoever was there couldn't see in. Moving silently, I went out the back and up the ladder. I moved softly across the top, careful not to rock the boat. As I reached the bow, I saw Romy below turning to walk away.

"Hey," I said softly. I held the gun slightly behind me, out of her sight.

She turned and looked around, then finally up at me.

"Oh, hey," she said. "Did I wake you?"

"No," I lied. "Hold on, I'll come down and let you in."

I replaced the pistol where I keep it, then moved to the bow. I pulled the blackout curtains and let her in.

I turned on a lamp and she sat on one end of the couch. I sat on the other.

"I'm sorry," she said. "I couldn't sleep and I thought I'd see if you were back."

"Just did get in," I said.

"Did you find out anything?"

"Not much," I said. I told her about the meeting with Mendoza and the warehouse. I didn't mention Blackhawk, the El Patron or big Bobby.

"So," I said, "I didn't hear from Mendoza, which makes me assume the black and white found nothing at the warehouse."

"So what do we do now?"

I shrugged. "Mendoza's having one of his people check Missing Persons but he says there is a legion of girls like

Lucinda out there. If she doesn't want to be found and if she doesn't want to go home, there's not much we can do."

Romy put her face in her hands, elbows on her knees.

"Can I get you a drink?"

She shook her head, face still in her hands. Then she stood up and looked at me. I stood. She came to me and put her head against my chest. I put my arms around her and she held me tight. Her voice was muffled, "I just want someone to hold me."

I pulled her tight against me and we stood like that for a long moment. Finally she slowly raised her face and we stared at each other for a long moment. Then I slowly lowered my face and kissed her. At first it was just a kiss and then it turned to something else. Her back arched and she pressed herself against me. Her mouth opened and one hand came up to the back of my neck. Still kissing, I reached down and picked her up, my left arm cradling her legs. I carried her down the hallway and sat on my bed, with her on my lap. She pulled her mouth away and again we were looking at each other, scant inches apart. She slipped off my lap and stood. She unbuttoned her blouse and let it drop to the floor. In a uniquely feminine move, she reached her hands behind her and unsnapped her bra. She held it for a moment, watching me, then she let it drop. She stepped out of the flip flops she wore, and hooking her thumbs into her waistband, she slid her shorts and panties down and kicked them off. She stood completely and delightfully naked. I thought this was a little one-sided. I stood and she hooked her thumbs into the waistband of my swim trunks and slid them down.

Now we were even. For a second we looked at each other, then she came to me and I fell back and we stretched out on the bed.

I had not been with a woman in a long time, so the first time was urgent and rough, using all of the big bed, rolling with first me on top, then her, coating us both with a fine sheen of perspiration as we tasted the salty skin and held the slippery bodies. It was the exploring and trying and finding time, and we were soon out of breath and reaching that final peak. She groaned her pleasure and I'm pretty sure I hollered "yippee!" The second time took much longer.

Chapter Fifteen

Father Jorge Correa was round. If Friar Tuck were Mexican this would be the guy. We were sitting in a small cramped office in a non-descript building within a couple miles of El Patron. It had no signage except for a simple sign beside the door that read *Safehouse*. He had led me to the office after I had introduced myself and had dropped Lieutenant Mendoza's name.

He excused himself.

"I have a new girl coming in, and I want to make sure she's taken care of. I'll be right back." He pointed at a half-full coffee pot. "Help yourself to some coffee. There are cups and Sweet and Low in the top drawer. I'll be right back."

I sat waiting for a while. When he didn't come back right away, I got up and found the cups and Sweet and Low and some powdered creamer. The cups were small Styrofoam and held about a third of my cup on the boat. I didn't see any stirrers so I put the sweetener and creamer in first, then poured the coffee. While I stood there with my back to the door, I opened the second file drawer. It was jammed with manila folders, each with a woman's first name written on the tab. First names only. It was on the bottom drawer that I got to the L's. There was no Lucinda. When he did return I was sitting where I had been, the coffee almost gone.

"Sorry to keep you," he said. "I appreciate your patience." He seemed to be in a constant state of happy. It sure didn't seem to be the kind of place that induces happy, but maybe that is what it takes to do what he does.

"I'm interrupting your day," I said. I had Lucinda's photo in a manila envelope. I opened it and handed him the photo.

As he took it, he pulled a pair of reading glasses from his pocket. He was dressed in a blue striped button-down short sleeve shirt and khakis. Well-worn tennis shoes were on his feet. Looked like the average Joe. No way to tell he was a priest.

He studied the photo, taking his time. Finally he looked back to me.

"She a relative?"

I shook my head.

He handed me the photo, "I don't recognize her as one of mine. Why are you looking for her?"

I hadn't really intended to go into great detail. I knew I'd have to tell him something, but his eyes were so genuine and his interest so palpable I said, "I live on a boat at Lake Pleasant. A couple of days ago two guys that looked like gang dropped her weighted body into the lake beside my boat. I got to her in time and pulled her out. A woman that also lives there took her in. When she recovered, she said her name was Lucinda and she didn't want the cops and she didn't want any family. She had been on the streets and had hooked up with a gang called the 7th Avenue Playboy Diablos."

"Roland," he said.

I nodded, "Yes, Roland. He had her hooking and she lived in some kind of commune deal."

"In a warehouse."

"You know him. She couldn't bring herself to believe they were the ones that dumped her. She took off. I'm thinking she got a hold of Roland or someone and they came and got her. I'm not convinced they won't dump her again."

"Why did they try to kill her to begin with?"

I shrugged. "No idea."

He was sitting at his desk in a secretary's chair. He was swiveling gently back and forth. He was looking out the door and down the hall. I waited.

He looked back to me. "The Playboys troll the internet for young girls. They reach out with social media, Facebook, Twitter and the like. They become friends. They really are quite sophisticated. They search Facebook for a certain age and certain key words. Looking for the troubled ones. The ones unhappy at home. The abused ones. The majority of them have been abused by then. They start off by meeting up with them at a mall and after a while the girls think they have found their new best friends. From there it's easy to have the girls run away and join them. That's when the girls find out they are expected to pay their way by hooking."

"They just put them on the street?"

"Easier than you would think. They all have such low self-esteem and almost all of them have been sexually active, either by choice or not, so sex with a stranger is no big deal."

"How do you know Roland?"

"I don't really know him. I know of him. I've had four girls come here for help that were involved with the Playboys. In the broad scheme of things, the Playboys are small potatoes. They cook crack and have their girls hooking. Not major drugs like some of the others."

"What happened to the four girls?"

"Three went back to the streets, one went to relatives in the Midwest."

"Not a very good percentage."

He shrugged, "I don't have the money for long-term fixes. We do what we can."

"I'm sure that you do. You ever hear of Frank Bavaro?"

"Doesn't ring a bell."

"I'm told he is an attorney that is hooked up with a drug cartel."

"He's out of my league. Mostly I just get the castoffs here."

I had made several copies of Lucinda's photo, so I said, "Would you keep the picture and if she shows up give me a call?"

"Certainly," he said. "What's your number?"

I told him and he wrote it on the back of the picture.

"I'm sorry I'm not much help," he said. "Would you like to see the facility?"

"Sure," I said.

He led me out of the office and down a small corridor. We passed a room where the smell of cooking wafted through the air. I glanced in and saw a very thin man in a hair net and a soiled apron stirring a very large pot of something.

"That is our kitchen. All volunteers. Unfortunately, we don't have the money for a paid staff so we are blessed by volunteers."

"How about the food?"

"There is a local grocery chain here in town and the owner has generously endowed us with food stuffs that have reached a sell-by date." He smiled at me. "Not to worry, sell-by dates are well before the stuff actually goes bad. It's funny that as our society has become more politically correct, we have become more concerned with the appearance of things, like the sell-by date, than whether the food is actually bad. Most food is good long after the sell-by date. I think these grocery chains are more afraid of being accused of impropriety instead of actually being improper. I don't know how my grandmother survived."

"Good to know," I said. "How about the shelter itself? How do you pay for it?"

"Donations from some of the larger churches and God's grace. I'm constantly scrambling for money."

We moved through a door and now were in a corridor that reminded me of a hospital hallway. Every few feet was a door. Most were open. As we walked along, I noted that most of the rooms were filled with a bed and dresser, a chair and piles of personal belongings. They were mostly empty.

"Most of the girls and their children are in the community room this time of day."

He stopped at one room. Inside was a very young girl with a baby nursing at her breast. She was humming and rocking and had her front and the baby discreetly covered. She looked up smiling. Her hair had been dyed blonde but now the roots were a couple of inches long. It was long and straight but looked clean. She wore no makeup and her eyes had dark circles. She looked like she was twelve years old and couldn't have weighed ninety pounds.

"Hello, Melinda," he said. "How is young Hayden today?"

She smiled up at him. "He's hungry, Father."

"Meet Mr. Jackson," he said indicating me.

"Hi, Mr. Jackson," she said.

"Hi Melinda," I said. "How old is Hayden?"

"Three months and seventeen days," she said brightly. "And growing every day." She pulled the cover away from the baby, exposing the baby suckling at her breast. "Look how big he's getting."

"You make sure you get plenty to eat. You're eating for two," Father Correa said. He moved on down the hall.

"Nice meeting you," I said but she was humming to the baby. I followed Father Correa.

The community room was filled with young women and children. There was a television on at one end but no one was watching it. Most of the women were sitting on the floor playing with the kids.

Father Correa looked at me, "Are you a man of faith, Mr. Jackson?"

"Depends on 'in what?'"

"Faith in a higher power? Faith in the role of God in our lives. Faith in eternal love and eternal life?"

"Faith in a holy cause is to a considerable extent a substitute for the lost faith in ourselves."

"Eric Hoffer, I believe. I see you read, Mr. Jackson."

"I also fish," I said.

"Some of the Apostles were fishermen. Does that mean you have no faith?"

"I'm not sure I'm smart enough to figure such things out. But I am a practical and pragmatic man, Father. I think the first time I questioned an adult's statement of fact was when I was about five years old. I find it difficult to believe any man understands the thinking of a God that made the sun, the moon and the stars. Let alone made this world."

He smiled.

"But Father, I do have faith. In things I can count on. I have no blind faith."

"How about in the goodness of men's souls?"

I moved my hand to indicate the room before us.

"Most people, including you, probably think these young women have a bad time of it."

"Most come from a bad life," he agreed.

"I was once at an orphanage run by nuns in the middle of Africa. It was in the path of rebel forces hellbent on destruction. I arrived too late. The nuns were raped and mutilated. The little boys had their throats slashed. The little girls were taken to be sold into slavery. No, Father, I don't have any illusions about the goodness of men's souls."

We stood silently for a long moment.

"Did you ever find the little girls?" he finally asked.

"How do you know I looked?"

"You are looking for one now."

"My team found them but we lost half of them on the extract."

"My God," he said.

"Yes, he probably is," I said.

We watched the mothers for a moment longer, then I followed him back down the hallway.

He walked me to the door.

"Thanks for stopping by, I will keep you and the girl in my prayers," he said.

I had nothing to say to that. He watched me walk away.

Chapter Sixteen

I was sliding into the Mustang when the phone in my pocket began to vibrate. It made me jump. I took it out and looked at it. It took me a second to remember how to answer it.

"Hello," I said.

It was a female voice. "Is this Jackson?"

"It is."

"This is Detective Boyce. We met in Lieutenant Mendoza's office."

"I remember. You were the one with the great big badge."

"We all have big badges," she said. "I ran your girl by Missing Persons. They don't have anything on her."

"Nothing?"

"Not unusual. A lot of the families of these street girls are happy they are grown up enough to go away."

"It takes a gang to raise a child."

"Yeah, something like that. I'll keep my eyes open."

I thanked her and hung up. I lay the phone on the seat beside me and it began to vibrate again. I picked it up.

"Hello."

"Frank Bavaro is a senior partner in a Phoenix law firm, Phelps, Gutierrez and Tamoso," the colonel said without preamble. "But I had already told you that. Office is in the Esplanade, 24th and Camelback. You will never find him there. If he owns property in Arizona it's not in his name. Best I can find is that he only has one client, the Kamex Corporation out of Mexico City. It's a multi-national company that has holdings in dozens of smaller companies, mostly in the Americas. Mostly construction. The dirty little secret that everyone knows is that it is a front for the Dos Hermanos drug cartel, but you would never be able to prove it. Dos Hermanos is one of the two largest cartels in the California and southwest area. They have been known to use MS13 as their hired guns. Bavaro is an untouchable, protected by layers of subordinates between him and the brothers."

"Who is the other cartel?"

"It is run by the Valdez family. This is a real shadow outfit. Not much known about it."

"Is there any motive for him to ice the girl?"

"Mr. Bavaro is married to east coast society and gets a lot of political protection because of it. But it appears it is mostly a marriage of convenience. If Bavaro wanted a girl he could snap his fingers."

"The wife's name's Romy Grandberry?"

"I won't ask how you know that. Grandberry's old east coast. Ambassadors, senators, old money."

"Thanks for the info."

"Be careful," he said and the phone disconnected.

I laid the phone on the console and headed for the freeway. I stopped and shopped for groceries, and when I got to the marina I found the Moneypenny all buttoned up. I was stepping on board the Tiger Lily when I heard my name.

"Hey Jackson!"

I looked to the lake side of the boat and there was Captain Rand Crowe. Rand was a guide for hire and sometime Captain of the River Belle. The River Belle was a huge two-story boat that was owned and used by one of the large tech companies in town. When MicroSensor wasn't using it, they rented it out for weddings and such.

Rand was tall and lanky with parched and tanned skin that comes only from years in the sun. I guessed he was in his fifties, but he was sun dried and would probably look like this the rest of his life. He sat in his twenty foot runabout, the one he used for private guides. I met him a year ago when he came alongside me and demanded to know who I was and why was I following him. I told him who I was and I was following him because every time I fished where he fished I caught fish. He had thought I was a competitor. Next time I saw him I gave him a case of Dos Equis. We have been friends since and once in a while I'll crew for him when his normal kid can't make it.

"Captain Rand. How you doing?"

"Fair to middlin'. Hey, they just pulled a girl's body out of the water across the lake."

I looked across the lake where he was indicating and could see the flashing red and blue lights of police cars by the shoreline. There was a Sheriff's Lake Patrol boat sitting off in the water with its lights flashing.

I felt like the bottom of my stomach had fallen.

"I went over to see what was goin' on and was talkin' with one of the sheriff's lake guys," he continued. "And this lady cop came up and asked him if he knew anyone named Jackson that lived out here. Maybe I shouldn't have opened my pie hole but I said I knew you and she asked me to come over and invite you to the party."

"Lady cop?"

"Yeah, hope I didn't cause you a problem. You gonna come?"

"Sure. Give me a ride?"

"Sure, hop in."

"Let me stick the milk in the frig." A moment later I was on the stern.

Rand maneuvered the skiff in close and I hopped down into it. Ignoring the no-wake zone, he put the throttle down, and in seconds we were skimming across the water. A minute later he roared past the *no wake* signs on the other side and came ripping into the shoreline. At the last second he cut the throttle and came gliding into the shore. Five feet out, he hit reverse and braked us to a gentle bump as we hit the ground.

It was Detective Boyce. There were several crime scene people there, plus the coroner's office and Lake Patrol. Various spectators were sprinkled along the shoreline. She was standing next to an ambulance gurney that had a covered body on it. She watched us come into the shoreline, then walked over when I jumped from the boat onto the shore. She wore a tailored suit that almost hid the pistol on her hip. She was wearing her great big badge on her belt where it gleamed as she walked. She had on aviator sunglasses and you couldn't see her eyes, just the reflection of yourself.

"Detective Boyce," I said.

"Seems like you are known around here."

"Looks like a big lake but it's not." I indicated the gurney, "Is that my girl?"

"Take a look," she said. I followed her over.

I put my hand out to pull the cover back. "It's not pretty," she said. "Been in the water a while."

I hesitated a brief second, then pulled the cover back.

It wasn't Lucinda.

For just a second I thought it was Melinda, the young mother at Safehouse. Small like her, the facial features pretty well gone. This one had been in the water a while. There were marks where the turtles had worked on her. Her hair was plastered against the small skull and one of her ears was missing.

"You know her?" Boyce asked.

I shook my head, "Should I?"

"I've been a cop a long time," she said. "Too long to believe in coincidences. Two girls in the same lake in the same week. I tried to call you."

I pulled my phone out and it showed a missed call. I showed her the number. "That you?"

She took it and looked at it, nodded and handed it back to me.

"Sorry, I didn't hear it. You mind if I take a picture?"

"Fine," she said. "You got any idea about these girls?"

"Not a clue."

"Who is the picture for?"

"Do you know Father Correa at Safehouse?"

"Yeah," she said. "Good guy." She studied me for a moment then said, "Don't get in the way." She turned and walked over to some of the other policemen and began talking with them. I took some pictures with the phone then waited for a couple minutes. I could see Captain Rand was getting antsy.

When she looked at me again I said, "Anything else?"

She shook her head. "Stay in touch," she said.

Chapter Seventeen

It was two in the morning and Blackhawk, Nacho, the singer Elena and I sat in the main bar of El Patron. We were drinking coffee. Elena was sipping a tiny glass of Grand Marnier. Her sips were so genteel I wasn't sure the stuff actually touched her lips.

The place was closed. I had stopped at the storage locker I rented, located just a short distance from the marina, and retrieved a Mossberg 500 shotgun, a Remington model 870 shotgun and an automatic weapon, a Spikes tactical compressor SBR-300, An AK styled weapon with sound suppression. When it is fired it sounds like someone spitting. They were on the bar along with ammunition. Like every weapon I had, they were untraceable.

"Looks like you have everything except your white horse," Blackhawk said.

"You don't have oats," I said.

"White horse? You have a white horse?" Elena asked.

Blackhawk laughed. "He thinks he's a Knight of the Round Table. Sir Gawain, or Lancelot."

Elena looked puzzled, "Who?"

"King Arthur," Nacho said. "You know, King Arthur and the Knights of the Round Table."

"Never heard of him."

Nacho snorted, "You never heard of King Arthur? Where the hell have you been?"

"In Mexico asshole. You ever heard of Octavio Paz?"

Blackhawk laughed again.

Nacho shook his head, "He a fighter?"

"Nacho, you need to let it go. You're in over your head," Blackhawk said. He turned to me, "When we going in?"

I looked at my watch. "In an hour, sound right?"

"I don't know if I like this," Elena said.

"If someone asked you who you were? What makes you tick, what would you say?" Blackhawk asked.

"I'm a singer," she said. "It's what I do."

"This is what we do," he said.

"What do I do?" Nacho asked.

"You are Sancho Panza," I said.

"Who?"

"Never mind," Blackhawk said and drank some more coffee.

An hour later, with Nacho driving and Blackhawk in the front passenger seat and me in the back, we parked Nacho's Jeep a block away from the Diablo's warehouse in the shadows of an alley behind an old machine shop. We all wore dark hazmat one piece coveralls, rubber soled shoes with cloth booties and we had rubber surgical gloves on. We each had a dark blue stocking cap which we could pull down to a ski mask. We were watching the line of the roof top of the warehouse. The streets were empty and deserted. There was enough residual glow from the streetlights to illuminate the top of the warehouse. There was no movement.

Nacho and I had the shotguns, Blackhawk the SBR-300. Nacho and I pumped a round into the chamber, then we moved quietly along the fence line of the machine shop yard. As we got closer to the warehouse I could see a dark SUV parked across the street from the warehouse.

"Empty," Blackhawk said softly. We stood for several minutes in the shadows watching the vehicle. Finally Blackhawk was satisfied and he moved toward the shadows of the building. We followed. He led us around to the back. There was a landing with a door. There was an overhead light but there was no bulb in it. Blackhawk pulled a small cylindrical combat light from his pocket and held it cupped in his hand so that just a thin sliver of light escaped. He put the light on the lock.

Nacho was staring at the lighted lock and Blackhawk whispered, "Don't look at the light. You'll be night blind. You watch behind us." Nacho turned. I pulled a small pick kit from my pocket. The lock was an old standard Yale dead bolt. I had it open in less than fifteen seconds. I pushed the door open and followed it moving to my left, shotgun ready. Blackhawk came in and moved to the other side. The door had opened to a large echoing room. Blackhawk shined the light around. It was completely empty. The only things in the room were old cigarette butts and dirt. Thirty feet across was a doorway with no door. Blackhawk's light showed a staircase landing.

I looked back out the door and Nacho was still standing, watching the way we had come. I whistled softly and he turned. I touched the cheap walkie-talkie I had clipped to my belt. We all had one.

"You on channel eight?" I asked softly.

He nodded.

"If someone comes, click the talk button twice, then wait five seconds and do it again. One of us will click back." I looked around. "Stay over there up against the wall in the shadows." He nodded and moved off. I went back in. Blackhawk was across the room in the stairway. I moved up beside him.

The warehouse was only three stories high, so the first set of stairs led to a landing, then turned and went up to the next landing.

"You cover," I said. Blackhawk squatted down against the wall and covered the top of stairs. I went up two at a time, then covered while he came up behind me. At the top of the next set of stairs was a door. I started to move up when…

BAM BAM, then BAM BAM again! Gunfire exploded behind the closed door at the top. Instinctively Blackhawk and I dropped to a crouch, covering the top of the stairs. It sounded like just one weapon. Whoever it was, they weren't shooting at us. Suddenly the door at the top flew open, slapping against the wall, and with a high keening sound, a slight figure fell through the lighted doorway. Blackhawk had the light lined up with his weapon and it was a girl. She tried to make the stairs but couldn't do it and tumbled down. I tried to catch her. She landed at my feet. Blackhawk put the light on her. She had been shot in the head. Her hair was matted with blood. She was gone. I had never seen her before. There was a sound behind us and Blackhawk almost shot Nacho as he came up the stairs behind us.

"Shit, man!" Blackhawk exploded. "I told you to cover our backs."

"I thought you were in trouble," Nacho said.

"Go back and cover us. Me and Jackson got this." Nacho headed back down the stairs.

I laid the girl's body down, her blood slick on my rubber gloves. I wiped what blood I could on my coveralls so my hands wouldn't slip on the shotgun. Blackhawk had the light and his weapon on the doorway and I went up, moving rapidly, flat against the wall. While I covered the door, Blackhawk came up. The room was lit and I went across the doorway to the other side. I could see bodies on the floor. With Blackhawk in place, I squatted low and looked into the room for a target. Someone watching the door would be watching head high. Being low gives you another half second of reaction time. Nothing moved. When I didn't react to anything, Blackhawk peered around the door jamb, then looked at me and shook his head.

"On three," I said in a low voice. "One, two" and we moved simultaneously into the room. There was some kind of hip hop music coming out of a speaker in the back. There was a very large screen TV, a pool table, a foosball table, several couches, and a mini-kitchen with stove, microwave, refrigerator and a long table with metal chairs.

There were three bodies. One of a girl sprawled in front of the couch and two men on the floor by the TV. The girl wasn't Lucinda. The girl had been shot center chest. Both men in the head. One of the men had a handgun lying beside him. The other had a nine in his pants. I looked at their faces. Not Roland. Not the two guys that dumped Lucinda in the lake.

We moved carefully to the three doors that opened up from this room. All the doors were open and all the bedrooms were empty. A hallway led back to a utility room that opened into a back stairs. There was no door and we listened for a long time. There was no sound. We went back into the main room.

Blackhawk looked at me, "Four shots," he said.

"Four shots," I agreed.

"Shooter was good. Four targets not close together. Three head shots and a center chest."

I nodded. The shooter was good.

Blackhawk was looking closely at the head wound of one of the men. He gently lifted his head and looked at the back. He gently returned the man's head to the original position.

"Most likely a .22 caliber. Probably a long. Might have been a target pistol."

"Unusual for a gangbanger."

Blackhawk nodded, "Guy was good."

"Or girl," I said.

He smiled at me, "Or girl."

I stood very quietly and studied the room, letting everything in. Trying to absorb every detail. I had been trained for it and I had a knack for it. Dirty dishes, filled ashtrays, beer cans and pizza cartons tossed in a corner. Smells of cigarettes and dope. Marijuana and crack. A regular playground.

Blackhawk took the walkie-talkie off his belt. "Nacho," he said into it.

There was a crackling sound, then Nacho's tinny voice, "I thought we weren't supposed to talk in these things."

Blackhawk ignored him, "Where are you at?"

"Where you told me," Nacho said.

"Go to the corner and look in the street at that SUV that was parked there. Is it still there?"

There was a moment, then Nacho's voice. "It's gone," he said.

Blackhawk looked at me, "You get the license number?"

"YLT something."

"1410," he finished. "You outta shape?"

"Probably," I said.

That's when I saw it. I walked around the kitchen table and picked up the book of matches from the floor. Pleasant Harbor on the cover.

Blackhawk was watching me. "Still bored, Kemo Sabe?"

Chapter Eighteen

It was after five by the time we had returned to El Patron, dumped my gear and weapons, and I drove the Mustang back to the warehouse. The streets were just coming alive with the early morning shift. It was still pitch black. This time of year it didn't get light until closer to 7. I parked in a conspicuous place in front and made my way to the back. I went up the stairs silently and on edge. Someone might have come back in the thirty minutes I'd been gone.

I passed the dead girl on the stairs and carefully entered the room. Nothing had changed. The room had taken on an old familiar odor of drying blood. I read somewhere that it smelled like freshly sheared copper. How they knew that I wouldn't know. Smelled like drying blood to me and I had smelled a lot of that.

I carefully looked around. Satisfied, I took out my new cell phone and redialed Boyce's number. She answered on the third ring.

"Hello," she said, her voice full of sleep.

"Detective Boyce," I said. "It's Jackson. I'm sorry to call so early."

"That's okay," she said. "I had to get up to answer the fucking phone anyway."

"I'm at the Diablo's warehouse. It's full of dead people."

There was a short silence on the other end, then, "What? Wait, hold on." I could hear a rustling over the phone. "Okay, I'm awake now. What the hell did you just say?"

"The warehouse where the Playboy Diablos hang out. I came looking for Lucinda and what I found was a bunch of dead bodies."

There was a deep silence on the other end, then, "You think this is funny?"

"Not a joke. Two girls and two guys. Each's been shot. Not Lucinda, I just found them."

"Okay, okay," her voice was urgent now. "What you do is nothing. Nothing. Don't move, don't touch anything, don't move anything, just stand still, you hear me?"

"Yes ma'am," I smiled.

"There'll be a black and white there shortly. I'm right behind. Don't touch anything, okay, repeat what I just said!"

"Don't touch anything."

"Right, don't touch anything."

"I got it."

She hung up.

It took less than five minutes. I heard the patrolmen coming up the stairs and could see the light swinging up the stairway. I heard one of them say "Oh shit!" when they saw the girl.

I stood with my hands out from my sides.

They came through the door like they'd been trained.

The one with the flashlight put it on me and they both put their sights on me.

"Freeze, asshole," the one with the light barked. I stood very still. The other came over and began to frisk me. When he finished they looked around.

"Jesus, look at this mess," flashlight said.

The other one unhooked his handcuffs and said, "Turn around with your hands behind you." I complied and he cuffed me.

Flashlight unhooked his radio and moved out on the landing. I could hear him talking, just not what he was saying. Soon I heard others arriving. A crime scene team came in carrying the tools to their trade. They didn't look like they had just been rousted out of bed. If the scene bothered them they didn't show it. They set to work quietly and efficiently. They all wore booties over their shoes and rubber gloves. They didn't have the ski mask or the hazmat coveralls I had worn earlier so I was up on them. One of them, a short, heavy Hispanic woman came over to me and started testing me for gunpowder residue. She asked me to slip out of my shoes so she could test them. My prosthetic confused her. I couldn't unfasten it with my hands behind my back. Finally she leaned down and took a swab of it. She didn't offer to help me take off the other shoe. When I got it off, she picked it up in her gloved hand and swabbed it. A young man with an expensive looking camera started taking pictures from all different angles.

A few moments later, Mendoza came through the door, followed by Detective Boyce. He looked at me and nodded, then slowly made his way around the room taking everything in. Boyce came over to me as the technician finished. She looked at the technician.

"He's clean," the tech said, unceremoniously dropping my shoe on the floor.

"Jackson, what the hell are you doing here?" Detective Boyce asked.

"How about taking the cuffs off?"

She nodded to the uniform and he unlocked the cuffs.

"I thought if I got here early I could..," I started. She held her hand up to stop me.

"Wait, the lieutenant will want to hear this," she said.

"Can I move around now?"

She pointed at the couch. "Go sit there."

I dutifully complied. I took my shoe with me. The couch was vinyl and cracked and worn. I sat and it sank like the part I was sitting on was the side where all the heavy people sat. That wouldn't be any of the dead ones. They were all stick thin and emaciated. Crack does that. I slipped on my shoes and watched with interest as the pros went about their work. Once in a while Mendoza would talk to one of them and they would answer his questions. Detective Boyce mostly watched him, standing to the side. He studied the bodies closely, lifting their heads and studying their faces. He moved their clothing to examine their wounds. Finally, he came to me.

"You are a very concerned citizen, Mr. Jackson."

"Just Jackson," I said. "Concerned about the girl, yes, I am."

"And yet she is nothing to you? No relative, no friend?"

"She's somebody's daughter."

"They all are. Tell me your story."

"I know you sent a black and white here and they found nothing, but our mutual friend Nacho suggested that they always have someone up top. A sentinel. So I decided to pay a visit early. Try to catch them off guard."

"These are punks, Jackson, but they are dangerous punks. They would shoot you as readily as lighting a cigarette."

"I guess I took a chance, huh?"

He looked at me for a long time, then looked at Boyce. She shrugged.

"Tell me what you did and when you did it."

So I told him I had just got there, parked out front, found the back door open and came up to find the girl in the stairway.

"I had Detective Boyce's number in my phone, so I called her."

"Not 911?"

"Gosh, I didn't think of that."

"Gosh?" Boyce said.

I gave her my best Boy Scout smile.

Mendoza looked at Boyce. "Residue test?"

"He's clean," she said.

"Do you know who they are?" I asked.

"Don't know the girl in the stairway, but that one," he said nodding toward the girl's body on the floor, "is Jaunita Rodriquez. Been with them a couple of years. Picked her up a couple times for soliciting, but no one would sign the complaint and she was smart enough not to fall for a sting. The guy over there was the one they called Dog. Name of Ruben something. Ortega, I think. Been in and out of the joint his whole life. The short one there was Pedro Bernal. Called him Petey. He hasn't been out long. The girl on the stairs?" He shrugged. "I don't know. We'll have to see if she's in the system."

"What if she's not? Lucinda wasn't."

"Same thing. Check with Missing Persons. If we don't get a hit we'll go out on the street with a composite, see if anyone recognizes her."

"A composite?"

"A drawing. Sure can't send a photo the way she looks now."

"Who do you think did it?"

He gave me a long cool look, "That's the sixty four thousand dollar question. At first look I would say a pro, but that is so unlikely."

"A pro?"

"You a shooter Jackson? Hunter? Go to the range?"

"I was in the service."

"Looks like the shooter used a small caliber weapon. Unless they discover more bullet holes, it appears the shooter hit where he wanted to hit each time. There are no shell casings. The shooter either picked them up or used a revolver."

"And that makes him, the shooter I mean, a pro?"

He shrugged, "Gang bangers are sloppy. They don't care.

They would have sprayed the room with a semi-automatic assault rifle."

"So you think these kids were targeted?"

"Right now I don't think anything. I know you think they are someone's children, but society didn't lose a lot today and I doubt seriously there will be any parents grieving. This could be anything. Drug deal gone bad. Revenge. Turf war, anything."

Detective Boyce looked at me, "Anything else you got for us?"

I stood, "Not really except—"

"Except what?"

"It's probably nothing, but when I got here and I was parking the Mustang at the front curb, a black SUV like a Chevy Tahoe came around the corner real slow like they had come from the back parking. But they could have just been on the side street. What was funny is how slow they were going, like they weren't in any hurry. It was almost like they were checking me out. Kinda made me nervous."

"I don't suppose you got the license number?"

"Yeah, YLT something, maybe 1410."

Mendoza's eyebrows went up. "You remember the license number on a car passing by at 5 in the morning?"

"I bought my first car when I was fifteen and the letters on my license were YTL," I lied.

"And the 1410?"

"I might be wrong on that."

"You said 'they'?" Boyce said.

"I might be wrong on that too. I don't know if there was

one or more. The windows were tinted and it was dark."

"Chevy Tahoe?"

I shrugged, "Not sure about that either. I'm a Ford guy."

"But you think there was more than one?"

I shook my head, "No, not really. It was just a figure of speech."

"You got any more little tidbits for us?"

"I don't think so."

One of the techs gestured at Mendoza. He nodded, then turned back to me. "Why don't you give your car keys to Officer Maloney here," he said, indicating flashlight. "You can ride with Detective Boyce downtown to make a statement. Officer Maloney will follow with your vehicle."

I handed the keys to Officer Maloney. "Don't let her get away from you. She has a mind of her own," I said, but he was already turning away.

Chapter Nineteen

By the time I got back to the marina it was ten-thirty in the morning. Everything was overly bright and my eyes were grainy and tired. The coffee I'd had at the station had left a fine coating of sludge in my mouth. When Officer Maloney had finally showed up with my keys he was grinning. "Sweet, sweet ride," he had said.

I parked the sweet ride at the top parking lot of the marina and pulling the canvas cover from the trunk, I covered and battened her down. I stopped at Marina Market and picked up a six pack and some eggs and cheese. The usual teenager had been replaced by a rangy old man. Eddie was an eighty year-old fixture around the marina. He lived aboard an old thirty-foot wooden scow that had a small sleeping area and a utility kitchen below decks. He had to use the public restrooms and the restaurant let him use the showers they had in the back for boating customers. Mostly he used a garden hose he attached to the water supply for personal hygiene. He was a very handy guy and made his pocket money fixing whatever was broken for those that needed something fixed. I had used him when I bought the Tiger Lily. We had dry docked her and had spent a long, sweaty summer day scraping off the barnacles. We gave her a new coat of paint. He was old but he was a worker.

Besides odd jobs, I was told he received Social Security and a police pension from the city of Chicago. Every day, rain or shine, he could be found on the water, slaying crappie and bluegill and the very occasional striper, but stripers only when they were hitting so voraciously he couldn't resist. That was it. Those were his species. He was very particular. He had fried me some little bluegill filets once. They were so small, the size of the tip of your little finger. Like popcorn shrimp. They were delicious.

"Hey Eddie," I said, placing my items on the counter. "You so bad off you had to get an honest job?"

"All honest work is honorable, young fella." He rang up my purchases. "Kid called in sick. Kids don't know what real work is. Heard you pulled a girl outa the water. Saved her life."

"That what you heard?"

I gave him some bills and he made my change. "Small town, this marina," he smiled. "When we going out again?"

"Sooner rather than later, my friend."

"Well, watch your topknot."

"Watch your'n," I replied moving out the door. This from our finding out we both enjoyed an old Robert Redford mountain man movie.

Carrying my packages, I went through the security gate and moved down the dock. When I got to the Moneypenny,

I saw the curtains were drawn back about halfway and the sliding glass door was open. I set my packages down and stepped on board.

"Hello, the Moneypenny," I sang out.

I could see into the dimness of the interior, but didn't see Romy.

I came to the door and sang out again, "Romy, it's me, Jackson."

I didn't enter but did move to the threshold of the door. From my left, a man stuck a pistol in my face. "Don't move," he said. Or at least that was what he was going to say. I was born with a whole lot of quick, and hours and hours of close-quarter training took over. This man, like most in this kind of situation, thought he was in charge. Because of this, the last thing he expected was for me to instantly react. Before he could get the words out, I had moved my left hand palm out up to grasp the pistol, bending it back against his fingers. At the same time, my right hand came across and I slammed him in the face with my elbow as I placed my thumb between the hammer and the firing pin. If it had been a hammerless pistol, I would have wrenched his thumb back toward his wrist and broken it. My body slammed against him as he let out a yelp and bounced against the wall. I pulled the pistol from him and now I had it.

"Stop!" Romy cried.

The man was down on one knee, leaning against the wall with his dislocated index finger down between his thighs. He was making a high keening noise.

"Jackson, it's okay, he's a friend."

"Sorry," I said, my adrenaline ramped up a little. "I guess he startled me."

"Startled you? What the hell would you have done if he downright scared you?" she said looking at me, shaking her head.

She came over to the man and helped him up. He was looking at his damaged finger. It was definitely out of the socket.

I tossed the pistol on the couch, noting that it was a 9 mm Taurus.

"Let me help you," I said. "I've had medic training."

"Stay the fuck away from me," he snarled.

"Let him help, Diego," she said, almost like a command.

The man looked at her, then gathering himself, he nodded. I reached out and took his hand. He instinctively tried to pull it back but I held on, looking him in the eye.

"It's okay, I've done this before."

"What are you going to do?" And before he finished the sentence I pulled the finger out and around and snapped it in the socket.

"Jesus Christ," he yelped, jumping back. He stared at his hand, then he slowly closed his fist, then opened it and closed it again.

"Feel better?"

He looked at me, "Yeah, it does."

"What do you think you are doing?" Romy scolded him. "This man is a neighbor, there was no need to pull your damn gun!"

She looked at me. "Diego is an associate of my husband's.

He thinks he has to be my protector." Now Diego was watching her. "Frank sent him to check on me, see if I needed anything. We were just getting ready to head to the store, pick up some things."

"Sorry I interrupted," I said. "If you want to, come by later and have a drink." I looked at Diego, "You too. I have to get some shut eye, I was up all night."

"Sure. Why were you up all night?"

Diego was watching me, his dark eyes impassive. "I was night fishing," I lied, not sure why I was doing it. Just seemed right.

I stepped out onto the bow, then onto the dock. They followed me out. I picked up my things.

"I'll get out of your hair," I said. I looked at Diego, "Sorry about the finger."

Romy said, "See you later."

I nodded and turned and walked down the dock toward the Tiger Lily. I could feel Diego's eyes on me. I glanced over my shoulder; they were going back into the boat. I could still hear them.

"That was stupid," Romy was saying.

Chapter Twenty

Blackhawk, Nacho and I were sitting at the main bar at the El Patron. It was late afternoon and the doors weren't open yet. Nacho had opened three bottles of Dos Equis and we were slowly drinking them. Earlier I had taken a shower and stretched out on the couch and had slept till about two in the afternoon. I had gotten up, taken a swim, showered, got a bite and gone down to the Moneypenny. It was battened up tight, so I headed for the El Patron.

So I took another drink of the beer and it was cold and delicious.

"The colonel says Frank Bavaro is hooked to the Hermanos cartel."

"Those are some bad dudes," Nacho said. "Kill you soon as look at you. Cut your fucking head off."

"And Bavaro is married to the woman on the boat?" Blackhawk asked. "What's her name again?"

"Romy," I said.

"Romy, kind of an odd name."

"Like Blackhawk."

He smiled, "Had to earn mine, son."

"Didn't we all. I met one of Bavaro's boys today."

"Yeah?"

I told them about Diego and his gun.

"What'd he look like?" Nacho asked.

"Hispanic guy. Long dark hair, about my height, wears contact lenses. I'd guess he runs one eighty or thereabouts. Expensive suit and shoes. Probably spent a grand on the suit. Tailored to carry a shoulder rig. Had a Taurus nine."

"Broke his finger?"

"Just dislocated."

"And you just a boat bum," Blackhawk said, setting his bottle on a coaster.

"Yeah, I know. I reacted before I thought."

"And you think Mendoza thinks you are just a guy so dumb as to walk into the Diablo's warehouse all by yourself."

"Had to be a part of it so I can talk with him later about it, or whatever I need to talk to him about if I need to."

"Huh?" Nacho said.

"He wanted to open an avenue to Mendoza," Blackhawk explained. "If somebody else found the bodies, Mendoza would have no reason to talk to him about it." He looked at me, "So what do we do now?"

"Find Roland. He'll take us to the girl."

"You think Roland did those kids at the warehouse?" Nacho asked.

I shrugged, "Don't know. Maybe. But I can't think of any motive, especially as it relates to the girl."

"Yeah, I doesn't make sense," Blackhawk said. "They

were his gang. As long as he had them, he was somebody. And you can bet your ass that if he didn't do them, he's running right now. The question is 'where's the girl?'"

"Probably with Roland, or maybe the shooter took her."

"Why?"

"Yeah, there is that. There's a whole lot that doesn't make sense." I looked at Nacho. "Was that his whole posse?"

Nacho shook his head, "Naw, there are more than that."

"So we find someone that knows Roland and shake them a little and find out where he would run to."

"The girl mentioned someone named Roberto."

"Just Roberto?"

"Yeah. Probably a lot of Robertos out there. Mendoza probably knows who he is."

Suddenly a female voice echoed through the room, "Hello."

We all turned, and Detective Boyce was standing in the double doorway.

"Your lips to God's ears," Blackhawk said.

She walked in and came to the bar and sat next to me.

"Can a girl join this boys' club?"

Nacho slid off his seat, "What can I get you?"

"Ginger ale," she said.

Nacho moved behind the bar to find her a ginger ale.

She was still wearing the same jacket and trousers she had worn that morning. Her jacket hung open exposing the badge on her belt.

"Thought I'd run by and take a look at your joint," she said to Blackhawk. She made a show of looking around. "Nice."

She looked at me, then back to Blackhawk, "Your hero here tell you what he found in the wee hours of the morning?"

Blackhawk smiled his bemused smile, "Yeah, must have been an awful sight."

She reached into her jacket and pulled out a pack of cigarettes.

"Okay if I smoke?"

"I thought it was illegal to smoke in a public building in this town."

She lit a cigarette as Nacho placed a ginger ale and an ashtray in front of her. "Yeah, it is," she said. "Probably ought to call a cop."

She blew smoke out the side of her mouth away from us. "I saw your Mustang out front. We got an ID on the girl we pulled out of the lake."

"Anyone you know?"

"We had her in the system. Rosemarie Medina, one of the Diablo Playboys. Picked up for soliciting and being drunk in public, heavy user. Had tracks up and down her arms, between her toes, behind her ears. Coroner says she was dead of an overdose before she hit the water."

"How long?"

"In the water?"

I nodded.

"Coroner says hard to tell, but more than a week."

"Somebody cleaning house?"

She shrugged. "We don't know that the overdose was related to the shooting. Same gang but that's all we have."

"You know any Robertos that hung at the warehouse with Roland?"

"Roberto? Yeah, that would be Bobby Benitez. Little fucking jitterbug that gets his kicks beating on the girls. Especially the new ones. Why?"

"Lucinda mentioned him. How about that Roland? Any word on him?"

"He's either dead or hiding from whoever did his posse."

"Anything on that?"

".22 cal, four shots, four dead. Had to be a pro, just don't know why. We're pulling in our informants, see if we can get a read on it. I did get a line on that SUV you saw."

"Yeah?"

"Yeah, your Chevy Tahoe was a Cadillac Escalade. Turns out it is registered in Mexico. Belongs to a company called Morales Trucking." She grinned at me. "You sure you're not going to say "gosh" or "golly", or "shucks ma'am that sure was good work?"

I shook my head, smiling, "Shucks ma'am, you going to move on that?"

"Fuckinay," she said taking a deep drag on her cigarette. "Go round up all the motherfuckers at Morales Trucking and drag'm downtown. Charge them with driving on a public street early in the morning. That should clear up a number of warrants."

Nacho snorted and Blackhawk smiled. I had to laugh.

"Who owns Morales Trucking?" Blackhawk asked.

She looked at Nacho, "You wanna take this one?"

"Ain't simple, bro," he said. "They don't keep records

and shit down there like up here. You don't just get on the corporate commission's website, find out who owns what. Even if you got to the clerk that keeps those records down there, you have to go down there and lay some cash on him."

Boyce stubbed out her cigarette and slid off the stool.

"Thanks for the good time, boys," she said.

"You hear anything on Roland will you let me know?"

She looked at me, "Oh hell, yeah. I will consider that my life's calling, keeping the Boy Scouts in the loop. Please, you sit by your phone day and night. I'll be sure to call you before I do any more police business." She made a slight dismissive wave with her hand, "Off to preserve and protect," she said. She turned and walked out.

All three of us watched her rear until she was gone. It's what guys do.

Chapter Twenty-one

The next morning I was on the stern dangling a line straight down with a shrimp on the hook and reading a Robert B. Parker book. The sun had been up a while and I had a steaming cup of coffee next to me. My phone went off. Careful not to damage the spine, I laid the open book down and went inside to find it. It was under a dirty shirt.

"Hello," I said.

"Jackson?"

I don't know why but I recognized the voice. "Father Correa."

He laughed. "You have caller ID?"

"No, I'm afraid I'm not that technologically advanced. I just recognized your voice."

"Well, I'm flattered. Listen, the reason I'm calling is about that girl you were asking me about."

I got that feeling in the pit of my stomach. "Did she come in?"

"No, unfortunately not. But I did get another visitor looking for a girl. He had a picture also, but the name for the girl was different. I think it is the same girl. His picture was of a girl a little bit younger, but it could be an old picture."

"What did you tell him?"

He laughed nervously, "Well, I guess that's the thing. I've been around a while and I have seen all kinds. Sometimes I just get a gut feeling. Something about this guy gave me reservations."

"Like what."

"Nothing to put a finger on, but he didn't seem to be real interested in the girl herself. Like he was hired to find her or something. He was just colder, more detached. Unlike you. I could tell you were truly interested in the girl's best interests. I'm not sure he was."

"What did you do?"

"Took his card, kept the picture and told him I'd be in touch if I saw the girl. I thought you might want to look at the picture."

"I'll be there in an hour."

It was after rush hour. All the minions had made it to their offices on time and traffic was light. I found a spot on the curb about a block and a half from Safehouse. I pulled in and locked the car. I looked around. Up and down the street. There was nothing unusual.

Father Correa was in the community room. He was seated in a wooden rocker with a baby on his lap. It was Hayden. Melinda sat on the floor at his feet, staring up with adoration at the child. The room was active with young women and their babies. Father Correa had that beaming, happy look he always seemed to have. He saw me standing in the doorway and waved. He stood and handed the baby to Melinda. She never took her eyes from the child and I couldn't help but hope that adoration was still there when the boy turned fourteen. Especially if he were raised in the hood.

I followed the good Father back to his office and took his offer of coffee. He didn't offer any condiments, his mind elsewhere. I sipped it black. He opened a desk drawer and pulled an 8 x 10 photo out with a business card attached to it. He handed it to me. I pulled the business card free and looked at the photo.

It was Lucinda.

It was Lucinda a couple of years and ten more pounds ago. She was quite pretty, her hair long and in curls. She wore a school uniform of some kind. She was smiling pleasantly and she looked so innocent it hurt.

"Look on the back," Father Correa said. I turned it over and written in a very neat cursive was the name *Gabriela Vallentina Amado Revera*.

I looked at the card. It was of good quality with raised lettering. Beige with a matte finish. It was very simple. It said *Santiago Escalona*. In the bottom left corner were the words *Attaché,* then below that *Consulate General of Columbia.* It listed an address and suite number on Adams Street and a phone number. It also had an e-mail address.

I stared at the card for a long time, then the photo. It was definitely Lucinda, except it appeared that Lucinda was Gabriela.

"Do you have access to the Internet?" I asked.

Father Correa put a pair of reading glasses on his nose and swung his computer monitor toward him. He hit a few keys, then looked at me. "I'm on."

"Google who the consulate general of Colombia is."

He hit a few keys, then went back and hit a few more, then he looked up at me.

"The consulate general out of Los Angeles is Jairo Soto Armado Revera."

"Revera," I said, studying the picture.

Chapter Twenty-Two

We were at the El Patron. Elena sat between Blackhawk and myself with Nacho behind the bar. She had a laptop computer open in front of her. I could hear a vacuum cleaner through the opened double doors as the hired cleaners were working on the other two bars.

Elena said, "How do you spell it again?"

I looked at Nacho and made a writing motion. He reached under the bar and handed me a pencil. I took a napkin and wrote *Jairo Soto Armado Revera,* then moved the napkin to Elena. She began typing on the keyboard, the tip of her tongue showing at the corner of her mouth as she concentrated.

She looked up at me, "Wikipedia?"

"Sure."

She read through the first part, then began to paraphrase. "Ambassador from Colombia. Graduated from Harvard. Born in 1938. Married, has three children, two boys and a girl. One of the boys and the girl are in Colombia, the other boy, who is a man now," she smiled, "is working for him at the consulate. Between them he has five grandchildren. Doesn't say which child had what or if the grandchildren were boys or girls.

"Let me see," I said and she slid the computer over to me. I read it and didn't find anything else from what she had told me. I slid it back to her.

"See what you can find on a law firm, Phelps, Gutierrez and Tamoso."

She hunched over the keyboard and began typing.

"You want anything to drink?" Nacho asked.

I shook my head.

"Got some donuts," Blackhawk said. "Want one?"

"Be a fool not to."

Nacho reached under and pulled up a box of Krispy Kreams. I took one and munched on it.

"Phoenix law firm," Elena said. "Specializes in international industrial law. Corporate stuff. Has an office on Camelback."

"Does it say who the managing partners are?"

She typed some more. "Seems they have five of them. Edgar Grebe, Roberto Gutierrez, William Phelps, Chase Brophy and Frank Bavaro."

"What's the address on Camelback?"

She rattled it off and I wrote it on the napkin.

"Look this up, Columbian Consulate on Adams in Phoenix."

She typed, then typed some more. She turned the computer screen toward me. I copied the address down and saw the name Santiago Escalona, Attaché.

Blackhawk was watching me.

"What now, oh great white hope?"

I put the napkin in my pocket.

"Let's go see what this guy Escalona knows about the girl."

Chapter Twenty-Three

We had to park the Mustang three blocks away in a public parking garage. We were on the fourth floor before we found a spot. We took the stairs down. Since the shooting at the warehouse I had been carrying a Kahr .45 caliber snuggled in a holster just off my hip. Along with my Wrangler jeans and New Balance running shoes, I had on a black tee shirt and a blue chambray long sleeve shirt unbuttoned in the front and the shirttail out to cover the pistol. I knew Blackhawk had the ankle gun and probably something else, but you couldn't tell it. He was resplendent in a Georgio Armani suit that probably cost as much as my boat and a pale blue silk shirt opened at the throat. As we walked the street I could see the shop girls giving him the sideways glance.

The Consulate office was in a high rise, and after checking the directory in the foyer we took the elevator to the fifth floor. We stepped off into a corridor and immediately to our left were glass doors with the Colombian insignia engraved on them. Behind the doors was an open area with the Colombian flag and expensive looking leather chairs for waiting. This was presided over by a very attractive young dark-haired woman behind a waist-high counter. She wore a white blouse that had reached its limit, a dark skirt and a headset.

I held the door and Blackhawk went through and I followed. The woman looked up and smiled at Blackhawk. When she got to me I could sense an air of disapproval.

"May I help you?" she said brightly to Blackhawk.

He turned and looked at me.

"My name is Jackson," I said. "I'm here to ask for a minute of Mr. Escalona's time."

The disapproval deepened.

"Do you have an appointment?"

"I'm afraid not, but I'm sure he will want to see me."

"I'm afraid Mr. Escalona is tied up and will be for a while. Why don't you call later today and set an appointment?"

I smiled my most beguiling smile, "Why don't you ring up Mr. Escalona on your headset there and ask him if he'll see me."

"Sir, I am so sorry, but I'm afraid...."

"Tell him it is about Gabriela," I interrupted.

She looked startled.

"Gabriela?"

I just kept my most beguiling smile at full wattage.

She glanced at Blackhawk, then back to me. She took off her headset.

"I'll be right back, sir. Please take a seat."

We didn't take a seat, but instead moved back and leaned

against the wall. Blackhawk looked at me, then nodded toward the ceiling. In the corner a very small security camera was mounted. It didn't look like a camera but that's what it was.

One, then two, then three minutes went by and the girl didn't return. The phone began to chirp but no one answered it. Then the girl came back out followed by a rather large man. He was completely bald and his suit didn't fit him. The arms and legs were bulging.

The girl said, "Mr. Escalona will see you now. Please follow Emil."

Emil looked at us without any expression, his eyes dark pools of nothing. He abruptly turned and started down the hallway. He didn't look to see if we were following. His bullet head sloped directly into his shoulders with just a roll of fat where the neck should be. He walked with the rolling gait of a man who worked with weights. A lot.

He led us into a spacious office with a window view of the downtown area. A man that fit the description Father Correa had given me was sitting behind a large ornate wooden desk. The office was finely furnished with plants and original oils. The desk commanded the room, but at one wall there was a smallish leather couch. At the other wall were two chairs, one on each side of a table and lamp. He didn't offer us any of that.

"Who are you?" he said without any pleasantries.

"And so nice to meet you, also. So kind of you to invite us into your splendid office."

"Who are you, and what the fuck do you want?" he said

with that soft slurring accent that Lucinda/Gabriela had.

I looked at Blackhawk. "Gets right to it."

Blackhawk shrugged. He was looking at Emil. Emil was looking back.

"My name is Jackson. This is my colleague Blackhawk. We are looking for a girl and I have reason to believe that you are looking for the same girl."

The man looked at me for a very long time. Then he leaned back and waved a hand at Emil. "Shut the door," he said.

Emil left, pulling the door shut behind him.

Escalona studied me coolly, then looked at Blackhawk.

"What are you doing here?"

Blackhawk nodded at me. "I do his light work."

Escalona almost smiled. "Tough guy?"

"Very," I said. I took Lucinda/Gabriela's photo out of the manila envelope and handed it to him. He studied it for a long moment, then lay it on his desk and leaned back in his chair.

"What makes you think I'm looking for her?"

I took out his business card and held it up.

"You're looking in the same places I am."

He picked the photograph up again. "She's lost weight."

Looking up, he said, "Can I keep this?"

I nodded.

"The official word is that Gabriela has gone back home with her mother."

"The unofficial word?"

He shrugged, "Your phone number?"

"On the back of the picture," I said.

He stood and moved around the desk to the door. He opened it. "If I hear anything I'll be in touch."

We left.

Chapter Twenty-Four

"So the question I have," Blackhawk said, sipping some Wild Turkey bourbon. We sat on the top of Tiger Lily as the sun was setting.

"Is this girl more important since she has turned out to be an ambassador's granddaughter rather than a strung-out street whore?"

I looked at him and smiled.

He laughed.

"Of course not. The gallant knight rides despite the damsel's station."

"From the lowest scullery wench to the princess of the realm. You remember the whorehouse in San Lorenzo?"

"Looked like a church?"

"Yeah. You remember the little whores there. Looked like they weren't thirteen until you looked close."

"I remember. A short people, almost tiny," Blackhawk said.

"Do you remember their eyes?"

He thought a minute.

"Dead," he said. "Dead eyes. All blank and used up."

"Just waiting to be discarded. We did our job and then left them behind. This girl wasn't like that. She was too new at it. She still had a spark inside. I could see it."

"So you want to find her before the spark goes out."

I nodded. "Yeah, that is exactly what I want to do."

The sun was putting on one of its spectacular shows and the bourbon was good when the gate to my pier opened. It was fifty yards away, but we both heard it, and we both turned and looked. Three men came through the gate. Even from the distance I could see it was Santiago Escalona, Emil and an older man. The older man had snow-white hair and a mustache and beard. He looked like Zorro's father. Escalona led the way with Emil taking up the rear. They were all dressed in dark suits, ready for the office, not for the pier.

Escalona and Emil had their jackets unbuttoned. I assumed they both were carrying a firearm. Better to assume they did and not be surprised. Blackhawk stood and moved his chair away from me. No sense in bunching targets.

They came to a halt at my bow, the older man and Escalona looking up at us. Emil was looking out at the water. The sun was bright on their faces and I knew we were silhouetted against the sky.

"Mr. Jackson," Escalona began formally.

"Just Jackson," I said.

"Yes, of course." He indicated the man next to him, "May I present his Excellency, Jairo Soto Amado Revera."

"How do you do," the old man said.

"How's it hanging?" I said. Blackhawk smiled.

The Ambassador gave Escalona a puzzled look and Escalona explained what I had said in low tones we couldn't hear.

The old man chuckled, then smiled up at me, "Yes, yes, very good thank you." He paused a moment, studying me. "Would it be possible to speak with you inside?"

I stood. "Yes, of course." Then I saw what Emil was watching. A boat just off my stern with two men in it. Captain Rand and Eddie. Eddie had a shotgun across his lap.

"How's it going?" Captain Rand called up.

I waved a hand. "Doing fine. Just entertaining some new friends."

"Want us to hang around?"

"I do appreciate it," I said, "but no need."

Eddie waved, and Rand moved the boat around and putted back down the line of boats.

Blackhawk and I went down and I opened the sliding door as Blackhawk moved across the room to lean against the wall beside the bar.

The three men stepped aboard. The boat moved under Emil's weight. I waved them toward the couch and chairs.

"Please, have a seat."

The Ambassador was looking out the port window, watching Captain Rand and Eddie move away. He looked back to me.

"It is good to have cautious friends."

"Yes," I agreed.

Emil stood by the door looking at Blackhawk, who was

looking at him. The Ambassador and Escalona sat on the oversized couch.

"Would you care for something to drink?"

The Ambassador nodded, "In the gesture of friendship I will accept. Do you have cognac?"

"I believe I do," I said. "And for you?" I said to Escalona.

"Nothing for us," Escalona said.

Blackhawk moved behind the bar and looked through the bottles.

"Remy Martin okay?" he asked.

"Yes, completely," the Ambassador said.

Blackhawk looked at me and I nodded. He poured a small amount in two glasses and set them on the bar. I picked them up and handed one to the old man.

"Saludar," he said, raising the glass. I lifted mine in return. The tiniest bit touched his lips and he set the glass aside.

"You are here about the girl," I said.

"Yes," he said. "Right to business." He motioned to Escalona and Escalona pulled my photograph of Gabriela from his inside jacket pocket and handed it to the Ambassador. The old man unfolded it and gazed at it for a moment, then held it for me to see.

"This is my randdaughter, my Gabriela. She means the world to me."

"Where are her parents?" I asked.

He shrugged with a weariness you could feel.

"Family is not always an easy thing, Mr. Jackson. Gabriela is young and headstrong. Gabriela's mother is sensitive and has gone back to Columbia to be with her family. My son is also headstrong. He does not have the age nor the wisdom that I have, and he does not see anything, except the girl will not bend to his will. He forgets that he also was a problem when he was younger." He shook his head ruefully, "He has washed his hands of the girl."

"And you want to find her."

He clasped his hands together and looked down at them for a long time. When he looked up his eyes were moist.

"Mr. Jackson," he started.

"Just Jackson," I said.

"Yes. Jackson then. Jackson, I have had a long life. During the course of my life I have had great success. I have gained much power. I have many young men and women who will do exactly as I ask. I have powerful friends. And I have powerful enemies. Gabriela is my granddaughter and I hold her deep in my heart. She will come through this rebellious period and she will be a true and great person. But this cannot happen if she is lost. I must find her." His eyes turned harsh, "And I must find her before others do. If the others find her first, they will try to force me to do things I will not do."

"I understand," I said. "I know something about you," I continued. "I know you have very powerful friends. I know that some of your friends have a lot of influence on the gangs that are on the streets. I believe your granddaughter is with one of these gangs. Surely your friends can help you find her."

He smiled. "You speak of the Valdez family. Regretfully

my association with them is innuendo and rumor. But if I did have such an alliance I would call upon them in the name of friendship. The same as I am calling upon you."

"What can I do that they can't?"

He shrugged and stood. Escalona stood also.

"You have friends they don't have. Influential friends. But I have told you how much the girl means to me and so I will not leave any stone unturned."

He moved to the door and turned. He held out his hand and I took it. It was warm and firm.

"Jackson, I am willing to pay a very large sum of money to get my granddaughter back. A very large sum."

He stepped out the door and Escalona and Emil followed. On the pier he turned back to me.

"Anything you find, I will be grateful if you contact Mr. Escalona immediately."

He turned and they went back down the pier. At the gate, Emil turned and raised a hand.

I looked at Blackhawk and he was smiling. "A very large sum," he said. "Maybe enough to get a new white horse." He looked at me, "Influential friends?"

"Mendoza," I said. "How did he know about Mendoza?"

Chapter Twenty-Five

I was sound asleep when my name came reverberating through the boat and into my ears.

"Jaaackson."

The green LED alarm clock showed two forty-two. It was almost like I had dreamed it, when again, "Jaaackson".

I swung out of the bed, pulled on swim trunks and attached my utility foot. I made my way forward. I pulled the curtains back, unlocked the door and stepped out on the bow. At first I didn't see her, then it was just the top of her head. I leaned over the railing and Romy sat, her feet dangling in the water.

"You okay?" I said and she giggled, squinting up at me, the faint light glistening off her hair. "Oh boy," I said softly.

"Come on in, the water's fine," she said, slightly slurring her words.

I stepped off the boat and moved to sit beside her. I pulled my foot off and set it on the pier before I put my legs in the water.

Romy reached over and picked up my foot.

"Poor ol' Jackson," she said. "Got no foot." She started laughing. "Can't put it in your mouth if you don't have it." She draped an arm around my neck and leaned against me. "Thas a joke," she said. She looked up at me, "Hey, how 'bout you buy me a drink."

"Let's go inside," I said. "It's chilly out here."

"Good ol' Boy Scout Jackson," she said.

I took the foot from her and attached it. I stood and helped her up. She stumbled against me as she stood, and I put my arm around her waist to steady her. I helped her up the gangway and into the main lounge. She pulled away from me and went behind the bar. She set up two glasses and poured vodka into one of them.

"What you havin', Jackson ol' boy?"

"Don't you think you've already had enough?"

She leaned across the bar glaring at me. "Fuck you, Frank. You don't tell me what to do." She downed the vodka. "All you men think you can tell me what to do. Stand here, stand there, wear this, wear that. Don't you worry your silly little head. Fuck you all. I'm doin' this my way." She splashed more vodka into the glass and tossed it down.

She put her head down, then looked up at me and laughed, "I meant Jackson. Good ol' Jackson. I said Frank and I meant Jackson. Fuckin' Frank. Don't you want a drink?"

"No, thanks," I said.

She came around the bar carrying the empty glass. "I think I want to sh'it down," she said, then she giggled. "Sh'it down, I said. I mean sit down." She giggled again, "Shit down." She shook her head, "Tha's funny."

She went over to the oversized couch and sat. "Good ol' Jackson," she muttered. She slouched back and rested her head on the back. I sat in the chair and watched. After a moment she closed her eyes. A few minutes more and she began to buzz softly and the glass rolled out of her hand. I reached over and picked it up and placed it on the bar. I got a pillow and blanket from the guest room. I gently lifted her legs up on the couch and got the pillow under her head. She mumbled and muttered but didn't wake up. I spread the blanket over her. I locked up, turned off the lights and went to bed.

When I opened my eyes Romy was sitting at the end of the bed. It was light out.

"You got any aspirin?"

"I'll get you some," I said, sliding out of the bed.

When I came out of the head with four aspirin, Romy was in the galley seated at the breakfast nook ,her head in her hands. I set the aspirin in front of her.

"Let me fix you something to wash them down with."

"God," she said rubbing her temples. "I didn't know my head could hurt like this. I still feel numb."

I poured tomato juice in a glass, cracked an egg into it, added tobasco and worcestershire and stirred it all together. I put the glass in front of her. She looked at it dubiously.

"Just drink it down."

"It looks awful."

"It'll help. It's an old Marine recipe."

"Let the old Marine drink it."

I moved the glass closer. "Just drink it."

She took the aspirin and put them in her mouth, then with her eyes clenched shut she drank the concoction. She got most of it down. She set the glass down.

"God that was awful."

"If you keep it down, you'll feel better."

She looked at me. "If I keep it down?"

I smiled. "Just a joke, you'll be okay."

She put her head in her hands. "I don't know if I will ever be okay again." She rubbed her face with her hands. Not looking at me she said, "I woke up on your couch."

"Yes."

"So," she said.

I waited.

"So," she was still not looking at me, "did we…?"

I laughed. "No, I'm sorry to say, things didn't make it that far."

Now she looked at me, "It would've been okay," she said. "But, you know, I would like to remember something like that."

"Maybe another time," I said.

"Yes," she said. "Another time." She paused, then, "Have you found out anything about Lucinda?"

I stood. "Would you like some coffee?"

"Please," she said.

"Do you like it strong?"

"Stronger the better."

I grind the coffee fresh every day and keep it in a container above the coffee pot. I put several scoops in the little basket, poured filtered water in the reservoir and pushed the button.

I sat down. "I went downtown and talked to a Lieutenant Mendoza and a woman detective name of Boyce. They are in the section that is involved with the gangs. They knew the Seventh Avenue Playboy Diablos. They knew where they hang out."

"Is Lucinda there?"

"I decided to look. So I went to the warehouse they hang out in really early in the morning, to catch them unawares."

"Was she there?"

"The only ones there were dead."

"Dead? What do you mean dead?"

"Two guys, two girls, each shot once."

She stared at me, "Shot? You mean, like murdered? Oh my God. Was it Lucinda?"

"I found no sign of her, but she had been there."

"How do you know?"

I reached over and picked up the book of matches I had found at the warehouse. I showed them to Romy. "Recognize these?"

She shook her head, "Matches?"

"Remember I bought Lucinda cigarettes?"

She nodded.

"These are the matches I gave her, on your boat."

"But they were there where the dead people were?"

I nodded, laying the matches on the table.

She was silent, then, "You called the police?"

I nodded again.

"But you didn't tell them about the matches?"

I shook my head.

"Why not?"

I shrugged. "I also went to see a Catholic priest named Correa. He runs a shelter for abused women." I told her about Father Correa and Santiago Escalona.

When I finished she said, "Gabriela. Her name is Gabriela? Why did she tell us her name was Lucinda?"

I shook my head. "Her name is Gabriela Vallentina Amado Revera. And I have no clue as to why she told us what she did except she didn't want to go back to family."

"I can understand that," she said.

"The other thing I learned is that her grandfather is the Consul General from Columbia. He came to see me yesterday."

"Whoa. Hold on," she said. She rubbed her temples. "This is going too fast. Revera? I think I met him once at a reception with Frank. Old guy, white beard. Why did he come see you?"

"I guess he wanted to know what I know."

"Did you mention me?"

I shook my head. "No need."

She looked relieved. "Good." She looked up at me, "I have enough trouble with Frank as it is."

I waited, but she didn't offer more. I wasn't sure I understood how trouble with Frank was connected to Gabriela's grandfather.

"How does Frank know Revera?"

"If you are anybody that is anybody in Columbia, Frank knows you."

We sat silently for a long moment. Finally I asked, "How is your friend's finger?"

"Who?"

"The gentleman I met on your boat."

"Oh, Diego. He's fine, and believe me, he is no gentleman. Frank sends him around to check on me. He thinks he is *the* Latin lover." She brushed the hair from her face, "He always has to make a run at me. He doesn't go too far because he knows if I told Frank, Frank would have him shot or something."

"Shot?"

She smiled, "Well, maybe not shot. But you have no idea what Frank is capable of."

We sat in silence for a moment, then the coffee maker beeped.

"Still want coffee?"

"Can I borrow a cup and take it with me?"

I got up and poured two cups.

"Cream and sugar?"

"Please, two sugars."

I fixed the coffees and set them on the table.

"It's hot," I warned.

She blew across the top of her cup.

"So Frank is a lawyer and he has a tough guy like Diego around to run his errands."

"Frank is a lot of things and lawyer is probably the least of them."

I sipped my coffee. "What else is Frank?"

She shook her head, then ran her fingers through her tousled hair. "Hell, I don't know what he does. He's always in some kind of meeting or flying here or flying there. He won't even talk on the phone if I'm in the room. I know he's on the board of several corporations."

"Like what?"

"The biggest is Kamex."

I shrugged. "Don't know it."

"Mexican construction. Nothing gets built in Mexico unless Kamex has a piece of the pie."

"So that makes Frank very powerful."

"And very rich."

"Why is Frank's wife living on a houseboat instead of in a penthouse?"

She gave me a fierce look, "Because he is a total cold stone bastard."

She stood. "I have to sleep now. God my head hurts." She handed me the coffee cup. "Sorry, I guess I don't want this after all."

"No problem," I said taking it and setting it in the sink.

"I'll get rid of the headache and we'll talk some more," she said.

"Sounds good."

She moved through the boat and out on the deck. With a little wave she was gone.

My phone rang. I went to the master stateroom and found it under a pile of clothes.

"Hello," I said.

"Jackson, its Father Correa. Melinda and Hayden have been taken, and the police can't do anything, and I didn't know who else to call."

Chapter Twenty-Six

"I tell myself that there is only so much I can do."

We were sitting in Father Correa's office. I had fought the rush hour traffic all the way down the Black Canyon and found a parking spot two blocks from Safehouse. He had coffee waiting.

"You can't force her to stay here."

"No, but he can force her to leave."

"Tell me who *he* is."

"Hayden's father. His name is Darryl Maupin. I don't know much about him. Street punk, deals crack, petty theft, works the system for welfare and food stamps."

"They married?"

He shrugged. "Don't know. In the street culture, marriage is just a piece of paper that has no worth."

"So he came and took them?"

"Well, he came and they left with them. She's over eighteen, she can do what she wants. But yes, he took them. The other girls said she was frightened to death."

"Eighteen," I said. "Lord, she looks twelve."

"I know."

"And short of physical force, there was no way for you to stop it?"

"As much as I want to sometimes, I don't beat people up."

"Tell me about Melinda."

"First time I saw her, she came in here, was pregnant and about to pop. She had been beaten badly, one eye swollen closed. Bruises up and down her arms. She was a mess, and she came here because she was desperate and feared for her life, and she wanted to have her baby."

"Did he try to stop her?"

He shook his head, "No, she didn't have the baby then, so he didn't give a damn. According to her he was already with another girl."

"So he wants the baby now."

"And her to care for him. In the welfare system, the baby is valuable. And then there is the macho thing about Hayden being a boy."

"And the police can't help her?"

"It's the rock and a hard place," Father Correa said. "If she puts forth a complaint she eventually gets the snot beat out of her and she runs the risk of Child Protective Services getting involved and taking the baby."

He wasn't looking as jovial as the last time I saw him.

"That's why I called you."

"What do you expect me to do?"

He took off his glasses and started cleaning them, "Care, I guess."

I studied him for a long moment. "I'm just a civilian. Why would this Maupin guy, or anyone else for that matter, listen to me?"

Father Correa leaned forward. "I've spent most of my adult life living with the garbage side of our society. Along the way I've learned many lessons and I've learned to be a pretty good judge of human character. I have a sense that you are just the kind of guy that would get Maupin to listen. That, and I just don't have anywhere else to turn."

"Where can I find her?"

"That I can help with," he said, perching the glasses on his nose and putting the handkerchief in his back pocket. He took a piece of paper off the desk and handed it to me. It had been crumpled. Written in pencil in a childish scrawl was an address. "I found this in her room. I think she left it behind so I would know where she was."

I looked at the paper, "Is this on the west side?"

"Yes, down close to McDowell and 59th Avenue."

"Is this where Maupin lives?"

He shrugged, "It's where somebody lives."

Chapter Twenty-Seven

"You are becoming a genuine royal pain in the ass!"

I was sitting at Detective Boyce's desk in the bustling and noisy squad room. I could see into Mendoza's office, and the light was off, and it was empty.

"I brought donuts," I said, opening the box for her to see. She studied them intently, then selected one with multicolored sprinkles.

"The one and only redeeming value that you have."

She held the donut with both hands and munched on it, looking at me over the top. "What do you want now?" she said with her mouth full. She had a sprinkle on the side of her mouth but didn't seem to notice.

I selected a cake donut with chocolate frosting. "You know Father Correa at Safehouse?"

She just watched me, waiting.

"When I was there looking for Gabriela," I continued.

"I thought you said her name was Lucinda," she interrupted.

"Yeah, I'll get to that, but while I was there Father Correa introduced me to a young girl and her baby son. Today the asshole father of the baby came and took Melinda out of Safehouse against her will and Father Correa fears for her safety.

"You sure her name is Melinda, not Wynona or Buffy?"

I laughed, "No, I'm not sure. She was introduced to me by Father Correa as Melinda."

Boyce selected another donut. "What the fuck are you, Jackson? The patron saint of lost little girls?"

"I don't know why he called me, but he did."

"How old is the girl?"

"Over eighteen."

She sucked the icing off of her thumb, "Eighteen? She's an adult."

"Maybe, but her baby isn't."

"Is the baby in danger?"

"I don't know."

"That's a Child Protective Services problem. What do you want me to do?"

"I was hoping that you and your big badge might scare this asshole into leaving Melinda alone."

She finished the second donut, and I watched her try to make up her mind about a third. She finally leaned back in her swivel chair. "And I get a harassment suit."

"There are no witnesses."

She cocked her head. "How do I do that?"

I smiled. "I do it."

Her eyes looked amused, but she didn't smile. "I'll say this, Jackson, you are damn sure of yourself."

"This punk is using her and the baby for government handouts. I think if he is pushed he'll figure the girl isn't worth the hassle."

She brushed the crumbs from her hands and wiped her mouth with the back of her hand.

"So you want me to drop all my extensive crime fighting duties to go with you and harass a civilian to get him to stop abusing a girl that you have no proof is being abused?"

"Yeah, that's about it."

She stood and took her jacket from the back of her chair. "Well, let's get going then."

She had me go out the front and wait on the steps of the public building while she checked a car out of the motor pool. I waited about ten minutes before she pulled to the curb. I grabbed the passenger door handle but it was locked and she had to hit the automatic lock switch. I slid in, and she slid away from the curb.

"You know where we are going?" she asked.

I pulled the crumpled paper from my pocket and read her the address.

"Brown town," she said. She maneuvered the Crown Vic expertly through the traffic, judging the lights and the other drivers.

"That a racist remark?"

"Probably." She turned her head slightly to look at me. "So what's going on with the other girl you are looking for? You *are* still looking?"

"Still looking," I said. So for the second time this day, I told the story of Father Correa, Santiago Escalona, Lucinda aka Gabriela Vallentina Amado Revera and the Consul General of Columbia.

"Jesus Christ!" she exclaimed when I finished. "What the hell have you got yourself mixed up in?" She was silent a moment. "Christ, I'm going to have to tell Mendoza about this." She looked across at me again. "Mendoza is going to shit a brick. You know he'll have to bring the Feds in on this. This Revera guy is a diplomat. This is international bullshit. What the hell do you think you are doing?"

"Trying to find a girl," I said.

"Jesus," she said under her breath.

She drove in silence for quite a while, then she said, "So this Melinda. I suppose she's the Crown Princess of Taipei or something."

I laughed, "I don't know. The way it's going she could be."

"You're funny as a crutch." She caught the freeway at 7th Street and headed west. We drove in silence as she maneuvered through the westbound traffic. We turned on the 59th Avenue off ramp and turned north. A few minutes later we were at McDowell.

Sometime in the last century, a guy that owned vast acres of empty land on the west side of Phoenix began building little 1200 square foot concrete block rectangles with a carport and sometimes a block archway to make it look less of a rectangular box. He sold them with creative financing for lower class families. He sold thousands of them. The address was one of these.

Boyce pulled the unmarked car to the curb, boxing in a

twenty year old brown and white Ford truck that was in the driveway. The truck was parked behind a rusted old Hyundai that was in the carport. The trash and cobwebs built up around the flat tires of the Hyundai attested to how long it had been sitting there.

Boyce slid out of the driver's seat and I watched as she adjusted her jacket, touching her weapon on her belt and then touching her badge. She didn't seem to be conscious of doing either. I followed her to the door. She rang the doorbell without hesitating. Without waiting, she rang it again. A moment later the door opened.

"Can I help you?" Melinda said. She had Hayden on her hip. She squinted out into the bright light.

"Are you Melinda?"

Melinda shielded her eyes with her free hand.

"I'm Melinda," she said hesitantly.

Boyce pulled her jacket back to show the badge on her belt.

"May we come in?" She didn't wait but moved forward, forcing Melinda to step back. I followed her in. It was gloomy dark inside and it took my eyes a second to adjust. The place was cluttered with boxes, dirty clothes and tabloid magazines. The television against the wall was on, tuned to a daytime talk show. The place smelled stale and sour: a combination of cigarette and marijuana smoke, spilled beer and dirty diapers. The garbage hadn't been taken out in a while.

"The place is a mess," Melinda said.

She started to pick up the clothes on the tattered couch

when a tall, young white man with cropped hair and two arms filled with tattoos filled the doorway to the kitchen. He had that weightlifter look, with bunched muscles under his sleeveless tee shirt. His neck was thick and his thighs were like tree trunks.

"Don't be picking that shit up. They ain't gonna be here long enough to sit down."

Melinda dropped the dirty clothes like they had burned her.

"What the fuck do you want?" the man demanded.

"I am here to talk with Melinda," Boyce said.

"She don't want to talk to you." He turned to Melinda, "You want to talk to her?"

Boyce leaned forward, her eyes bright and intent, "Shut the fuck up. I'm here to talk to Melinda, not to you."

"Who the fuck are you? You think you can come in a man's house and start telling him what to do just 'cause you have a badge."

Boyce pulled handcuffs from the back of her belt and held them up for him to see. "You shut up or these are on your wrists and you are downtown charged with obstruction."

The man said, "You got no right to pull that shit," but he was beginning to deflate.

"Go back to what you were doing and shut the fuck up," Boyce said. She turned to Melinda, "This man been harming you? He beat you? Treat you rough?"

Melinda was looking at the floor, the baby was beginning to fuss and she gently bounced him on her hip.

"I've been told," Boyce continued, "you don't want to be here."

Melinda continued to stare at the floor.

"Look at me!" Boyce demanded.

Melinda reluctantly raised her eyes.

"I'm here to see if you want to go back to Safehouse. If this man is holding you here against your will I will put him in jail. If you go back to Father Correa's and this man continues to harass you or threaten you in any way I will put him in jail." Boyce looked at the man. "I *will* do these things, and I can start right now."

The man was staring at Melinda. Melinda was looking at the floor again.

"What are you waiting for?" the man said. "Tell her you are just fine. Tell her to get the hell out of my house. Tell her!"

Melinda smoothed the fussing baby's hair. "I'm fine," she said.

"I'm here to help you," Boyce said.

"I'm fine," she said again, this time a little louder.

"Now get the fuck out," the man said triumphantly.

Boyce looked at me and shrugged. She turned to Melinda, "This man mistreats you or the baby, you call 911 and they will notify me, and I will come and take this man out of your life, you understand?" Melinda wouldn't look at her. "You understand me, Melinda?"

Melinda nodded.

Boyce looked at me, then turned and went out the door. I stood a moment.

"Don't I know you?" Melinda said, looking at me.

"Who the fuck is he?" the man asked.

I looked at him. "Darryl Maupin," I said.

"You know me? Who the fuck are you?"

I stepped toward him, "You muss a hair on this girl's head and I'm your worst nightmare."

He made a dismissive gesture, "Get the fuck out."

I stood a moment longer looking at him, then I turned and went out. He didn't seem very intimidated.

Chapter Twenty-Eight

Once we returned to the police station, Boyce had me come back up to her desk. Mendoza was in his office and she pointed at a chair next to her desk for me and went in. I sat down. I watched her talking to Mendoza and knew what she was telling him, but his expression didn't change. Once he looked out and met my eyes, then looked back to Boyce. When she finished he said something and she turned and beckoned to me.

I went in and he waved at a chair. Boyce remained standing, leaning against the wall.

Mendoza lifted a pair of reading glasses from his desk and began to polish them with a tissue. He studied me for a long moment.

"Detective Boyce has told me about the girl, but I want to hear it from you."

"Which girl?"

Mendoza looked at Boyce. "How many girls are there?"

"Father Correa called him to help another girl with a problem," she explained. She looked at me. "Tell him about Lucinda aka Gabriela."

"Father Correa?" Mendoza said. "He called you? He called you, who the hell are you?"

"He thinks he is the patron saint of little lost girls," Boyce said.

Mendoza looked from me to Boyce then back to me then back to Boyce.

"Are we done playing games here?" he said, looking back to me.

"Yes, sir," I said. "The girl I pulled out of the lake told me her name was Lucinda. You remember the pictures I had taken of her?"

Mendoza nodded.

"I found out about Father Correa and his shelter for street girls, so I showed him the picture. He didn't recognize her so I thought it was a dead end. Then he calls me to say an attaché of the Colombian Consul came to see him looking for a missing girl. He showed him pictures of the granddaughter of the Consul General and it was the same girl. It was Lucinda, but her name really is Gabriela Revera. Gabriela Vallentina Amado Revera to be exact."

Mendoza leaned back in the chair, "So the girl you saved, the girl that is hanging out with the Playboy Diablos, the same Diablos of which four of them have been recently murdered, and this same girl is, you believe, back with Roland Gomez, a crackhead gangbanger, this same girl is the granddaughter of the Consul General of Colombia?"

"Yes sir."

He shook his head and started cleaning his glasses again. "Jesus."

"And he came to see me."

He stopped rubbing the glasses, "Came to see you?"

"Yes sir."

"The Consul General of Columbia came to see you?"

"Yes sir."

He set his glasses down on the desk top, "Well this is just better and better. Please expound upon this."

I shrugged, "He told me that his attaché had told him I was looking for the girl. I suggested that with his resources he would have a better chance to find her than I did. He suggested that he would leave no stone unturned. I was one of the stones."

"Or what was under it," Boyce said.

Mendoza swiveled in his chair and stared out the window. We sat in silence for a long time. He drummed his fingers on the arm of his chair as he thought. Finally he swiveled around.

"The attaché? Who was he?"

"His name is Santiago Escalona. He is in the Colombian office on Adams Street."

He looked at Boyce, "And we have no Missing Person filed on this girl?"

She straightened up. "I just got here, just found this out. Didn't have one under the Lucinda name.

I haven't checked the Gabriela name yet."

Mendoza cocked his head, "Well, why don't you do that."

"Yes sir," she said moving out the door.

Mendoza turned his gaze to me. "You have anything else to tell me??

"You find Roland yet?"

He shook his head, "Not yet. He'll show up. You can take the crack away from the crackhead, but you can't take the crackhead away from the crack."

"Meaning he'll have to feed the habit, so he'll have to find a supply."

"Or go back to the warehouse. I don't have enough resources to watch everyone out there selling crack, but we've got a sheet out on him and the girl. They'll show up."

"I don't think Boyce will find a missing person on Gabriela."

"Do tell?"

"There would be diplomatic consequences if it was known the granddaughter of the Consul General had run away to hang with crackheads and gangbangers. Also, why would Ambassador Revera personally come out to the marina to see me if he had the entire Phoenix police department looking for the girl?"

"That's a good question. What's the other one?"

"The other one?" He just looked at me. I thought a moment. "The other one is, if he or the girl's parents didn't file a Missing Person, why didn't they? This is no ordinary girl."

He smiled and nodded, "Very good. Not just another pretty face." He stood. "Why don't you go sit at Boyce's desk? I need to talk to some people. Sorry, the coffee's cold."

I did as I was told. He followed me out of his office and left the floor.

I settled my mind and waited. After a while I began to name the other detectives in the room. First was Curly, Larry and Moe. Then there was Dino, Barney and Fred. After a long while, after I had gone through Gilligan's Island, Scooby Doo and Seinfeld, Boyce came back and went into Mendoza's office and made a phone call. She came back out, came over to me and said, "Hang on, we have people that want to talk to you."

"Feds?"

She shrugged, turned and walked back out.

It was almost an hour before Mendoza came back. The room had almost cleared out, leaving Fred and Kramer. Mendoza was accompanied by Boyce, a thick man in shirtsleeves and two young crew-cuts in suits whom I named Tweedledee and Tweedledum. He beckoned me into his office. Boyce rounded up chairs for everyone. I was the last one in and Boyce shut the door behind me. Mendoza gestured toward a chair and I sat. Boyce resumed her position, leaning against the wall, the men sat.

Mendoza gestured to the man in shirtsleeves, "This is Commander Davis, our watch

commander." Indicating the other two, "This is Agent Cummings and Agent Pistorius of the FBI."

I nodded. Tweedledee was Cummings, Tweedledum was Pistorius.

"You were right," Mendoza continued, "There is no missing persons on the Ambassador's granddaughter. Commander Davis thought it best to bring the FBI in because of who the girl is."

"Lieutenant Mendoza has told me your story but I'd like to hear it from you," Davis said.

So once again I related pulling the girl from the lake, telling it up to her grandfather visiting the houseboat. Once again I omitted the reward. Didn't see any reason to talk about it.

"I understand you've lost a foot," Agent Cummings said.

I nodded.

"Lose it in the service, Iraq, Afghanistan?"

"Industrial accident," I said. "Got it caught in an auger."

"Sorry to hear that," he said. "The Lieutenant says you said you had been in the service."

There wasn't anything to say to that, so I didn't say anything.

"You own a houseboat out on Lake Pleasant."

I didn't hear a question so I didn't say anything.

"I want you to understand that you are in no trouble," Cummings said, "but what is funny is that I had you run through every databank available, and until you bought the houseboat you didn't exist. Where were you born?"

"In a hospital right next to my mother." I looked at Mendoza. "We done?"

He looked at Davis and Davis nodded.

I stood and Boyce opened the door.

"Stay where we can find you," Pistorius said.

"Am I under arrest?"

"Of course not," Mendoza said.

"Then I'll be where the hell I want to be."

Chapter Twenty-Nine

"Do you still get the headaches?" Blackhawk asked.

We were in Blackhawk's office. I was lying on his couch with an arm across my eyes.

"Not as much," I said.

"What you need is a woman," Elena said. She was across the room on a straight back chair with one foot hiked up on the seat of the chair opposite. She was applying a very bright shade of red to her toenails.

"You available?"

She snorted. "Am I available?"

She looked at Blackhawk, "Am I available?"

"Free as a breeze."

"There you are. When do you want to get married?"

I laughed, sitting up. "Now that's a whirlwind romance."

"I can't get this lug to marry me," she said switching feet, "might as well be you."

Blackhawk stood, "All right. Let's go get married."

She looked up, startled. "What?"

"You want to get married, let's go get married."

"When? Right now?"

"When better. Yeah, right now. We'll go downtown and get married."

"Well, uh, what about my family? I can't get married without my mother and my sisters. I don't even have a dress."

Blackhawk laughed. He looked at me as if to say- See! He laughed harder.

"You bastard," she spit at him. "You make fun of me!" She turned back to her toes. "Now I don't marry you at all."

"What about your friend Anita?" Blackhawk asked, sitting down.

She looked at him. "You want to marry Anita?"

He laughed again. "No, for Jackson. Fix him up with Anita."

"Hey, hey, don't do me any favors. I like my life the way it is."

Elena was looking at me with that light in her eyes.

"Yes, Anita. Anita would be perfect for you, Jackson. I will bring her over to introduce to you."

"No, don't do that," I groaned. "Please, I beg of you."

"You would love her," she continued as if I hadn't said a thing. "She is very sweet. Very kind. Everyone says she has a great personality and beautiful eyes."

"And fat," Blackhawk said.

"You shut up," Elena said. "She is not fat. Maybe just a little plump, but cute. Not some skinny, bony Anglo girl."

"Lots to love," Blackhawk grinned at me.

"Where's Nacho?" I asked, to change the subject.

"You are a coward like your friend here," Elena said, stretching a foot out and admiring her toes. "Anita deserves better."

"His day off," Blackhawk said, ignoring her.

I stretched my legs out, then I took the prosthetic off and began to rub my stump.

"Does that hurt?" Elena asked watching me.

"Mystery pains," I said.

"What's that?" she asked.

"Sometimes I feel like my toes are cramping."

"You don't have toes," she said.

Blackhawk shook his head, lowering his head to hide his smile

She was looking at me very sincerely.

"I know," I said. "But sometimes it feels like I do. That's why I call it a mystery pain."

She studied me a while, then said to Blackhawk, "Sometimes I think your friend is a little weird."

"You don't know the half of it," Blackhawk said.

"What does Nacho do on his days off?" I asked.

"I never thought of that," Elena said. "What does he do, go to chicken fights?"

"I thought he was more of a ballet or Museum of Modern Art kind of guy," I said.

"Yeah, the ballet," Blackhawk said. "That's why he keeps a tutu behind the bar. In case he has a sudden overwhelming urge to whip out an allegro."

"Or an arabesque."

"You two are so full of shit," Elena said, stretching her

other foot out for inspection.

Blackhawk looked at me. "I think he just chills out. Watches Telemundo and drinks beer."

"That ain't all bad," I said.

"You watch Telemundo?" he asked.

"You know I don't have a TV."

Elena looked at me, shocked, "You don't have a television?"

I shook my head.

She looked at Blackhawk, "He doesn't have a television?"

Blackhawk shrugged.

She looked back at me in amazement, "Man, you are weird. Everybody has a television."

"Not me," I said.

She cocked her head, her eyes narrowing, "You funning me?"

"I've been on his boat," Blackhawk said. "He doesn't have one."

"You must be rich, live on a boat," she said, not able to stay with the television discussion.

I laughed. "Just the opposite," I said. "I live on a boat because I can't afford a house."

"Weird," she said, shaking her head, going back to her toes.

The door opened and Nacho came in.

"Hey Nacho," I said. "What do you do on your day off?"

"Hey, guess what?" he said.

"What?" Blackhawk asked.

"I think I found that fucker."

"Which fucker?"

"That Roland fucker!"

Chapter Thirty

"So, where is he?"

Nacho moved across the room and poured himself a drink from the bar. He drank it down and poured another.

"You shouldn't drink so early," Elena said, still admiring both feet stretched out in front of her.

Holding the glass, Nacho pointed at her with his index finger. "That's the reason I'm not married," he said.

Not even looking at him, Elena said, "You're not married because you are so ugly."

"Don't start that married stuff again," Blackhawk said. "So where is he?"

"You remember Benny Yoon?" Nacho asked.

Blackhawk nodded.

"Did time with Benny Yoon," Nacho said to me. "He didn't learn the lesson. He's still out there using and abusing, so I went looking and sure enough found him down at that Margaret Hance Park, off of Central. I came walking up and that little band of stringers he had all got up and took off. He recognized me so he knew better than to take off. I asked him about Roland, showed him the picture but he didn't have to look at it. He knew Roland. At first he said he hadn't seen him so I asked him with a little more -." He looked at Blackhawk.

"Emphasis," Blackhawk said.

"Yeah, emphasis. That helped him to remember."

"What did he remember?" Blackhawk asked.

"He remembered that the same dude Benny got his stuff from was tight with Roland."

"A Playboy Diablo?"

He shrugged, "He didn't know. Thought so but wasn't sure."

"What's the dude's name?" I asked.

"Benny says Henry Cisneros."

"Does he hang at the warehouse?"

Nacho shook his head, "I went by there this morning. Still got police tape up. I sat down the street for an hour and a black and white went by twice, so ain't nobody using the warehouse."

"You know where we find Cisneros?"

Nacho finished his drink, "No, but Benny Yoon knows where he is. Says he doesn't, but I know he does."

"So we encourage Mr. Yoon to divulge that information," I said,

"We do," Blackhawk said, standing.

Chapter Thirty-One

The three of us crowded into Nacho's car again. This time I had more than the knife. I had the Kahr .45 in a hip holster and the .380 Ruger LCP in my back pocket. Both had the nasty little rounds in them that are sold under the description of *home protection.* Soft hollow point rounds that exploded into flesh and thoroughly wreck everything in its path.

Nacho drove us across Baseline to Central, then north. We parked behind the Irish Cultural Center on Central and walked down into the park. It was ripe with the scent of newly mown grass. A ribbon of sidewalk disappeared into the distance. It was alive with joggers and the urban dwellers walking their little yipper dogs. Little inbred balls of fluffy fur with high-pitched yips that would drive the Dalai Lama to murder. Psychotic dogs inbred at puppy farms and sold with large price tags.

As we passed one spandex-clad older woman with her little ball of white fluff, Nacho asked, "Know what we call those dogs back in Sonora?"

"What?" I bit.

"Bait," he grinned.

I laughed.

"Know why old women joggers wear skin-tight spandex?" he asked.

"No, why?"

"Keeps their Depends in place!" He laughed out loud.

I just shook my head.

"You're hilarious," Blackhawk said.

"You know what..," then he stopped, staring down the pathway. "He's not here," he said. He looked all around.

"You expected him to be?" Blackhawk asked.

"Yeah, I did. Guy like him doesn't have wheels. Sleeps in a crack house. Goes to a shelter every couple weeks to clean up, get a meal. He's somewhere close."

"Any shelters around here?" I asked.

He shook his head. He stood with his hands on his hips.

"There," he said nodding toward a clump of decorative bushes with a brick wall around them. A man sat on the wall.

"That Yoon?" I asked.

Blackhawk shook his head, "Not Yoon."

"It's one of the shitbags that was hanging with him earlier," Nacho said.

"He know where Yoon is?" I asked.

"Yeah, probably," Nacho said, moving toward the man.

The guy looked half-asleep in the sun when we walked up on him. He started when he became aware of us.

"Hey," he said. "You got a cigarette?"

Nacho shook his head, "Don't smoke. Where did Yoon go?"

The guy tried to look dumb, which wasn't a reach. "Who?"

Blackhawk reached over and grabbed a handful of his long stringy hair and jerked the guy to his feet. He gave him a shove and the guy went back, tripping over the brick wall and falling into the bushes.

"Hey!" he yelled. He didn't try to get up. "You didn't have to do that." His voice had the whine of someone used to being shoved around.

"Answer his question," Blackhawk said softly.

The guy stared at Blackhawk, then said, "He's up on his corner."

"What's his corner?" Blackhawk asked.

The guy waved a hand toward the south, "He works the light rail stop."

Blackhawk turned and looked at me, then started back toward where we had parked. Nacho and I followed.

"Hey, you got any spare change?" the guy called after us.

When we got to Central, Blackhawk and I crossed the street. Nacho stayed on the west side. We could see people standing at the light rail stop. Blackhawk spotted Yoon from a block away.

"That's him," he said, nodding toward a raggedy looking man with a long coat and a knit cap. He was on Nacho's side of the street. Yoon was working the cars stopped at the light. Then when the light rail stopped and the passengers stepped off, he worked them. He was carrying a tin can to collect the money and a cardboard sign. Most of the people shouldered right past him but there was always some sucker to stop and put money in his can, usually a young woman. As we got closer I could read the sign. The childish scrawl across it declared him to be a homeless Vietnam veteran. He looked like shit, but even so he didn't look nearly old enough to have been in Vietnam, unless he had done his tour as a five year old.

Yoon spotted Nacho about ten steps before Nacho reached the corner. He turned and bolted across the intersection with honking cars in his wake. He ran right into our arms.

"Hey Benny, long time no see," Blackhawk said.

"Shit!" Yoon said.

The crowd discharging from the light rail streamed around us. No one made eye contact. In the downtown big city no one gets involved.

We walked him down a side street without resistance. Blackhawk had a hand on the back of his neck like they were old buddies. There was a closed club that had outdoor seating. The chairs were stacked up against the wall. I pulled three out and Blackhawk shoved Yoon onto the one in the middle. Nacho had headed back to get his Jeep Cherokee.

Yoon pulled a pack of cigarettes out of his jacket. He shook one out, his hand shaking. He offered it to Blackhawk, then to me. We both shook our heads.

He put it between his lips and lit it. His hands shook so badly he could hardly strike the match.

"Hey, Blackhawk," he said. "How's it hangin'? Ain't seen you in a coon's age. So you still got that nightclub?" He was nervously rattling. He had a line of spittle running from a tooth to his lip. I couldn't look at him. "Nice place. Always did like that place though it was a Mex place. What's the name? I forgot the name."

"El Patron," Blackhawk said.

"Yeah, Patron," he said, dragging on the cigarette like it would be his last. "Like the tequila. Always liked that place. I lived closer, I'd be in there regular."

"You come in there," Blackhawk said, "I'll have Nacho break your leg."

"Hey, that ain't no way to be."

"Shut up," I said. He looked at me, was about to say something, then decided to shut up.

We sat silently until Nacho pulled to the curb. Each of us took an arm and moved Yoon to the car. Blackhawk opened the back door. Nacho said, "Get rid of the fag. You'll stink up my car bad enough without it."

Yoon flipped the cigarette and Blackhawk moved him into the back seat and came in behind him. I got in the front passenger and Nacho pulled away from the curb.

"Where we going?" Yoon asked.

"We're going to see Henry Cisneros."

Yoon's eyes widened. "Shit, man. What you gonna do that for?"

I took Roland's picture out of my pocket.

"You know this guy?"

He barely glanced at the photo. I pulled the Kahr from the holster and rapped him across his nose.

"Goddamn man! What you do that for?"

I shook the photo. This time he looked at it.

"Yeah, like I told Nacho, I seen him around. I don't hang with him or nothin'. He's hooked up man, outa my league."

"What's his name?"

"Roland something. Guy's hooked up with some serious bangers. MS-13 and shit."

"Where we going?" Nacho asked.

"Where we going?" I said, lifting the Kahr.

"Whoa dog, ain't no reason for violence," he said pronouncing it *vi-o-lence*.

"Where we going?"

"Chill now," he said, lifting a hand to ward me off. "He usually down off Encanto, down in the hood below the Shamrock Farms factory. They gotta house down there. Diablo's and shit. That's where I gotta go to get shit when I can't find it down at the park."

"What street?"

"31st Ave, but man, you gotta dump me before you get there. He see me and he'll fuck me up." He looked at Blackhawk. "Hey Blackhawk, you and me go back a long way. You gotta keep me out of it. That motherfucker will fuck me up, man."

"Shut up," Blackhawk said.

"He'll fuck me up, man."

"Shut up," Blackhawk said more softly.

Yoon's jaw clamped shut and he hunched back into the corner, his eyes flitting all over the place.

After a while Nacho made a couple of turns and the Shamrock factory loomed on my left.

"Where now?" Nacho asked.

"Go on down past Encanto," Yoon said. Now he scrunched down in the seat, so only the top of his head was above the bottom of the window.

"Take us past it," Blackhawk said.

Yoon peeked up, "Go two blocks and turn right."

Nacho drove two more blocks and turned right. All the houses past Encanto were little block houses with carports. About every fourth one was clean and neat, but the rest had rusted cars in the knee-high weeds with old sofas and ratty chairs on the front stoop as lawn furniture. A half a block ahead there was one of the more junky ones with a half dozen young Hispanic men sitting around the front porch.

"That's them," Yoon groaned.

"Which is Cisneros?" Blackhawk asked.

"He's the big dude on the couch in the checkered shirt, oh shit." He slid down to the floorboard.

"Go on by normal speed," I said to Nacho.

Blackhawk slumped down and I turned my head, not looking at them.

As we went by Nacho said, "Man, they're giving us the skank eye."

"Go on a couple blocks, then turn back toward Encanto," I said.

He drove two blocks, then turned.

"Go a couple more blocks, then pull over," I said.

"You think he saw me?" Yoon asked.

"Your nose was buried in the floorboard, he might have seen your ass," Blackhawk said.

Nacho pulled to the curb at an empty lot. Blackhawk

looked at me and I nodded. He shrugged, then opened the door and stepped out.

"Come on," he said.

Yoon hesitated, looking out the back window.

"Get the fuck out of my car," Nacho said.

"Here?"

Blackhawk leaned down to look at him, "Now."

Yoon scrambled out, "Hey, can't you at least drop me at a bus stop?"

Blackhawk slid back into the backseat and Nacho pulled away. I watched Yoon watch us until we were a couple blocks away, then he pulled out a cell phone and made a call.

"He's ratting us out," I said.

"Yeah," Blackhawk said. "Too bad it isn't Mogadishu."

"What's Mogadishu?" Nacho said.

"That's where you could put two in the back of the head of a rat and dump them behind a dumpster," Blackhawk said, watching Yoon grow smaller out the back window.

Chapter Thirty-Two

I had Nacho circle back. From a block away we could see the porch was empty.

"Check the alley," Blackhawk said.

Nacho twisted the wheel and we shot down the side street. He slowed at the alley, but it was empty both ways. Nacho sped up, then turned right on the next street. At the next intersection, Blackhawk said, "There."

Cisneros in his plaid shirt and two others were nonchalantly moving down the street.

"Give him space," I said. Nacho sped up. "Go three blocks, then circle back to be in front."

"Cisneros know you?" I asked Blackhawk.

"Don't know why he would."

"He knows you," Nacho said. "Everybody knows Blackhawk."

I leaned down and unfastened my foot. "You still got that ball bat I saw in the back?"

"Yeah, under the blanket," Nacho answered. "I always have it there."

"Never know when a baseball game will break out," Blackhawk grinned.

"Get ahead of them, then drop me around the corner so they don't see your car. After you drop me, back up so they can't see you from the corner."

He sped down the street until I said, "Should be far enough. Let me out here."

He pulled to the curb and I swung the door open and hopped out. Holding the roof I hopped around to the back and opened the deck lid. I got the bat out and shut the lid.

"Okay," I said moving out of the way. Nacho backed the car up. Using the bat like a cane, I hobbled onto the sidewalk and toward the corner. At the corner, I could see Cisneros and his two buddies still a half block away. Cisneros was on his phone. The other two were laughing. I hobbled on a few feet and they hesitated when they saw me. I sat on the curb and lifted my stub and pretended to adjust the sock I had covering it, giving them a good look at the gimp. Then I struggled to my feet, and again using the bat as a cane, started slowly hobbling toward them. They were moving toward me again and I slowed, wanting them to reach me while I was still close to the corner.

They came sauntering up to me and Cisneros said "Hey bro, what did you do to your foot?"

I hit him in the crotch with the ball bat. He screamed and went to his knees, hands on his crotch. I pulled the Kahr and pointed it in the general direction of the other two. They were too shocked to react. Then Nacho pulled to the curb and Blackhawk was out of the backseat, a pistol in his hand.

The two took a step back, holding their hands out as if to fend off the trouble.

Nacho came around from the driver's side and shook them down, taking the automatics they had tucked in the back of their belts. He tossed the guns onto the floorboard of the front passenger seat.

Blackhawk looked down at the groaning Cisneros. "You've been kicked in the balls before. You know the pain will pass."

I pulled Roland's picture from my pocket and showed it to Cisneros's friends. "You know this guy?"

Both of them shook their heads.

"We find out you're lying we'll be back," Blackhawk said.

The taller of the two shook his head, "I ain't never seen that dude."

"Me neither," said the other one.

Blackhawk looked at them for a long moment.

"Get out of here," he said.

It was hard to retreat with dignity and they tried at first, but after a few feet, the shorter one took off running and the taller one hesitated, then followed.

Cisneros was taking long deep breaths.

"See, it's getting better," Blackhawk said to him.

I sat on the passenger seat and refastened my foot. Blackhawk and Nacho helped Cisneros up and got him into the back seat. I turned in the seat and put the Kahr on Cisneros. Blackhawk remained outside the car.

After a while I said, "You better now? You can talk?"

Cisneros was gathering some of his old self. "Fuck you," he said.

Blackhawk reached in and grabbed his ankle and suddenly and viciously pulled Cisneros until he was lying across the backseat. I put the Kahr on his nose.

"This is a .45 caliber Kahr with hollow point rounds in it," I said. "Kahrs don't have safeties. There is a round in the chamber. The slightest pressure and this gun will go off and the back of your head will make an expensive mess in Nacho's car."

"Ah, man, don't do that," Nacho said. "Pull him out to shoot him."

Blackhawk put the barrel of his Sig Sauer in Cisneros's crotch.

"Take his shoe off," he said to Nacho.

Cisneros was wearing expensive basketball shoes. Nacho didn't bother untying them. He yanked on one till it and his sock came off. Every time he yanked, Cisneros tried to hold his head perfectly still. He was sweating.

Blackhawk took his pistol away from Cisneros's crotch and placed it on his little toe.

"I'm going to ask you a question," Blackhawk said softly. "If I don't like the answer, or I think you are lying, I will shoot your toe off. Then we go to the next toe. Comprender?"

I let up on the pressure of the Kahr. "Answer him."

He nodded.

"My friend here is going to show you a picture so there can be no mistake," Blackhawk said.

I showed him the picture of Roland.

"This is Roland Gomez," Blackhawk continued. "I know you know him and I know you know how to find him. Now you have to ask yourself, is this piece of shit worth one of your toes? So, where do we find him?"

Cisneros looked at me as I leaned over the backseat.

"Hey, man, I don't know...."

Blackhawk blew his toe off, the sound deafening in the car. Cisneros screamed and I shoved the Kahr into his opened mouth.

I leaned over, my ears ringing, my face inches from his, "I will give you a few seconds to compose yourself, then Blackhawk will ask you again."

Cisneros's eye were wide with fear and pain. I held the photo in front of him again. I shook it.

Blackhawk leaned in, "Where is he?"

Cisneros tried to say something, so I took the barrel of the pistol out of his mouth.

He swallowed hard. "Fuck," he said. He swallowed again.

"Where is he?" Blackhawk asked again.

"He has a sister," Cisneros gasped. "Somebody lit up his gang so he's laying low there."

"Where is there," Blackhawk asked.

"Up north, Bell Road."

"Give me his sock," Blackhawk said to Nacho. Nacho handed it to him.

"Sit up," Blackhawk said to Cisneros. Cisneros struggled up. Blackhawk handed him the sock. "Hold this tight on the toe, it'll stem the bleeding."

Nacho went to the back and collected the blanket. He brought it around to Cisneros's side and opened the door. He tossed the shoe on the floor. He handed Cisneros the blanket.

"Wrap your foot in this. Don't get your fuckin' blood on my car."

Nacho got behind the wheel and Blackhawk slid in beside Cisneros. It's hard to guard someone sitting next to them in the backseat. In the movies, the one being guarded is so afraid of being shot that he does nothing. In reality, the gun is so close that it just takes the slightest inattention and a quick move and gun can change hands. I scooted around with my left arm along the top of the seat, the Kahr in my right hand. Now he was covered.

"Bell Road and what?" I asked

Cisneros was struggling with the blanket.

"Bell Road between Cave Creek and 32nd Street." He was flushed and panting.

"How long did it take you to rehabilitate your foot?" Blackhawk asked me, not taking his eyes from Cisneros.

"Six months."

"Six months," Blackhawk said to Cisneros. "See, he loses his whole foot and six months later he's up and around." He pointed the Sig Sauer at Cisneros, "That's good news for you because if we get up to where you are telling us and Roland ain't there, I am going to shoot your whole foot off."

Everyone in the Jeep believed him.

Chapter Thirty-Three

Nacho took us up to I-10, then jockeyed across six lanes to catch the SR51 north. Cisneros was holding his foot, rocking back and forth and moaning. Blackhawk never took his eyes off of him. It took a good half hour before Bell Road started showing up on the exit signs. Finally Nacho took the Bell Road exit.

A large black pick-up, jacked up five feet off the ground, came swinging onto the exit in front of us. Nacho had to brake.

"Assholes," Nacho said. "Drive like assholes."

We caught the green at the top of the ramp and went west across the freeway bridge.

"Where to?" I asked.

"Man, my foot hurts like hell. You gotta take me to an emergency room. I'll tell them I did it myself."

"Where to?" Blackhawk asked softly.

"Shit," Cisneros groaned. "Go on past 32nd to, I don't know, a couple blocks maybe. I only been there a couple of times. His sister's a bitch. She don't like nobody hanging around."

"You know the house number?"

"Fuck no. It ain't a house, it's an apartment kinda thing."

"Kinda thing," I said.

"Cheap-ass place. One story about eight, ten units in a row. She's near the end."

We came up on 27th street and Nacho said, "Turn here?"

"Yeah," Cisneros said. When Nacho turned he said, "Go on down a couple blocks."

Nacho slowed down, and as we crept through the intersections, Cisneros would peer down the street to the right.

Finally he said, "There!"

Nacho had already gone too far to make the turn, so he went down to the next street and turned right. We went around the block and came at the apartments from the other direction. This put them on our left. As described, they were one story high, dirty yellow units, one after the other. There were ten doors, each having a slab of concrete in front that served as a porch. Most of the slabs had cheap lawn chairs on them. The height of urban living. The ground was bare dirt with patches of scrub winter grass. A couple of the units had rusty cars with flat tires pulled up on the dirt.

"Which one?" I asked. Cisneros didn't answer, so I rapped his shin with the Khar.

"Next to last," he said hurriedly. "With the open door."

Connected to the wall of the last unit was a seven-foot concrete block wall that went to the curb. Somebody's spite fence that blocked this property from the next one.

"Door open, they'll see us," Nacho said.

"Bitch don't pay her electric," Cisneros said.

"Pull up short on that side of the street," I said. "So they don't see us."

Nacho pulled to the curb facing the wrong way. I stepped out of the car, followed by Blackhawk and Nacho. Cisneros huddled in the back.

Blackhawk went around and opened his door. "Get out."

Cisneros reluctantly climbed out. I had the Kahr in my hand. Nacho had one of the confiscated pistols in his back pocket and was carrying the ball bat. Blackhawk put the Sig Sauer on Cisneros.

"You lead," he said.

Blackhawk walked Cisneros ahead of him, between him and the door. I went to the front wall next to a door three down from the open one and moved along the wall, the Kahr pointed at the empty space. Nacho came along behind me. We got to the door at the same time, and without hesitation Blackhawk shoved Cisneros through the opened door and I went in low and moved left. Blackhawk came in to the right. Nacho stayed outside.

The living room was tiny with one chair and one filthy sofa and a small flat screen TV on the otherwise blank wall. It was empty. Cisneros was on his knees, hands covering his head like he was expecting World War Three. With my free hand, I pointed at Blackhawk, then at the kitchen, and pointed at myself, then at the hallway that led to the bedrooms. He nodded, and we moved at the same time. There were two tiny bedrooms and a bathroom. The first bedroom had a bed covered with soiled clothes and blankets.

The second was empty except for cardboard boxes filled with various junk. No one was in the bathroom. I don't think I've seen a filthier toilet bowl since the Mideast. It didn't have a seat.

I moved back out into the hallway and Blackhawk came out of the kitchen. He shook his head.

"We have company!" Nacho yelled, stepping inside.

Blackhawk moved out of my sight toward the front door. I stepped back into the bedroom and looked out the window. To the left I could see the nose of a black Cadillac Escalade peeking out in front of the block fence. Suddenly two men with automatic rifles stepped around the fence and moved out into the middle of the street. They opened fire. I recognized them. They had dumped Gabriela into my lake.

The assault rifles chattered a fusillade of rounds across the front of the house. I fell back into a corner, getting as low as I could. Thank God the rounds were a light caliber, and though they were chewing the concrete on the outside, they weren't penetrating. There was enough damage as they ripped the window and windowsill to splinters. It went on for a long time, then abruptly ceased. Their clips were empty. They were reloading. I came up to the window looking for a target. The window was in glass shards and I couldn't rest my arm without slicing it. I took a bead on the big Mexican when suddenly –*Bam!* Outside and to my right was the concussive explosion of a high powered rifle. The big Mexican exploded into a mass of blood and flew backwards into the street. The other shooter yelped and dove behind the concrete fence. Ba*m!* A second report and a huge chunk of concrete exploded from the wall, leaving a jagged hole. There was screaming behind the wall, then the sudden squealing of tires as the Escalade yanked backwards out of sight. I could hear it racing off in reverse. It went racing around the corner, then it was silent.

I moved down the hallway to the living room. Blackhawk and Nacho were rising from the floor, brushing glass and debris from their clothes. I looked into the kitchen and Cisneros was gone.

"What the hell?" Nacho said.

I cautiously went to the front door, squatting, I put my eye around the jamb. I couldn't see anything. I slowly went out the door and onto the slab until I could see down the street. Blackhawk came up beside me.

A block away a Lincoln Town Car was sitting sideways in the intersection. Behind the hood Emil stood, his massive bald head gleaming in the sunlight. The big Mexican lay sprawled in the middle of the road, blood pooling under his body. Emil raised a heavy caliber rifle over his head in salute. I raised my hand. He tossed the rifle in the back seat, then got in the car and drove away.

"What the fuck was that?" Nacho said.

Blackhawk and I looked at each other.

".50 Cal," we said simultaneously.

Chapter Thirty-Four

Nacho parked his Jeep around the side of the El Patron next to where the other employees parked. The sky was still bright and streaked with clouds and contrails. The air was warm. It was still early enough in the day that the bar wasn't open for business yet, but the double doors were propped open. Next to the entrance, to the side of the doors, there was an ash can the size of a small garbage pail filled with sand and overflowing with cigarette butts. Because of the no smoking ordinance, this is where the smokers came.

Nacho led us in and we went through the foyer and down the hallway. The doors to the smaller two bars were opened and as I passed each door I could see a bartender inside each room stocking for the evening. I could hear a vacuum cleaner but couldn't tell where the sound was coming from. The smell of stale beer and humanity was becoming familiar.

In the big room, Jimmy was readying things for the night. As we came in, he was rolling a keg of beer behind the bar. We sat down and Nacho put the two confiscated pistols on the bar. One was a Smith and Wesson and the other a

Glock. They were both worn, with nicks and scratches.

Jimmy jockeyed the keg into place and quickly hooked it up, then came down to us.

"Didn't you read the sign?" he said to Nacho. "No firearms."

"Fuck you," Nacho said.

"Want something, Boss?" Jimmy asked with a grin, wiping the bar in front of us.

"Have someone empty that ashcan out front," Blackhawk said. He looked at me, "You want something?"

"Beer sounds good," I said.

"Three beers," Blackhawk said. "And three shots of Arta'."

Nacho was taking the pistols apart.

"Assholes don't take care of their weapons," he said.

"Where's Elena?" Blackhawk asked Jimmy.

He nodded toward the stairs. "Taking a nap, she's singing tonight." He expertly poured the three beers, set them on napkins in front of each of us. Snatching three shot glasses from the overhead rack, he poured the three tequilas.

I took a small bite of the tequila and washed it down with the beer. Nacho knocked his back all at once. Get'er done.

"You want lime with that?" Jimmy asked Blackhawk.

"Too late," Nacho said putting the barrel of the Smith and Wesson up to the light and peering down the barrel. "Barrel's pitted," he said to no one in particular.

Blackhawk shook his head to the offer of lime and drank a little of his beer. He swiveled around on the stool to face me.

"Cisneros set us up."

"Or Benny Yoon."

"Yoon doesn't have the cajones. Yoon knew if we survived we could find him if we wanted. Cisneros could disappear if he had to."

"He has to," I said.

"But Yoon," Blackhawk continued, "has got no place to go."

"So we find Cisneros again, before he disappears?"

Blackhawk shook his head, "Wouldn't do any good. Roland is long gone now. He'll go in deep."

"So we are worse off than we were," I said. "Except," I added, "Roland has lost five Playboy Diablos now."

"You'd think that would piss him off."

"Yeah."

"So what does a pissed off gangbanger do?"

"Get revenge," Nacho said, wiping the hammer of the pistol with his shirt sleeve.

"Against who?" I asked.

"You," he said.

"Why me?"

"Because," he said, turning to look at me, "You are the little white bread turd that he was going to take out. Simple little drive-by, and instead he loses another boy. You are the gnat that keeps buzzing around his ear and he'll want to swat you."

"Yeah," Blackhawk smiled. "The little white bread gnat."

"So, he'll try again?"

"Oh yeah," Nacho said, blowing down the barrel of the gun. "He's gonna try again."

Blackhawk said, "So, did Emil surprise the hell out of you, or was it just me?"

"Me too," I said. "That girl is important to somebody."

"How'd he know where we were?"

I shook my head, "Only three possible ways. One is too improbable to consider and that is he just happened to be in the neighborhood which, of course, doesn't answer why he would help us. That leaves, he followed us or he's following a separate thread that took him to Roland's sister and showed up the same time we did."

"Don't like coincidences," Blackhawk said. "So he followed us. He must be very good, or we are getting really sloppy."

"We weren't driving," I said, swallowing more of the beer. "It's not hard to tail an inexperienced man."

Without looking away from the pistol, Nacho said, "You know I'm sitting right here."

"Ninety percent highway," Blackhawk said, meaning that it is exponentially easier to follow someone unseen on a busy highway than on city streets.

"Still, should have spotted him."

"We didn't think about being followed. No reason to think about it. But now we think about it. Why would he follow us?"

"Why don't you just ask him?" Nacho said, still working on the pistol.

Blackhawk and I looked at each other, then we laughed.

"Mouth of babes," I said.

Chapter Thirty-Five

The sun was behind the western mountains when I parked the Mustang and walked down the hill to the pier. The store was closed and the sensor lights were just coming on.

A man was standing in the shadows of the overhang and I put my hand on the butt of my pistol. As I reached the bottom of the steps, I turned to face him and he stepped out of the shadows. It was Eddie.

"What are you doing skulking around in the dark?" I said.

"You got company. Thought you might like to know."

I looked down the pier. It was empty.

"What kind of company?"

"Kind with badges," Eddie said.

"How many?"

"Four. Three guys and a female cop. She's the one that was here when that girl got pulled outa the water."

"Boyce," I said. "The men?"

"One's a city cop, I'd bet. The other two smell like Feds."

I looked down the pier a long moment thinking.

"Thanks Eddie, I'll get you an old dog to kick."

"Had an old dog," he said. "Could use a six-pack though."

I fetched a ten out of my pocket.

"Store's closed," I said, handing it to him.

He grinned, the overhead light highlighted his missing teeth. "I got a key," he said. "But I don't take nothin' I don't pay for."

"I know you don't."

"You want I should back you up?"

I smiled, "I'm good, but thanks."

"Watch yer top knot," he said and went around the side to the door of the store.

I went by the Moneypenney and there was a faint glow coming from the back. I kept going.

They were on top of the Tiger Lily. I came up to the gangway and leaned to see the alarm LED light. It was blinking red. I stepped on board and turned it off where they couldn't see me. No one on top said a word. I unlocked the sliding door and went in. I went to the refrigerator and collected five beers. I carried them out the back and up the ladder way to the top.

Of course, it was Boyce and Mendoza and the huckleberry twins, Cummings and Pistorius.

"Comfortable?" I asked, handing each a beer.

Mendoza said, "Thanks." The others didn't say anything. Boyce just looked at me with her grey slate eyes. Yeah, I could see them in the fading light.

I hooked another chair and moved it to where the lights were in their eyes and behind me.

"Isn't it wonderful that we can all get together like this?" I said.

"Cut the bullshit," Pistorius said, twisting the cap from his beer. He started to toss it overboard.

"Don't do that," I said.

"Do what?" he said, the cap still in his hand.

"Don't throw your garbage in the water."

He looked at me like he didn't have a clue as to what I was saying.

"Why not?"

"It's shiny and a fish will think it is food, and it will kill that fish."

Cummings snorted, "Jesus Christ, what are you, St. Francis of Assisi?"

"It's my boat," I said to Pistorius. "If that cap goes in the water, so will you."

"I'm a federal agent," Pistorius said with heat, leaning forward.

"And I'm St. Francis of Assisi," I said.

"Let's take it easy," Mendoza said, his voice firm like a father talking to two boys tussling in the backseat. "Leave your shit in your hand," he said to Pistorius.

He turned to me. "We have some questions."

"Always a pleasure to see you, Detective Boyce," I said.

She suppressed a smile and drank out of her bottle.

"Ask away," I said, taking a drink myself.

"Where have you been today?" Cummings asked.

I took another drink, then leaned forward a bit.

"See, the problem is, Agent Cummings, I think you are

a class A, genuine asshole and whatever you say and however you say it, you will just piss me off. So I think it is best if Lieutenant Mendoza asks the questions."

Boyce ducked her head into her chest.

Cummings started to reply, but Mendoza held up a hand and stopped him.

He looked at me. "We have a street guy that gives us information once in a while. He tells us that you and two others, presumably your friend Blackhawk and our mutual friend Nacho, grabbed him off a downtown city street and forced him to reveal the whereabouts of a man by the name of Cisneros. Then we have a man by the name of Cisneros showing up at the Paradise Valley Hospital ER missing his little toe. With gunpowder residue all over his foot."

"Guns are very dangerous. You really have to be very careful."

"He said he lost the toe to a lawnmower."

"Lawnmowers are dangerous, too."

Mendoza sat and looked at me. Boyce was staring out across the darkening lake, a half smile on her face.

"Then," Mendoza said, "A member of the Seventh Avenue Playboy Diablos was literally blown apart by a very high powered rifle just blocks from that same ER. The rifle had also blown serious holes in a concrete wall next to an apartment that had been rented by the sister of Roland Gomez. She had moved, by the way. Which is a good thing since someone chewed the place to pieces with semi-automatic weapons."

"Do you know where Roland Gomez is?" I asked.

Mendoza set the untouched beer down. He shook his head, "Not yet. Cisneros says he doesn't know him."

"He's lying."

"I know."

"Anything on the girl?"

"We talked to Mr. Escalona."

"And?"

"Mr. Escalona didn't know what we were talking about," Boyce said, speaking for the first time. "He insisted that Ambassador Revera's granddaughter was with her mother in Columbia. I showed him a copy of the picture you took of the girl and he said he didn't recognize her. Said it didn't look a thing like Gabriela Revera."

"He's lying."

"I know," Boyce said.

"He's lying," I said to Mendoza.

"I know," he said.

"How's Melinda?" I asked.

"No 911 calls," she said.

"Who's Melinda?" Pistorius asked.

"Unrelated issue," Mendoza said.

"So, where were you today?" Cummings asked.

I looked at Mendoza, "This street guy. He pressing charges?"

Mendoza shook his head no.

"How about that fella with the missing toe?"

Again, Mendoza shook his head.

I stood. "So what is it this little get together is supposed to accomplish?"

Mendoza stood, he looked at Cummings and Pistorius, "About what I thought it would."

Boyce chuckled, sipping her beer. "We were hoping that the sheer weight of the federal government coming down on you would start you whining and blubbering and then you'd sign a full confession," she said.

"Don't be a smart ass, Detective, one is enough," Cummings said.

"What is it I'm supposed to confess to?" I asked.

"Damned if I know," Mendoza said turning to the stairway. "Let's go," he said.

Cummings and Pistorius stood, giving me that hard federal agent look. Boyce stayed seated. The two agents reluctantly followed Mendoza down the ladder way. Boyce didn't move. I watched the three men move down the pier toward the lights by the store. I looked at Boyce who was studying me.

"I'm kinda hoping you have your own wheels," I said. "But I could give you a ride if needed."

"I have my own wheels," she said.

Seeing she was in no hurry, I sat down.

"So how's tricks?" I asked.

"Would you really have done it?"

"Done what?"

"Throw an FBI agent off the top of your boat because he threw a bottle cap into the lake?"

"It could kill a fish."

"You kill fish all the time."

"Most of them I eat, some I let go. I don't kill something for no reason."

"So would you have done it?"

"Only way to know is if he threw it in the water. But he didn't."

She nodded, "Yeah, you would have done it."

We looked at each other for a long moment.

She set her beer aside and pulled a cigarette out of a pack she had in her jacket pocket.

"Mind if I smoke?"

"Yes."

"Tough shit," she said, lighting the cigarette.

"You really don't have a lead on the girl or Roland?" she said exhaling a double stream of smoke from her nostrils.

"Are we on the record, Detective Boyce?"

"No," she said. "You can call me Boyce tonight."

"Off the record, I was told that Cisneros could take us to Roland."

"That how he lost his toe?"

"I'm told it was a lawnmower. But what he did was set us up."

"Us?"

"Me."

"Were you there for the firefight?"

"Yeah."

"Did you shoot the gangbanger?"

I shook my head.

"What were you doing while the bullets were flying?"

"Crouched in a corner, whining and blubbering."

"Who shot the dude in the street?"

"Long-range rifle shot. I saw him hit. Blew him into vapors

of blood and guts. Fifty caliber I'd guess. Didn't see the shooter."

"Yeah," she said. "Forensics called it a .50. Did you have a weapon?"

"I'm just a regular citizen worried about a teenaged girl. Why would I have a weapon?"

"You mean you don't have one, like the one you don't have on your hip right now?"

"Yeah, like that."

She studied me a long moment, "Don't you think you are in over your head?"

"Probably."

Finally, she stood finishing her beer.

"Another beer?" I said.

She moved to the stairs, "Another time; Mendoza will be waiting for me."

She turned to look at me. It was full dark now and the dim lights of the marina played like highlights across her hair. The low lighting softened her face, making her even more attractive. "I was talking on the phone today to a Mexican detective I met a couple months ago at a cooperation conference."

"Yeah?"

"Seeing if I could get a line on that Escalade you saw at the warehouse. Owned by Morales Trucking."

"Yeah?"

"He says Morales Trucking is one of many holdings of Kamex Corporation."

"Kamex."

"Yeah, like being owned by General Electric. Probably no help."

She went down the stairs, then turned to look up at me.

"Yeah," she said after a long moment. "You'd have thrown his ass in. Damn, I wish he would have thrown that bottle cap."

Chapter Thirty- Six

I pulled a tall glass from the cupboard and filled it with ice. I poured in some Ballantine's and added some club soda. I filled it to the top and had to lean over and sip some to lower the level. I liked the color of it. Some scotches were too dark and some too light. This was just right.

I carried my drink out to the bow and was standing there sipping it, looking down the pier. Romy came out of the Moneypenny and stepped out on the dock. She was carrying a drink and held it out away from her, careful not to slosh it as she made the transition from boat to dock. I sipped my drink again and watched her come toward me.

As she reached my walkway I said, "Hey."

"Oh," she said, her hand coming up to shade her eyes. "You startled me. I didn't see you. May I come aboard?"

"Of course," I said, moving over to take her free hand and help her onto the deck. She wore a sleeveless blouse tied in a knot just above her navel. She had on very short white, jean shorts.

"Would you like to come inside?"

"It's a beautiful night, can we sit on top?"

"Sure," I said.

She held onto my hand until we reached the stairway. I followed her up, admiring the tight muscles moving under the white jean shorts.

She stopped at the top and turned and looked down at me. "Are you looking at my ass?"

"Be a fool not to," I said.

She laughed.

I stacked the chairs from earlier and pulled two chaise lounges over toward the side for a better view of the lake.

"What are you drinking?" I asked.

"Gin gimlet," she said. "Want a taste?"

I shook my head. "Doesn't mix with scotch."

"I started to come over earlier, but you had company."

"Nothing important."

"They looked like the police to me. The woman is attractive, in an authoritarian way."

"I didn't notice."

"Yeah, right," she smiled. "What did they want?"

I shrugged, "Another one of the Diablo Playboys was killed in a drive-by shooting, and they wanted to know if I knew anything about it."

"Why would you know something about that?"

"They know I was looking for Roland." I decided to change my construct of the Lucinda/Gabriela thing and just stick with Gabriela. "And they know I'm looking for Gabriela."

"Lucinda?"

"Yeah, Gabriela."

"Have you found anything? I assume if you had found her, you would have told me by now."

"Of course. Unfortunately, I haven't found anything."

"Nothing?"

"Not much. A friend knew a guy who knew a guy that was supposed to be in tight with Roland, but it was a dead end."

"So what do you do now?"

"Roland's a crackhead so he'll surface eventually to buy some. The girl cop, Boyce, has people looking for him."

"Maybe you should give up. Let the cops do their thing. The girl made her choice."

"I remember the choices I made when I was her age. They usually weren't good ones."

"People are getting killed. I'm not just worried about her, I'm worried about you."

"You shouldn't."

I could see her searching my face in the dim light. For the second time inside a few minutes, I was sitting here looking at a very attractive woman with the dock lights playing across her hair, and the moonlight trailing across her body. I was on a roll.

"Yes," she said. "You have a very self-confident air, Jackson. Like a man with a solid center, but these are crazy people. They kill each other for a half ounce of dope. They'd kill you for your watch."

"I don't have a watch," I said.

She shook her head. "You know what I mean."

"You sound like you know these people."

"Not really, but I know they exist."

"And you say your husband isn't around dirt bags like these."

"Frank tries to be what he isn't. But he came from a background like theirs. Some of it had to rub off."

"Why did you marry him?"

"He was exciting and completely different from anyone I knew. He too had a very self-confident air, and you can't move his center with a bulldozer."

She stood and moved to me. She straddled the chair and sat on my lap. She put her arms around my neck and kissed me lightly on the lips.

"In fact he's the reason I came to see you tonight."

"Your husband?"

She kissed me again, this time a little longer. She put her forehead against mine.

"He's been making noises about wanting me to come back to live in his house. Not be married, but be where he can control me. That's why he sent Diego to see me."

"Ah, Diego?"

"You remember, the guy whose finger you dislocated."

"I remember, so how is the finger?"

"Up his ass probably."

"So, are you?"

"Am I what?"

"Are you going back to Frank?"

"No."

"No?"

"No, but I did come to say goodbye. At least for a while."

"You just can't tell him no?"

She smiled, "Nobody tells Frank Bavaro no. It's inconceivable to him. An invitation from Frank is a command."

"Are you afraid of him?"

"You have to be seriously stupid not to be afraid of Frank."

"Where will you go?"

"Away. I just have to be away for a while, until he has other things to think about."

"Other things?"

"Diego says there is trouble coming. Okay by me. Let him think of something else. Anything but me. I don't know if I will ever be free of Frank."

"Maybe I can help."

She kissed me longer.

"That kind of thinking can get you killed. I can handle Frank, but if he finds out about you then you become leverage. He says do what I want, or Jackson gets killed. Then what do I do?"

She began to unbutton my shirt.

"Probably should be my decision."

She pulled my shirt off then began kissing my chest.

"I don't like this," I said.

"You don't like this," she said kissing my chest again.

"No, I like that a lot. I don't like you going."

"Shush," she said.

She slid back and worked her way down, kissing my

nipples, then my stomach. When she got to the navel, she unbuckled my belt and unzipped my pants. She pulled my underwear and trousers down to my ankles. She began kissing my thighs and then I felt her mouth on me.

I don't know how you do back flips while lying on your back, but I did. There was a huzzah in there someplace.

Chapter Thirty-Seven

At daybreak, she quietly slid out of my bed and put on her clothes. She leaned down and kissed me, then was gone. I had been right. I didn't like that much. I rolled over and tried not to think. I dozed off.

When I awoke I put on trunks and my foot and padded down to the Moneypenny. It was battened up and deserted.

I came back to the Tiger Lily and ground some Columbian coffee. I filled the reservoir with filtered water, put in the coffee and turned it on. While it was perking, I put on my swimming foot and swam out to the far buoy and back. The water was cold but I'd been trained to ignore it. I started for the buoy again. Once into my rhythm, the muscles began to stretch and I felt good. I poured it on coming back, and when I reached the ladder I was taking in great gulps of oxygen.

Back on board, I poured a cup of coffee and carried it into the oversized shower. I took a long shower, brushed my teeth and dressed as I sipped the coffee.

I put a small skillet on the burner and turned the heat to

medium. I poured some olive oil in and let it heat. While it heated, I chopped a fresh mushroom, a small vine-ripened tomato and a piece of white onion. I separated the meat of the tomato from the juicy part, then put the tomato meat, the mushroom and onion in the skillet to cook. Leaving in the juicy part of the tomato makes the whole thing too soggy. I took two extra-large eggs out of the egg tray in the refrigerator and cracked them into a small metal bowl. I took some shredded cheddar and put it in the bowl, then poured a dollop of half and half in. I whisked it all together, then when the mixture of vegetables was mostly cooked I turned the heat down and scraped in the eggs with a spatula. I put a slice of whole wheat bread in the toaster. When it popped up, I buttered it with real butter and the eggs were done. I had breakfast.

I was in the galley washing the dishes when I felt the small thud as a boat bumped into my stern.

"Hello, the Lily," Eddie called.

I dried my hands and went to the back. I pulled the curtains back and stepped out on the stern.

"Morning," I said. He was in his old skiff, holding on to the boat with one hand. The day was a bright one; it would be warm.

"Stripers are hitting anchovies thirty to fifty by the dam."

"I'm in," I said. "Give me a second, I'll grab my pole and tackle. I have a fresh pot of coffee. Want a go cup?"

"Boy howdy," he said with his crooked, semi-toothless smile.

I grabbed my gear and put on a worn ball cap. I grabbed

my sunglasses. I handed the tackle down to him.

"I'll get the coffee," I said.

I poured the coffee into two plastic cups with screw on lids and carried them back. I handed them down, then swung over the rail onto the ladder and stepped onto his skiff.

The boat was an eighteen-foot by four-foot wide aluminum Arkansas Traveler with a 35 horse Johnson pull start motor attached to the back. There was a foot operated trolling motor attached to the bow and a depth finder attached to the side where he could watch it while he fished. He claimed the skiff would float on a heavy dew and I believed him. He had extracted the middle bench and had a five-gallon bucket there he used as a live well. He called the boat *Lucille.* Named it after the line by George Kennedy in *Cool Hand Luke* where when asked how he knew the buxom girl washing her car was named Lucille he replied, "Anything looks that good gotta be named Lucille". It had been owned by a kid who got drunk and pushed it into the rocks at the mouth of Bartlett Lake, busting the prop and the lower shaft. The Sheriff's office had impounded it and the kid never claimed it. When the obligatory waiting time had passed, a friend had told Eddy about it and he bought it at auction. He fixed it up and has used it ever since. The only time I get nervous with it is in the middle of the lake in a high wind. It's a great fishing boat but not so much for ocean going.

I pushed us off. He pulled the rope on the motor one time and it roared to life. He grinned at me, proud of that motor. He swung us around and headed for the dam.

The water was still glassy and we skimmed along with less than a foot of the boat in the water. I let my hand trail along and the water seemed warmer. It would get windy later, as it did almost every afternoon, but now it was calm and flat.

He got to where we were going and cut the motor. Pulling the release rope, he dropped the trolling motor into the water. I stood and pulled the swivel seat from its fitting, put the extension pole in, placed the seat on top and now, setting up, I was ready. I had grabbed the pole I had rigged for drop shot and I baited it with the anchovies Eddie had brought in a large coffee can. I had two hooks, three feet apart with the weight five feet below them. I had marked the line with a knotted piece of heavy line every ten feet, so once I was baited I dropped the line over and counted the knots until I was thirty feet deep.

Eddie was studying the depth finder.

"Thirty feet, maybe forty," he said. "See a lot of activity."

He dropped his line over and immediately had a hit. Some guys are like that. You can sit right next to them with the same rig and the same bait and they'll pull five to your one.

"Whoa," he yelped. "I think I got a twofer." And he did. He pulled his line up and had a nice striper on each hook.

Then I got a hit.

It went like that for another hour, then as it happens, it stopped. Eddie trolled around trying to pick them up again. A large cigarette boat came roaring by with a twenty foot plume of water shooting straight up in its wake. Cigarette boats are long and loud and the cockpit seats two. It is made for speed and that is all it is made for. They got the name by smuggling cigarettes and other contraband from Cuba. They were low and fast and really hard for the Coast Guard to catch.

At least those in Florida had a purpose. This one was just going fast with a stereo system cranked as loud as it could get.

"Goddam idiots!" Eddie shouted, shaking his fist at them. "Goddam fuckers, don't they know that's the kind of shit a man is trying to get away from out here."

"I don't think they care," I said.

"Hell no, they don't care. You ever seen a stupider boat in your life? Go fast! Now turn around and go fast back where you started. Yahoo, what fun! A hundred dollars in gas later, you put in on the trailer and go back to bein' a stupid rich guy."

I agreed with him but he made me laugh.

Eddie trolled around for a while before he gave it up. We headed into the camping area where there was a fish cleaning station. In another hour I was back to the Lily wrapping some nice fillets and putting them in the freezer.

I took another shower to get rid of the fish smell, put on a black tee shirt with an old worn cotton shirt over it and a pair of clean jeans. I slipped the Ruger LCP into my hip pocket and battened down the Tiger Lily and walked up to the Mustang.

Forty minutes later I was sitting two houses down from Melinda's house. The brown and white truck wasn't there. I had brought an old Elmore Leonard western and I slouched down in the seat and read with one eye on her house.

Two hours later, I was getting hungry and I was starting to feel cramped when there was movement behind the house.

I started the motor and slowly cruised by, leaning down to look out the passenger window. Melinda was in the backyard hanging some clothes from a makeshift clothesline. She looked okay.

I went around the corner, did a U-turn and went by again. Now she had the baby on her hip and was picking at some tall weeds in the dirt yard. I pulled away and drove downtown.

Chapter Thirty-Eight

Boyce wasn't at her desk but Mendoza was. Downstairs there had been no one at the front desk so I just kept moving like I belonged and went up the staircase.

I walked into Mendoza's office and sat down. He looked up from a report and frowned.

"Make yourself to home," he said.

"Thanks," I said.

He looked at me steadily for a moment.

"Can I get you some coffee or maybe a scone?"

I chose to ignore the sarcasm.

"Coffee would be good."

He looked at me another long moment, then cocked his head toward the coffee pot on top of the file cabinet. It was half full and the light was on. I got up and filled a Styrofoam cup, added some dry creamer and a packet of Sweet and Low that was beside the pot. I indicated his cup with the pot in my hand.

He nodded and I filled his cup.

I replaced the pot and sat down, gently sipping the hot coffee.

He sipped his.

"You are becoming a pain in the ass," he said.

"One of my finer qualities."

"You here just for the coffee?"

I set my cup on the edge of his desk and he opened a drawer and took out a

napkin and handed it to me. I took it and put it under the coffee cup.

"Where are Frick and Frack the junior G-men?"

"You want to be careful with them," he said. "They're a little thin-skinned and if you push them too far they can make trouble for you."

"Yikes."

"But luckily for you they've been pulled back to do other things. Your friend Santiago Escalona, who speaks for the ambassador, insists the girl is not missing. Without something official they have nothing to do."

"You believe him?"

"No, for some damned reason I find myself believing you."

"Can you help me?"

"I still don't like the idea of you meddling, but no one else is doing anything, so I guess I'll do what I can."

"Can you help me find Roland Gomez?"

"You still think he has the girl?"

"For lack of anything else to believe, I guess so. I know for a fact the ambassador's granddaughter is missing. I can't think of anywhere she would be but with her family or on the streets with Roland or someone like him."

"Punks like Roland will surface eventually," Mendoza said. "The girl on the other hand, I don't know. Depends on what she is to him. If she is somebody to him then maybe he'll keep her. If she isn't, then he'll use her till she's too strung out to produce and he'll dump her."

"Think he'd kill her?"

He shook his head, "Can't think of why. Hundreds of girls on the streets. Dump her and find another."

"If you really wanted to find Gomez, what would you do?"

"Well, I really do want to find Gomez. I still have four bodies in the morgue. Murders that he could be a material witness to."

"Any line on the shooter?"

"Had to be a pro. Just don't know why."

"Looking for Gabriela."

"Could be."

"Ambassador Revera has ties to the Valdez Cartel. Could be one of theirs."

Mendoza sipped his coffee and studied me over the rim. He studied me for a long time.

Finally he said, "Who the fuck are you? How do you know that?"

I shrugged.

"Don't give me that *interested citizen* bullshit. Very few people outside of this squad room know of any connections between the Valdez people and the Ambassador."

"I am truly trying to help," I said. "How can I find Roland?"

He set his cup down. "Each shift his picture and the girl's picture are handed out to our patrol officers. I have a black and white check the warehouse twice a day. It looks as if the Diablos have found someplace else to smoke their crack."

"Where?"

"Haven't found that yet."

"Anything else on Cisneros or Bennie Yoon?"

"Bennie Yoon? I don't remember disclosing his name to you."

I grinned, "Heard his name in the squad room as I came in."

He frowned at me, "Don't try to be too smart, it'll come back and bite you on the ass."

I leaned over and took a pen that was one of many in a coffee cup. He had a pad of post-it notes on his desk. I took one and wrote the colonel's phone number on it.

I stood.

"I'm going to trust you with this," I said. I lay the post-it note on his desk. "The man at this number can tell you what you want to know about me. He may choose not to. He probably won't want to. So, you tell him number ten said you could be trusted."

"Number ten?" he said, not picking the note up.

"Yes. That will tell him that indeed you got his phone number from me. He knows who you are."

I turned and walked across the squad room to the stairwell door. When I glanced back he was still watching me. He still hadn't picked up the post-it note.

Chapter Thirty-Nine

It was mid-afternoon when I parked the Mustang on the far shady side of El Patron. You can tell someone that lives in Phoenix. They'll park a half block away if it is in the shade. There were a handful of cars in the parking lot, including Blackhawk's Jaguar and Nacho's Jeep.

The front doors were open and the cigarette trash can had been emptied. The sounds of Elena and the band filled the hallway. I came into the big room and a Hispanic couple was mopping the floor. I came into the main bar and Jimmy pointed upstairs.

I moved to the stairs and Elena waved at me, then continued the motion by waving the band to a stop.

"No, no, no!" she admonished them. "I tell you again. From E minor to D then to the bridge! Now again!" Girl was in charge. No doubt about it.

The foyer at the top was empty as was Blackhawk's office. I went back out into the hallway and moved to the first door on the right. I rapped on it and a moment later Blackhawk opened it.

"Hey," he said. "Come on in."

This was where he lived.

He was wearing a black tee shirt and jeans. Not just jeans. Probably cost $400. He was barefoot and had a hand towel around his neck. It was a larger room than you would expect. A huge television covered most of one wall and he moved over to an extra-large leather couch and picked up the remote and shut it off. He waved at an overstuffed chair that matched the couch.

I sat down and unstrapped my foot and began rubbing my stub. Blackhawk had good taste. The walls all held original oil paintings. One was huge, framed with an ornate gilded frame. It depicted a massive mountain range, wild and brutal looking with storm clouds among the mountains and sunlight trying to break through. In the foreground there was a dark, deep lake and on this bank were an Indian mother and child bathing. Two teepees nestled into the woods off to the right. On another wall was a disgruntled ballerina huddled in a front lit rustic corner. She had her hands in her hair on both sides of her head looking very upset.

"Elena's favorite," Blackhawk said.

"I can see why."

"Something to drink?"

"Later, maybe," I said. It felt good to massage my leg.

He went into his oversized kitchen and opened his oversized refrigerator, and took out a normal sized bottle of Amstel. Somehow, I expected it to be a quart. It seemed everything of his was bigger than life.

"You sure?" he asked, holding the refrigerator door open.

"Yeah, thanks."

He rummaged in a drawer and found a church key and popped the lid off the beer.

"Don't those unscrew?"

"I'm old fashioned," he said coming back into the room and sprawling on the couch.

"When I was a kid," I said, "I had a friend named Leroy. His Pap brewed his own in the basement. Saved all the quart bottles of Falstaff he and his buddies bought and refilled them. First beer I ever drank was his home brew. We'd sneak down there and shift the bottles all around so he couldn't tell if one or two were missing. We'd go back out to the alley and open the bottles with our teeth just to prove how tough we were."

"That why you had the Marines do all that dental work?"

I laughed.

"My brother gave me my first beer when I was twelve," he continued.

"How old was he?"

"Twenty-two."

"Where is he?"

"Doing life in Florence."

I nodded, with nothing to say to that.

Blackhawk took a drink of his beer and shrugged. "Sitting in a bar on Cave Creek Road with his ex-wife Bernadine and some guy she had picked up. Took objection to something the guy said, went out to his truck, got a .44, came back in and blew the guy off his barstool. Six witnesses.

Because he went to the car for the weapon it was premeditated. Done deal."

I didn't have anything to say to that either.

He drank his beer, looking across the room at the wall.

"I was thinking about what Nacho said," I said.

He looked at me, waiting.

"About asking Emil why he helped us out."

"Good question," Blackhawk said.

"You up for going with me?"

Before he could answer, Nacho came through the front door. "Hey boss!"

"Jesus, Nacho, can't you knock?"

"Sorry, boss. Thought you'd like to know that jock we threw out of here the other night is back."

"Which jock?"

"You know. The one Jackson smacked with the shot glass. He's asking if Jackson is here, or gonna be here."

I strapped my foot back on. "He looking for trouble?" I asked.

He shrugged. "Don't act like it. Just asked calm like. Not pissed or anything."

"Drunk?"

"Don't act like it."

I looked at Blackhawk and he shrugged.

"Well, let's go see him," I said.

We came back down the stairs, Nacho leading.

Big Bobby was sitting with a friend at the corner of the bar. Though the bar wasn't opened yet, they each had a beer in front of them. Jimmy diplomacy. They were watching the band practice. Blackhawk and Nacho came at them directly, while I moved around so Bobby's buddy was between him and me. I slid up on a barstool one removed from his buddy. The buddy looked at me, then nudged Bobby. Bobby leaned over and looked at me. His ear still looked red and angry.

"How you doin' Bobby," I said pleasantly.

His buddy leaned back so Bobby could see me better.

"Hey," he said. "I've been looking for you."

"How's the ear," I said.

"Hurts like a sonofabitch," he said.

"What do you want?" I asked.

"I want to buy you a beer," he said turning to look at Blackhawk and Nacho. He held his hand up, palm out. "No trouble." He turned back to look at me. "Just want to buy you a beer."

"That's awfully nice of you, Bobby. To what do I owe this distinction?"

"Me and Jed, here," he said jerking a thumb at his buddy, "play football for ASU."

"How wonderful," I said.

"We got a shot at the Rose Bowl this year," he continued.

"Congratulations," I said.

"Yeah, thanks. If we win the Rose Bowl I could turn pro. But see, when we were in here the other night we were breaking the coach's curfew. So after you hit me with whatever the hell you hit me with, we went back to the dorm. Coach pulled a surprise inspection. If I hadn't been there, he'd of kicked me off the team. So I guess, the way it worked out I'm still playing and I owe you a beer."

I looked at Nacho, "Dos Equis," I said.

He pointed at Jimmy and Jimmy nodded. He brought the beer and set it on a napkin in front of me. He took one of the bills sitting in front of Bobby, made change and brought it back.

"Thanks for the beer," I said.

He slid off the barstool, "Got practice, gotta go. See you around," he said. He turned to leave then turned back, "What the hell did you hit me with anyway?"

"He hit you with a shot glass," Nacho said.

"Shot glass?"

"You are lucky," Blackhawk said. "He hit you with the base of the glass. If he'd hit you with the rim he'd of cut your ear off your head."

Bobby stood looking a Blackhawk a moment. He turned and looked at me, "What's your name?"

"Jackson," I said.

"Sorry, I was drunk, Jackson. I don't normally pick fights. Usually drunks pick fights with me. I'm the big guy, so they get drunk and feel they have something to prove."

"Bobby usually tries to stay away from trouble," his buddy Jed said. "When the pros look at you they look at more than what you did on the field. Guy gets a couple DUIs and you drop way down the draft or off the list altogether."

"You going to get drafted too?"

Jed smiled, "Naw, not me. I ain't good enough like Bobby."

"Good luck," I said to Bobby.

"Thanks," he said. "See you around, Jackson," and he turned and walked out, Jed trailing behind.

Nacho and Jimmy were smiling.

Blackhawk said, "Go figure."

Chapter Forty

The same young girl was behind the counter at Escalona's office. She was dressed, again, in a crisp white blouse that struggled mightily to contain her. As we came in, she looked up, then abruptly took off her headset, nodded at Blackhawk and turned and left the room. A moment later she was back.

"He'll see you," she said. "Please follow me."

"To the ends of the earth," I said.

She ignored me. I was getting used to that.

She took us down the corridor. She ushered us into Escalona's office. Escalona was perched on the corner of his desk. Emil sat across the room, his face impassive.

I nodded at Emil, but he was looking steadily at Blackhawk. Blackhawk moved across the room so we weren't bunched together. He was returning Emil's look. Both their faces could have been cut out of stone.

Escalona was coolly studying me.

"So," he said. "I am hoping you come with information about young Gabriela?"

I shook my head. "I'm afraid not."

I looked at Emil again, but he was still studying Blackhawk. "We found someone who we thought could take us to Roland Gomez. As we've discussed, this is who we think Gabriela is with. Instead it was an ambush and we were lucky to come out alive."

"Most fortunate," Escalona said.

"We had a guardian angel."

"Everyone can use one of those."

"And, you know, ours was Emil. He was following us. On your orders, we presume. So we come to say thank you."

He shrugged.

"But I have to ask, why?"

Escalona stood and moved around the desk and sat in his high-backed chair.

"His Excellency does not want you dead." He smiled, "at least, not until you have found Gabriela."

"Emil can find Gabriela. Probably faster than I can."

"You underestimate yourself. You have the police helping you. That is impossible for Emil."

"The Ambassador has very powerful friends."

He nodded, "Yes, you have brought that up before. I will admit the Valdez family," – he pronounced the name with a hard e – "has many resources, but there is a war coming. A war Valdez does not want. Dos Hermanos is like a powerful bully, full of itself and believing it can have whatever it wants. They are preparing to invade. They can be very brutal. And they are arrogant. His Excellency knows that a war will be bad for everyone. He doesn't want his granddaughter to be a pawn in this war, but if she is not found, she will be. If they have her, he will be forced to resign, otherwise they will hold her life in their hands and force him into actions that would be, let us say, detrimental."

"But it seems that they have her now."

"It seems that, but we have people inside Dos Hermanos and they tell us Dos Hermanos is looking for her. So, no, they don't have her yet."

"So who has her, Roland? He's not Dos Hermanos?"

"Gomez is a," he waved his hand, "how you say, a punk. Gabriela may be with him, but he isn't Dos Hermanos. This is why the police and you will probably find her first."

"What do you know about a black Cadillac Escalade?"

"There are many of those."

"How about Morales Trucking or Kamex?"

"Kamex is a very large company. Morales Trucking, I've never heard of."

"Frank Bavaro?"

"Bavaro? How do you know Bavaro?"

"I came across his name while I was looking for Gabriela."

"Is Bavaro connected to Gabriela?"

"Not in any way I can determine. The policewoman, Detective Boyce, tells me that Bavaro is connected to Kamex and Kamex is connected to Dos Hermanos."

"Sadly, this is true."

"On the night four of Gomez's gang were murdered at the warehouse, there was a black Escalade parked in front." I looked at Emil and now he was looking at me. "I know for a fact Gabriela was there when the shootings went down.

Lieutenant Mendoza says the four were assassinated by a professional. The Escalade is owned by Morales Trucking which is owned by Kamex. What kind of vehicle do you drive?"

Escalona smiled, "Emil drives me in a Lincoln towncar. It is owned by the Columbian government."

"Would Bavaro kill those four people?"

Escalona smiled again, "He would have them slapped like a mosquito but he wouldn't dirty his hands. You will never prove he had anything to do with it. He is a very careful man."

"Who drives that Escalade? Who killed those four people?"

Escalona stood, indicating the meeting was over.

"Mr. Bavaro employs some very deadly people, any one of which would kill four kids without blinking."

Emil stood and Escalona said to him, "See if you can find someone connected to Bavaro that drives an Escalade."

I stood and moved to the door, "License number YLT1410."

As I moved out the door Emil winked at me.

Chapter Forty-One

We were in Blackhawk's Jaguar and we decided to take a run by the Playboy Diablos' warehouse. It still had police tape up and no vehicles were in the lot or on the street in front. One of the windows had been broken out. It looked deserted. The Playboys had found a new home. I decided to call Boyce to see if she knew where. I found her number in my phone and hit redial.

As soon as it connected, Boyce said, "Dammit, Jackson, you know I have a real live job as a police detective."

"Yes ma'am, and a damned good one too. How'd you know it was me?"

"Caller ID, you moron. What do you want?"

"Playboy Diablos," I said. "A really good detective like you probably knows where they're hanging out now and I was hoping you would tell me."

"You still begging for a scumbag punk to gut shoot you with a zip gun?"

"I am cloaked in the invincible shield of truth, justice and the American way."

"You are cloaked in the shield of bullshit."

"Well, yes. But I was hoping you would still tell me."

"Haven't checked it out yet, but I had a black and white report they saw some of them at a dive on Broadway called the Brown Jug." She hung up.

I looked at Blackhawk, "Caller ID?"

He shook his head, smiling. "God, man, where you been?"

I shrugged, "She says a black and white saw some Diablos at a place on Broadway called the Brown Jug."

"Rat hole," Blackhawk said, turning the corner to head back the way we had come.

There were three cars in the parking lot. Blackhawk parked on the far side, not wanting to risk a ding. If Blackhawk ever had a child he wouldn't treat it any better than he treated this car.

We went in. The inside made El Patron smell like a rose garden.

The building was low, long and narrow. A bar ran down the left side as you entered, and there were booths on the right side. Two pool tables were at the end of the room. No one was playing.

Despite the three cars in the lot, there were only two men in the place. One was the bartender, and the other was sitting down at the end with a half-filled glass of beer in front of him. He was watching a hockey game on the television that was mounted up in a corner near him.

Blackhawk and I took two bar stools. The bartender came down and set coasters in front of us.

"What can I get you gents?" he said.

He had a long ponytail and a tattooed tear on the edge of his right eye. He wore a wife-beater tee shirt and his arms were a mass of tattoos. Looked like prison.

"I'm looking for someone," I said.

He looked at me and moved back half a step, "Ain't nobody here 'cept me and Jerry."

I laid a twenty on the bar. "I'm looking for Roland."

He didn't look at the twenty. He shook his head, "Don't know him."

"Henry Cisneros?"

He shook his head emphatically, "Nope."

"How about Dog or Petey?"

He looked at me hard. "You a cop?"

"Not me," I said. "I'm just trying to find some old friends."

He snorted, "Shit, you ain't never gonna find Dog or Petey."

"How do you know that?"

"Cause they're dead, man."

"So you do know Roland?"

"Never heard of him," he said. "So unless you got a badge, why don't you and Cochise get out of here."

I held up the twenty. "Last chance."

He turned away and began to wash some glasses. I glanced at Blackhawk and he was laughing.

"Cochise?" he said.

As we drove away Blackhawk said, "You white people don't realize that when you call someone like me Cochise, it is the ultimate compliment."

I asked Cochise if he minded running by Melinda's to check on her.

Maupin's truck wasn't in the drive. All the blinds were drawn.

The doorbell socket was empty so I knocked on the door. Blackhawk stood to the side where he couldn't be seen from the front window.

No one answered, so I knocked again, a little more forcefully. The blinds shifted slightly and Blackhawk said, "Someone is here."

"Melinda," I called. "It's Jackson."

Nothing happened. After a long moment I called again, "Melinda, it's Jackson. I just want to see how you are."

Another moment went by, then I heard the latch and the door opened a crack.

"You shouldn't come here," Melinda said through the small opening.

"Can we come in?" I asked.

She shook her head. "The baby's asleep."

It was dim inside. She was wearing a short sleeved blouse and a shaft of sunlight lit her bicep. There were bruise marks on it. I put the flat of my hand on the door and forced it open. She tried to resist but couldn't. She stepped back.

"He home?"

She shook her head. She looked very tired and strung out.

I reached over and lifted the bottom of her blouse to reveal her side and abdomen. There were yellow and ugly purple bruises. She began to cry.

"You'll just make it worse," she said.

"Where is he?"

She shook her head, wiping her nose on her forearm, "Please, don't."

"Look at me," I said, lifting her chin. Her eyes were closed. "Look at me," I said again.

She opened her eyes.

"He will not hurt you again, I promise. Where is he?"

"At the tavern," she said, her voice barely audible.

"Which tavern?"

"Tilly's," she said.

I looked at Blackhawk. He shook his head.

"Take care of Hayden," I said and stepped back. She softly closed the door.

In the Jaguar, Blackhawk pulled his phone and began fiddling with it.

After a moment, "On 56th Avenue," he said.

"What the hell is that?"

"You can look up places on your phone."

"Jesus," I muttered. "Does it wipe your ass too?"

"You have to download an app for that," he said.

Chapter Forty-Two

Following his directions, we found Tilly's in under five minutes. Maupin's brown and white truck was in the parking lot along with several other trucks and a couple of sedans. This was a much bigger dive than the Brown Jug, but it smelled just as bad. Unlike the Brown Jug, this place had customers. I never could figure out why two places that seemed the same could have such different success. Or lack of it. They say location is all, but this joint didn't seem to be much different than the other. The beer on tap was the same. The bartender could have been a clone to the other.

Tilly's had its bar on the right hand side and tables on the left. Again, there were pool tables at the back, along with dart boards and shuffleboard. Behind the pool tables were two doors. In faded and amateurish scroll one was labeled Gents, the other Ladies.

Maupin was playing pool for money. There were twenty dollar bills stuffed in an empty beer glass sitting on the edge of the pool table. He was intent on his game and didn't see us walk up. No one paid us any attention until Blackhawk sat a haunch on the corner of the table. I moved around till I was next to Maupin.

Now everyone stopped and looked at Blackhawk.

Maupin had been leaning over a shot. He straightened up, holding the pool stick.

"What the hell you think you're doing?" he said pointing the stick at Blackhawk.

Blackhawk said, "I'm here to see the fight."

"What fight?" Maupin said.

"Between you and me," I said and hit him in the mouth.

I hadn't put any real force into it, just enough to split his lip and knock him back a step. That was a mistake. I should have hit him harder. He recovered faster than I expected and he swung the pool stick at my head. I blocked it with my forearm. Luckily it was the small end and it snapped in two. He kept coming, swinging the stick back and forth.

Thousands of hours of hand to hand training, and the first thing I was taught was to choose the area of conflict carefully. I guess I was rusty because the crowded bar was not conducive to me avoiding his attack. So when I ran out of room, I had to step into the swinging stick and take a hit. I turned and took it on the muscle on my side, under my arm. I clamped my arm down on the stick, trapping it.

He let the stick go and tried to take me by the throat. He got my shirt in both hands and tried to knee me in the groin. I twisted and took the knee to my left thigh. Using that momentum, I swung my left arm over both of his wrists, trapping them and using my weight I pulled him off balance. I rapidly elbowed him in the face three times and he let go.

I grabbed a bar stool and swung it at him. It hit him in the forearm and he wrenched the stool from my hands and it flew across the floor, scattering the customers.

We stood four feet apart. He was bleeding heavily from his nose and his breath was coming in gasps. I knew parts of me would hurt tomorrow, but the blood was moving through my veins and my breath was even and I felt good. God, this was fun.

He stood with his ham hands clenched and sweat running into his eyes. He ignored it. His eyes were small and piggish and cold. I had shot at a charging wild boar once and the eyes were the same. Brutal, cold and murderous.

"I'm going to beat you to a pulp," I said. "I told you what would happen if you touched Melinda." I stepped in and snapped two straight lefts to his face and danced back. He let out a bellow and charged me, and I danced farther back, then lunged forward, meeting his momentum with two more lefts and an overhand right. It stopped him for a second and I danced back. There was a mirror behind the bar and I could see I had a clear twenty feet behind me before I ran out of room.

He came at me again, this time catching the point of my shoulder with a thunderous right. My arm went numb. He tried to wrap me up and use his weight advantage. I tried to slip away but got caught up in a high top table, and he got one of his massive arms around my neck. I worked on his hand and managed to separate his little finger. I was seeing spots. Running out of air, I kicked him in the shin as hard as I could with my prosthetic foot and at the same time, snapped his finger. He howled and let me go. I spun and he was looking at his broken finger, and I kicked him on the side of his knee and his leg bent a little funny and he stumbled back, struggling to stay upright but he fell down. Now he didn't know what to hold, his finger or his knee. I moved to the side and kicked him in the gut and all the air left him and he rolled to his side, curling into the fetus position.

I heard Blackhawk say, "Put it down."

He was still sitting on the pool table, but he had the Sig Sauer in his hand resting nonchalantly across his thigh. He was talking to the bartender. The bartender had a phone in his hand. He lay the phone aside and raised his hands.

I leaned down close to Maupin's ear and said, "You touch that girl again, I'll kill you."

One of the customers in the back said, "Jesus, I never saw anything like that."

Another said, "You better go ahead and kill him, mister, he ain't the kind that will let this go."

I stepped over to the bartender and leaned into him, "You never want to see me again, you let this go. You want to see me again, call the police."

Driving away, I was looking at my knuckles. They were beginning to puff.

Blackhawk said, "Have fun?"

"Yeah, you?"

"Not as much as you."

Chapter Forty-Three

We parked in my reserved spot and walked in the dusk down the ramp to my pier and out to the boat. We each carried a sack of groceries. The Moneypenny was deserted. Spiders had already spun webs across the gate opening in the aluminum railing that rimmed the bow. Spiders that live on the water are quick to claim their territory.

A half mile across the water, Captain Rand had the party boat out and the lights were on and the band playing. The whooping and laughter carried across the water and sounded like it was right next door. There were times the revelry was so raucous I would resort to wearing my sound suppression gun range earmuffs just to sleep. It was especially bad on the good weather weekends. All the boat owners that lived nearby would come down and fire up the gas grills and pour the cocktails and inevitably one or two would crank the music up, thinking the whole world was as enthralled with their music as they were.

My infrared warning light was green so there were no surprises aboard. I turned it off and stepped on board. Blackhawk followed me in. I began putting the groceries away and he made the drinks. I dialed the radio service to some Alison Krause. He filled two large rock glasses with ice, added a dash of bitters and a little over three fingers of Plymouth gin. We took the drinks up top. We sat in the captain's chairs at the cockpit and watched the evening find the water. The speakers up top had individual volume controls. I wasn't sure the rest of the world wanted to hear Alison Krause so I tuned it low.

The afternoons on the lake are usually windy, but with the sunset the wind dies to a mild breeze. The breeze kept what bugs there were at bay.

Blackhawk had a foot up on the rail and was watching me in his bemused way.

"What?" I said taking a bite out of my drink.

"That little girl."

"Melinda?"

"If she don't have, what's his name -"

"Maupin."

"Maupin. If not him, it'll just be another dipshit. Girls like that need to be taken care of. And they'll take a lot of beatings to get what they need."

"So I should just let it go?"

He shrugged. "Up to you. Here's the question –"

I waited.

"You doing it for her or for you?"

"Ah, Dr. Blackhawk. You think I have some psychological need to protect?"

"Don't know about psychological but that's all you been doing. And, yeah you are a male and we males are fixers.

Woman has a problem, we want to fix it. Man has a problem, the woman will hug him and nurture him and tell him it's going to be all better, then he's on his own to fix it."

"Doesn't mean she should be beat up."

"Men been beating up their women since the stone age."

"Doesn't make it right."

"No it doesn't, but it's our nature."

"To beat up women."

"Men have always been the hunter gatherers. We been stabbing, sticking and clubbing things since the beginning of time. Killing is a violent act. Women take care of the nest. They are the nurturers. No violence required."

"So I am predestined to violence and at the same time to take care of these girls."

"Pretty much."

I laughed. "Oh well, keeps me busy."

"Busy beating the shit out of people."

"Know anyone that needed it more?"

He shook his head. "Can't say I do. But we both know you were just toying with him."

I shrugged.

"Don't know if you were just bullying him or playing the punisher but you could have put him down immediately any number of ways."

"How can I kill thee, let me count the ways."

"Cue ball, cue stick, bare hands, beer bottle. Many ways. You baited him."

"But I didn't kill him. Finger will mend. He'll walk funny for a while."

"You told him you'd kill him."

"Yeah, there is that."

"Will you?"

I shrugged again. "Won't know unless he beats the girl. Then we'll find out."

"I know who you are," Blackhawk said. "Once you said it, it'll be hard to take it back."

The party noise moved farther away as Captain Rand's boat moved further down the lake.

"Yes, there is that," I said.

We were silent for a while, both thinking about that.

"Who we are now seems like we came from a faraway time in a faraway land," I said. "For God and country. Instead of for a little girl whose crowning achievement in her life is getting pregnant."

"The colonel always said to never let emotion get into it."

"Easy to do back then. Most targets were nameless."

"Harder now?"

"Yeah. Meet a little girl looks twelve in a place called *Safehouse* that she thinks is, but is not."

"What about the other girl?"

"She's out there somewhere."

"Hope is the poor man's bread."

"Hope is the thing with feathers – that perches in the soul. And sings the tune without the words, and never stops – at all."

"Wow," Blackhawk said. "You reading Dickinson again?"

"Never stopped."

"Unit always thought that was a little pansy."

"Reading Dickinson?"

He shrugged.

"No one ever said that to me."

"They weren't fools."

Now he grinned.

"What now?"

He took a drink, the ice cubes clinking.

"Seems like saving little girls is a weakness of yours." He tilted his glass at my prosthetic, "Starting with the little girl that cost you that."

"I should've been faster," I said.

Again we sat in silence. This time it went on for a while. It was one of the small things that had bonded Blackhawk and me. We didn't have to endorse our being together by talking. Neither of us minded the quiet.

Finally I said, "So, since we're males we are predisposed to beat our women?"

"Pretty much."

"So, you beat Elena?"

"You crazy?"

"Why not?"

"She'd kill me."

Chapter Forty-Four

"You hanging here or going back?"

"Owning your own business is like being married," Blackhawk said. "Spend too much time away and you start feeling guilty."

"How would you know?"

"I read it in a lovelorn column somewhere."

The temperature had dipped and we had moved back into the main lounge.

"I'll drive you back," I said.

We buttoned up the Tiger Lily and I activated the alarm. Walking down the pier I could see Danny Valenzuela, one of the security guys, with his two-seater golf cart at the end by the restaurant waiting on us.

"Saw you coming," he said as we drew close.

We piled into his cart and he drove us up the hill to the Mustang. Blackhawk tipped him with a fifty.

It was ten-thirty when Blackhawk and I pulled up to El Patron. The parking lot was packed. Both the side bars were crowded to overflowing with couples with drinks in hand lounging in the hallway or moving from one bar to the other. In the main room Elena and the band had the crowd in a dancing frenzy. I found a spot at the bar. Blackhawk went upstairs to do some bookwork. Since I intended to head right back to the boat, I had Jimmy give me a tonic and club soda with a wedge of lime. Nacho was nowhere in sight.

Elena was in full voice, her olive skin glistening with perspiration. Men sweat, women perspire. She was a joy to watch. The band was in sync down to the smallest move.

I was finishing my drink when two men came up on either side of me. They were both dressed in dark silk suits with silk shirts and dark silk ties. Took a lot of silkworms to dress them.

One was tall and broad, his features flat and ethnic like he had Indio in his Mexican blood. His flat black hair was oiled and combed straight back. He looked like Mike Mizurki from the old Bogart movies. He leaned forward, both hands on the bar, and the guy on the stool next to me looked at him, slid off the stool and moved away.

The other guy was his opposite. Slender with rusty colored hair. His eyes were pale and when he was younger he must have had really bad acne. It had left pitted scars across both cheeks. These guys weren't Feds.

I looked at Jimmy and he was watching. He reached under the bar and I knew he was pressing a button.

"Mr. Jackson?" Rusty asked, even though I was sure he knew who I was.

"In all my glory," I said. I swiveled, putting myself full face on him, figuring he would be the easier escape route. "I was just wondering how many silkworms died for your sartorial splendor?"

He looked puzzled.

"Mr. Bavaro would like a minute of your time."

This surprised me.

"Mr. Bavaro?"

"Yes sir. He is waiting outside."

I looked at him for a moment.

"Is Romy with him?"

"No sir," Rusty said with nothing in his voice. "It will just take a moment." He stepped back and indicated the way with his hand palm up.

I thought about it for a split second, then slid off my stool and followed him out. Mizurki was behind me. We made our way through the crowd. Rusty was very patient and polite, gently edging people out of the way. Mizurki didn't have any trouble. People just naturally got out of his way.

Duane, the part time bouncer, was manning the door. He nodded as we went out. The lot was surrounded with overhead lights that left dark shadows around each vehicle.

There was an itchy spot behind my right ear where I expected Mizurki to hit me, but he didn't. Rusty led me to the outer edge of the lot where a dark Cadillac Escalade sat. It had the wrong license number. As he reached it, Rusty leaned down and opened the back door.

The man that got out wasn't tall but he had the aura of power that some men have. He was dressed immaculately in a dark pin striped suit with a grey silk tie and matching handkerchief in the breast pocket. He was dark with dark eyes, a dark mustache and dark hair combed straight back from a pronounced widow's peak over a balding head.

He held his hand out to me.

"I am Frank Bavaro," he said without making it sound important.

"Jackson," I said taking the hand. His grip was firm and dry.

"Thank you for coming out to see me. Most men would think twice about coming out into the dark to meet a stranger."

"This is just a guess, but I'm guessing I didn't have much of a choice."

"There are always choices. Some just come with consequences."

"Well put, Mr. Bavaro. How's Romy?"

The lights that illuminated the lot also illuminated his face. He looked surprised. His face hardened slightly.

"My wife has nothing to do with us."

I shrugged. "What does have something to do with us?"

He smiled, but it wasn't warm, "I like that. You get right to it."

I had shifted in a natural fashion until the entrance was in my line of sight. Blackhawk, Nacho and Duane were standing by the door watching.

Long ago Blackhawk and I had settled on our signals and all I had to do was touch my nose.

"Why would you come here to talk to me?" I asked.

"I am told you are looking for a girl."

I didn't say anything.

"I am also looking for this girl," he continued. "She is the daughter of an old friend and we are all distressed that she is on the streets and may be in danger. I came to see what you have found out."

I thought about it for a second then decided it didn't make much difference.

"You speak of Gabriela Revera?"

"You know I do. What do you know of her? Do you know where she is?"

"The best I know is that she is probably with some of the Seventh Avenue Diablo Playboys."

"Do you know where?"

I shook my head.

"I am told that you are working with the police trying to find her."

"The police are looking for her, yes."

"You don't know where she is?"

"No," I said.

He looked at Rusty.

"How much cash do you have?"

Rusty looked a little bewildered, "Couple of grand maybe."

Bavaro held out his hand and Rusty dug a roll of bills from his pants pocket and handed it over.

Bavaro handed me the roll of bills.

"Consider this a retainer," he said. "Anything you find about Gabriela, you will call us and tell us immediately."

He took a business card and a pen from his inside pocket. He wrote on the card then handed it to me.

"You call the number on the card. I have written an extension number on the card also. That will get you directly to me."

He turned and climbed back into the back seat. Rusty closed the door and the window came whirring down. Bavaro leaned forward his face in the window.

"You call me first."

"You before the police," I said.

"Yes, after I have the girl you call the police. When you find her I will give you fifty thousand dollars for your trouble. Do we understand each other?"

"Yes, I think so," I said.

Mizurki got behind the wheel and Rusty walked around to the passenger side and got in.

As soon as he was in and couldn't see me, I stepped into Bavaro's blind spot and turned and pointed at Nacho. Then I pointed at Bavaro's vehicle.

Blackhawk said something to Nacho and Nacho took off in a run to his car. As Bavaro's Escalade moved out of the parking lot and onto the street, Nacho's Jeep was following.

Chapter Forty-Five

Blackhawk, Elena and I were in Blackhawk's apartment when Nacho returned. El Patron was closed and shut down. I had decided to stay until Nacho returned so I was sipping some Ballantine's and club soda with lots of ice.

Elena had showered and was wearing a pair of cut-off jean shorts and one of Blackhawk's tee shirts. Even with no makeup she had that healthy skin look with full eyelashes and full lips. She had the TV remote and was cycling from show to show.

I counted the roll of bills Rusty had in his pocket and it came to $1820.00. Hundreds, fifties and twenties. Elena looked at it and said, "What you got there?"

"Man gave Jackson a wad of bills," Blackhawk said.

"For what?"

"Wants him to find a girl."

"You give me that and I'll find you a girl," she said, tossing her hair. Her eyes went back to the TV screen.

Nacho came in without knocking, and Blackhawk threw him an irritated look. Nacho went straight to the bar and fixed a drink.

Twirling the ice with his finger, he came to the couch and sat beside Elena. He leaned back, throwing his feet up on the coffee table.

"Don't put your feet on the furniture," she said without looking at him. He put his feet on the floor. He took a couple of long pulls on the drink, then got up to fix another.

Blackhawk watched him, irritation just under the surface. I was trying not to smile.

Finally Blackhawk said, "Well, goddammit, are you going to tell us where they went?"

Nacho moved back to the couch. "I lost them," he said.

Blackhawk just stared at him.

"You guys wanna watch this Conan guy?" Elena asked.

Nacho looked at Blackhawk and got a sly look on his face.

"But I found them again."

Blackhawk put his elbows on his knees and buried his face in his hands. He rubbed his eyes and ran his fingers through his long hair. He looked up at Nacho.

"You tell me now or I will shoot you."

"Hey look," Elena said, "It's Paul Newman. I love Paul Newman. Wow, he looks like a baby. I wonder how old this is?"

"You told me Bavaro was working for Kamex, so when I lost them I realized that was the direction they were headed, so I just headed over to where Kamex has that big compound. You know, the place that used to be a cotton gin in the old days. And sure enough I picked 'm up again."

"Kamex has offices there now?" I asked.

"Yeah," Nacho said. "Place was lit up all around. Razor wire and security gates with guards. Fuckers had weapons."

"Where is this?" I asked.

"Down around 51st Ave and Van Buren."

"I've been by there," Blackhawk said. "Had some big structures on it. Used to dry the cotton."

"Been built up recently," Nacho said. "Has a couple of three story warehouses now. Big. My cousin works construction and laid the concrete there. I parked across the street and watched them. Guard had the gate going up before they even came to a stop. He knew Bavaro. There is parking all around, but they must have hit a door opener because this big frigging door opens up and they drive into the building." He took a drink. "Guess what was inside?" He got that sly look again.

Blackhawk said, "You are seriously going to make me ask?"

"No, no you gotta ask me," Nacho said completely pleased with himself.

"I am going to shoot you," Blackhawk said.

"What was inside," I asked.

"More black Escalades."

"More? More than one?"

"Yeah, I saw two or three more, but I'll bet that the one we saw outside the Playboy Diablos' warehouse is one of them."

"You see the license number?" Blackhawk asked.

Nacho finished his drink and got up to get another one. "No, I was too far away, but I'll bet anything it was in there."

Blackhawk looked at me, shaking his head.

I stood up.

"I'm going home," I said.

"Ain't anyone going to watch this movie with me?" Elena said. "Paul Newman is in this cracker prison camp and they keep making him dig this hole."

"What we have here is a failure to communicate," I said.

Elena took her eyes off the TV and looked at me, "What the fuck are you talking about?"

Chapter Forty-Six

It was late when I pulled the Mustang into its slot. The wind was coming up and the sky was full of clouds racing across the moon. I pulled the canvas cover out of the trunk and covered her up, tightening it down so the wind couldn't dislodge it. It was tough for one man but I finally got it done.

The warning light on the boat was blinking red.

I pulled the little flat and deadly Ruger from my hip pocket. I looked around at the sliding glass door on the bow. It was closed. No one had jimmied it. I silently moved down the side of the boat and slipped aboard on the stern. All the curtains were pulled tight like I had left them. The glass doors on the stern were locked up tight. This meant that either someone had come aboard, then left, or they were up top.

They were up top. Or, rather she was up top.

At first it was just a bundle of something but upon closer examination it was the fair Detective Boyce. She was asleep on a lounge chair.

I moved silently around her, put the Ruger away and sat

on a deck chair and watched her sleep. After a while I decided it was warm enough and I might as well let her sleep, so I stood to go back down and she opened her eyes.

"Oh," she said. She sat up. "I must have fallen asleep."

"Easy to do on a boat," I said.

She rubbed her eyes and shook her hair.

"What time is it?"

"I don't know. Late."

She took her phone off her hip and hit a button to illuminate it.

"Almost three," she said.

"Can I get you something?"

She yawned. "Coffee. You can get me some coffee if you have it."

"I can do that," I said.

She followed me down and plopped in a chair on the stern while I unlocked the doors. I went into the galley and started a pot of coffee. While it was going through, I came back out and sat next to her. She was looking out over the dark water. A breeze was gently rocking the boat and the small whitecaps were fluorescent in the moonlight. We sat in silence until the coffee pot dinged. I went in and came back with two oversized mugs on a tray along with a carton of creamer and bowl that had Sweet N Low and raw sugar packets in it.

I set the tray between us. We fixed our coffees. We each sipped.

"Good coffee," she said.

"Thanks."

"What is it?"

"Columbian roast I get at Costco. Buy a couple of pounds unground. Grind it fresh."

"It's good."

"Thanks."

We sat for a while sipping the coffee.

Finally I said, "So what do I attribute the pleasure of your company to?"

She didn't answer right away, then, "Tequila."

I smiled, "Tequila?"

She looked at me and grinned.

"Girlfriend had a birthday party. Girls' night out thing."

"Detectives get a girls' night out?"

"Leave the badge and gun in the car, they do."

"And tequila reared its ugly head."

"Fuckin' Sharla. Started doing shooters and I was real cool, but she kept ordering them till I had a line of five of them on the bar. Then it was a challenge match."

"Who won?"

She thought a minute.

"I don't remember. Sharla passed out and she had friends to get her home so I decided to call it."

"You drive home? How did you get here?"

"Well, wasn't going to. I went out front and got my badge and gun and called a cab, and a half hour went by and the cab still didn't show up so I said screw it and started driving. Got to the stoplight at Glendale and the Black Canyon and don't know what happened. It turned green and next thing I'm on my way out here. I think I yelled something like *screw it, let's go see ol' Jackson*." She sipped her coffee, looking at me over the rim. "But ol' Jackson wasn't home so I went up top to take a nap."

"Well, ol' Jackson is glad you stopped by."

"Seemed like a good idea at the time. Stupid."

"Not stupid. Late, but not stupid."

"So where you been?"

"El Patron."

She set her cup down. "Okay, this is bullshit."

"No, I really was at El Patron."

"That's not what I mean. Nobody is named Blackhawk! What the hell kinda bullshit is that? Blackhawk, for Christ sake."

I smiled.

"That's what he calls himself."

"But you know his name?"

"Blackhawk."

"Bullshit!"

"I will swear on whatever you hold dear that I don't know him by any other name but Blackhawk."

"So is Jackson your real name?"

I was quiet. Finally I said, "I was born with another name. But that name and that person are dead. For all intents and purposes, my name is Jackson."

We were silent for a while and her eyes just stayed on me. Finally she said, "So you think this mysterious bullshit works with the ladies?"

"Does it work with you?"

"No."

"Are you a lady?"

"Fuck you!"

Again we were quiet.

Finally she said, "So what you got on Mendoza?"

"What does that mean?"

"You giving him sexual favors or something?"

I just shook my head.

She set her cup down and turned to look at me.

"Just who or what the hell are you?"

"What you see is what you get."

"That's crap! Nobody is more by the book than Mendoza and all of a sudden he's telling me, no ordering me, to bring you in the loop on anything we find on the Revera girl. Mendoza doesn't like civilians nosing in police business and now he's telling me to bring you in."

"Things I can do, you can't."

"Like what?"

"Like break the law."

"You think cops don't break the law?"

"Sure they do, but you don't and Mendoza doesn't."

She picked up her coffee again. "Okay, I'll give you that." She took a sip. "Although I was driving under the influence all the way out here."

"There is that."

"But you haven't answered my question."

"Which was?"

"Who are you? Pistorius and Cummings couldn't find anything on you before you purchased this boat."

"Does it matter?"

"It matters to me," she said. She drained her cup. "Do you have more?"

"Sure," I said. "Would you like a little somethin' somethin' in it?"

"You join me?"

"Sure." I stood and took her cup.

"And then you tell me who you are."

"Sure."

She leaned forward, stretching her back out. She rubbed her scalp. "God, I smell like that damned bar. I feel like I'm covered with something sticky."

"Take a dip," I said.

She laughed, "Sure, I'd bet you'd like that."

I shrugged, "Suit yourself. Brandy okay?" I said, picking up my mug.

"Sure," she said looking at me.

I went back through the stateroom, down the hall to the galley. I poured the coffee, added a dollop of brandy to both and carried them back out.

As I stepped out on the deck the first thing I noticed was a pile of clothes on the deck. The next thing I noticed was Boyce, naked as an egg, perched up on the rail by the aft ladder.

"Changed my mind," she said and went over the side.

To my credit, I didn't drop the coffees.

Chapter Forty-Seven

Okay, I'm not gonna lie. Young men my age who are up late and have had a certain amount of drinks would have jumped in the water, and if a pastor were present, married the girl right then and there. Well, maybe not married the girl but at least made serious commitments. Or, at least done anything to reach a certain connubial arrangement.

And as I set the coffees down and was wondering the best way to strip down and join her without being awkward, her phone rang.

Her phone rang.

Right then.

And she heard it.

"Get me a towel," she called.

"Let it ring."

"I'm a cop, give me a towel!"

I went inside and found a big beach towel and took it back outside. She was treading water at the bottom of the ladder.

"Just drape it right there," she said, "and turn around."

"Now you are shy."

"Turn around, goddammit."

I did as she asked and I heard her come up the ladder, water running off of her body. I tried not to think about it.

After a moment she said, "Okay, you can turn around."

She had the towel wrapped around her and knotted just above her breasts.

"Hand me my phone," she said.

I took the phone from her jacket and handed it to her.

"This may just be the most ill-timed phone call in the history of phone calls," I said.

She smiled at me and hit the redial button. In the silence I could hear it ringing, then a tinny voice came on the other end.

"This is Detective Boyce," she said. "I just missed a call from this number." Then she said, "Oh, hi." She listened some more. I could tell from her demeanor it wasn't good.

"What's the address?" she asked.

She didn't ask for a pencil. She disconnected the phone and looked at me.

"That was the 911 supervisor. I told you that I'd asked them to contact me if there were any calls from Melinda."

"Is she hurt?"

"I don't know," Boyce said. "The call came in from a neighbor who heard loud voices and screaming. They have a black and white heading there now."

"I'll go with you."

"You go inside so I can dress," she said.

I went inside.

When I followed her car into Melinda's neighborhood, the street was awash with flashing red, blue and amber lights. There were a few neighbors standing at the curb, the women in their bathrobes, the men in tee shirts and pants. The flashing lights made long eerie shadows that stretched across the lawn.

Boyce double parked in the street, and I pulled around her and pulled to the curb beyond the fire truck and ambulance that were parked in front of Melinda's house. There were also three patrol cars. One in the drive. There was no brown and white truck.

Boyce waited for me and we went up on the porch together. A patrolman looked at me and Boyce showed her badge and said, "He's with me."

Inside there were two patrolmen standing back in the corners watching three of the paramedics working on a tiny body on a gurney. Melinda was across the room in a straight back chair, hunched over, covered by a blanket and sobbing inconsolably. The female paramedic was performing CPR on the baby. I could just glimpse Hayden's little face and it was blue from lack of oxygen.

Boyce beckoned to one of the patrolmen and he followed us back outside.

"I'm Detective Boyce, this is Mr. Jackson, what's going on?" she asked him in a low tone.

He shook his head. His eyes were old and tired even though he looked to be only in his thirties.

"Neighbor couldn't sleep and got up to get a drink and heard a baby crying and a man shouting. She said then the man and woman were shouting at each other, then suddenly the baby stopped crying and the woman started screaming and that's when she called 911."

"Baby looks dead," I said.

"The baby is dead," the cop said, "but the paramedics don't want to call it here so they'll take the baby into the ER and call it there."

"What do you think happened?" Boyce asked him.

"Same shit, different night," he said. "Guy that lives here was probably drinking or doping or both, and the baby wouldn't stop crying so he shook the shit out of the poor little thing and broke its neck."

"Was the guy here?"

"Just the girl and the baby and the girl's not talking, but the neighbor heard a man shouting so I'm thinking that the asshole saw what he had done and boogied."

Just then the phalanx of paramedics brought the baby out on one of those collapsible gurneys the ambulances carry. They moved across the lawn to load it into the ambulance. Melinda followed, climbing up with two of the paramedics who were continuing the CPR. She was still crying.

Boyce looked at me, "I'm going to talk with her at the ER."

"I'll follow you," I said.

Chapter Forty-Eight

The ambulance didn't use the siren as it wound its way through the deserted streets to John C. Lincoln hospital at Third Street and Dunlap. Boyce had a dashboard flashing blue light and I pulled in beside her in the no parking zone. The paramedics were unloading and now they didn't seem to be in a hurry. They were no longer working the CPR. When they pulled the gurney out of the ambulance, the body was completely covered.

Now the female paramedic was with Melinda, gently talking with her. Melinda had been sobbing so hard she had the hiccups. Boyce and I followed them in. There is something unworldly about an ER in the middle of the night. The light seems too bright, and it has a greenish cast that makes everyone's skin look sickly. They took the gurney with little Hayden, followed by Melinda and the female paramedic, through some double doors. One of the paramedics peeled off to talk with the admitting nurse.

Boyce said, "Why don't you wait out here," indicating the waiting room.

I nodded and as she moved through the double doors, I found a chair facing a nearly soundless TV tuned to CNN. There were magazines lying around and I found a Sports Illustrated, and spent twenty minutes reading about the wondrous giants of the NBA. It didn't take long for my eyes to droop and I could feel the tiredness of it all moving through my body. Finally, I pulled another chair around and put my feet up on it. I slouched down and rested my head on the back of the chair and it was uncomfortable, but I fell immediately to sleep.

Boyce woke me by shaking my good foot. I sat up and glanced at the clock on the wall. It had been an hour and a half.

"They are taking the baby to the morgue for an autopsy," she said.

"Foul play," I said, rubbing the crick out of my neck. "Murder?"

"Probably manslaughter. We have an APB out on Maupin."

"What happened?"

"Just like the patrolman said. Maupin had been at the bar all night. When he got home he decided to play with the baby, who was sound asleep. Melinda protested and Maupin took the baby anyway." There was a tiredness in her face that a night's sleep wasn't going to erase. "The baby started crying and wouldn't stop. Maupin became enraged and shook him and broke his neck."

I looked out the automatic doors at the dimly lit parking lot. There was a white heat coursing through my middle and up into my throat.

Finally, I asked, "Melinda?"

"I'm not sure what to do with her. She doesn't want to go back to her place."

"Father Correa," I said.

"Yeah, that's a good idea. I'm going to bring her out, why don't you be outside. She's pretty upset."

"Okay," I said.

"She's blaming you."

I looked at her for a long time. Her eyes weren't cop eyes now. They were the eyes of a woman that saw the pain in front of her. Finally, I nodded and turned and went out into the dawn.

I was leaning against my car when they came out. At first Melinda didn't look at me but once she was in Boyce's passenger seat, her eyes found me and they stayed on me. They stayed on me until Boyce had to turn the car and Melinda would have had to turn to look over the back seat to see me. She didn't turn.

I stood, leaning against my car for a long time. Boyce's car had long disappeared. I finally got into the Mustang and sat there for a long time. The white heat inside had turned icy cold. I pulled out of the parking lot and into the awakening city. I drove slowly home. On the Tiger Lily, I sat on the stern and sipped reheated coffee until the sun was well up. Finally I went inside and pulled the blackout curtains and lay down and tried to sleep.

Chapter Forty-Nine

I tossed and turned for about four hours, then finally gave it up and went fishing. I don't know if it was because my heart wasn't in it or it was just a lousy fishing day, but I didn't get a bite. Late in the day I gave it up.

I snugged Swoop back in her mooring and went back to the houseboat and took a shower. I toweled off and put on a soft chambray shirt and some khaki slacks and Teva sandals. I had spent the previous six months perfectly happy to spend my time alone on the boat, but for some reason, tonight I needed to be around people.

I tucked the Ruger in my back pocket and drove toward town. I guess I was headed for El Patron by way of Safehouse, but halfway down the Black Canyon I decided to run by the Diablo Playboy warehouse.

The police tape was gone and in the gathering dusk I could see a faint light coming from one of the upper windows. I pulled around the corner and parked. There was no one on the street. I opened the trunk and pulled out a jacket I kept there. Draping the jacket over my arm, I walked easily around the corner on the opposite side of the street. I walked with purpose, like I was heading someplace. I didn't see a sentinel on top of the building. I walked down two blocks, then crossed over, put on the jacket, turned the collar up and came back toward it. The master of disguise.

As I reached the building, I ducked into the deepening shadows and moved to the back. I pulled the Ruger and ratcheted a round into the chamber. The back door was ajar. I eased inside and let my eyes adjust. It was as if time had stood still. Nothing was different except the new dust.

I went up the stairs silently, pistol extended, hugging the wall. When I reached the middle landing, it was as if there had never been a body there except for a dark smudge that could have been dried blood. I went on up. I stood listening outside the door for a very long time. I could hear something but couldn't make it out. Finally, I realized it was the sound of someone humming.

I went in low, quiet and quick.

There was an old black man sitting on the couch with a Bunsen burner, heating up something in an old saucepan. This was generating the only light in the room. His back was to me. His hair was shot with gray and he wore a tattered Army surplus jacket. His bed roll and most everything else he owned was on the other end of the couch.

I stepped out into the room and he shot straight up, almost up-ending his cook pot.

"Oh, my my," he cried, scuttling back away from me. He was looking at the gun. He put a palm out to me, "I'm sorry boss! I'm sorry! Didn't know this belong to anybody!"

I lowered the pistol. "It's okay. I'm not here to harm you."

"Don't mean nothin' boss." He was terrified.

"It's okay," I said again. I tucked the pistol in my back pocket. "I'm looking for someone else."

He slowly relaxed, "Ain't no one here but me."

"How long you been here?"

"Couple of days, boss. That's all."

I walked around, looking at the place. There were still dark spots on the floor where the blood had been.

I looked in the utility room, then came back out. The old man was watching me. I realized he wasn't as old as I originally thought.

I moved past him, then turned back. I took some of Rusty's cash from my pocket and handed him a twenty.

"Gangs use this place. Hang out, smoking crack. If they come back they'll mess you up soon as look at you."

He took the twenty, bobbing his head.

"Yessir, boss. I stay away from them bad people. Thank you kindly."

"Don't be spending that on Thunderbird," I said.

"Oh, nossir," he said. "I ain't no wino," telling me he knew what Thunderbird was. "This here will get me a weeks' worth of beans."

"Those gangbangers come back, you get your stuff and go down that back stairs."

"Yes sir, I surely will."

I went back down the stairs and outside. The air was cooling so I left the jacket on. I walked back to the Mustang, dropped the magazine from the Ruger, ratcheted the round out of the chamber and put it back in the magazine, then put the magazine back in place. As I slid in, I saw a Lincoln town car drive by a block away. I couldn't see the driver but I smiled anyway.

I drove over to Safehouse.

I found Father Correa in the community room. The place still smelled like cooking.

Many of the mothers were rocking their babies. Some were feeding. All were gathered around the flat screen TV watching a rerun of NCIS. Father Correa, smile still firmly in place, was bouncing one of the toddlers on his knee. Not one baby was crying. Melinda wasn't in the room.

Upon seeing me, Father Correa handed the baby off and came over to me.

"Mr. Jackson, it's good to see you."

"I'm sorry for the reason. I came to see about Melinda."

"She's resting," he said. He put his hand on my shoulder and gently moved me to the door.

"Let's go to my office where we can talk."

I followed him back down the corridor. Midway down, he indicated a closed door. "Melinda's staying in here," he said in a hushed voice.

In his office he indicated the spare chair and I sat down. He indicated the ever present coffee pot. I shook my head.

"Have they caught the father?" I asked.

He looked surprised. "I would have thought that you would know that before me."

"Last I saw of Detective Boyce was at the hospital, early this morning."

"Yes," the Father said, taking his glasses from his face and taking a tissue from a box on his desk he began cleaning them. "Fine young woman. She was here with Melinda for an hour and a half, till Melinda finally succumbed to the medication the hospital had given her and fell asleep."

"She still sleeping?"

"Was a half hour ago when one of the volunteers checked her."

"I feel responsible for this."

He looked at me, surprised, "Why is that?"

"I misjudged Maupin. I didn't think the baby was in any danger, just Melinda."

He replaced his glasses and looked at me over the top of them, "I'm sensing there was something that transpired between you and Melinda and her baby."

"And the father," I said.

"Maybe you should tell me about it."

So I did. I softened the beating part, making it more just that I had threatened Maupin if he hurt Melinda. I left Blackhawk out of the narrative.

He listened carefully. When I was finished, he studied me a moment.

Finally he said, "I don't see anything wrong with taking the young woman's part. A man like Maupin is a slave to his own demons. I believe that whether you were in the picture or not, eventually he would have done something evil. Probably to both of them. Maybe you didn't save young Hayden but maybe you did save Melinda."

I thought about that.

Finally, I stood. "If she needs anything, you still have my number?"

"I still have your number, Mr. Jackson. I'll call if she needs something, but I think she will be safe here for a while."

"You are a good man, FatherCorrea."

"So are you, Mr. Jackson," he said. Been a long time since anyone had told me that.

Outside I sat in the Mustang for a moment, thinking about what the Father had said, then I drove to El Patron.

Chapter Fifty

I had too much to drink, so I spent the night in Blackhawk's spare bedroom. When I awoke the radio clock on the bedstand said it was 5:30. I felt a little fuzzy from the drink, but knew I couldn't sleep anymore.

I was back at the boat an hour later. I put on my swimming foot and swam to the buoy and back, then did it again to punish myself. By the second time, the blood flowing through my body pushed all the fuzziness out and I felt refreshed. Suddenly I was famished. I put a pot of coffee on, then fixed a three egg omelet with scallions, cheese and tomatoes. I pulled a wrapped parmesan bagel from my freezer, microwaved it for 15 seconds to thaw it, then cut it in half and put it in the toaster.

I took the breakfast out on the stern. Eddie went by with a fishing customer sitting in the bow of his skiff. He waved, and I waved back.

I finished breakfast and cleaned up. Anything to avoid thinking about the girl, Gabriela, and why I couldn't find her. It had been long enough that Roland should have surfaced somewhere.

I was reading on the sofa and had fallen asleep when my phone in my pants pocket vibrated and woke me up. It was Boyce.

I hit the connect button and before I could say anything she said, "Where are you?"

"At the boat," I answered. "You want to go swimming?"

"Shut up," she said with a laugh. "I'm at Seventh Avenue and the river bottom, how soon can you get here?"

"What is it?"

"Just get here," she said and hung up.

It took me just under thirty minutes to hit the Seventh Avenue exit off the Black Canyon, then another couple to get to the river bottom. I had been thinking that directions of just *Seventh Avenue and the river bottom* were pretty meager directions, but when I got there I had no trouble finding her. There were four squad cars, a fire trunk, an ME's wagon and couple of other official looking cars, including one that was Boyce's, most of them with their lights flashing.

I found a place to park and made my way down off the street. They were all gathered fifty yards away, down into the river. Of course, the Salt River bottom was completely dry and almost always was, unless Phoenix had a completely abnormal downpour.

Boyce saw me and waved. The ground was broken and jumbled with chunks of concrete and piles of river rock. At this point it had to be one hundred fifty yards across. The river was rocks, weeds and scattered trash. Because of my foot I had to walk very carefully.

They were all gathered around a blue plastic tarp that was

spread on the ground. There were flies on the tarp. When I reached them, Boyce said, "Got something to show you," and lifted the edge of the tarp. She was watching me as she did it, as were the other cops.

I don't know what she expected my reaction to be, but I had seen beheaded corpses like these before, so my reaction was slight. Rigor had set in on both bodies. One wore a long sleeve shirt over a ribbed undershirt. Both of these shirts had been torn open and there were burn marks on the torso. Strange as it was, the body seemed familiar. The other body had an undershirt only. It was not torn. Both wore expensive running shoes and jeans. The one without the shirt had a familiar eagle tattoo on his arm.

I looked at Boyce, "Roland?"

She nodded, watching me.

"Most people start throwing up now," she smiled.

"I didn't have a lot for breakfast; who is the other one?"

She squatted down and pulled a shoe off. He didn't wear socks and his little toe was missing.

"I know you say different, but I do believe you have made his acquaintance. This is what is left of Mr. Cisneros."

"You know him?"

"The toe kinda gives it away and the description of his tattoos is on file."

"Almost like having a bar code," I said. "How long?"

She stood, tossing the shoe aside. She indicated a short, balding man that had a real honest to God pocket protector. He was carrying a notebook and was making notes in it. "Smitty says a couple of days, anyway."

"At least two," Smitty said, without looking at me.

"Any other trauma besides losing their heads?" I asked.

Now he looked at me. "Just the burn marks you see and the missing toe which appears to have happened earlier, but nothing deadly, at least nothing that is apparent now. We'll know more when we get the bodies to the morgue." He looked at Boyce, "Which I'm hoping can be now, if the Detective is through with show and tell."

"All yours, Smitty," Boyce said. She nodded at the patrolmen and started back up the grade.

Smitty and his people began to body-bag the bodies.

I followed Boyce to her car. She leaned against the fender of the non-descript Impala and studied me.

"This isn't all," she said.

"What else?"

"There was a shootout at a Circle K in Tolleson last night. Three dead, no witnesses."

"Related to this?"

"Nothing physical to tie it, but my gut says yes."

"Do I know who died?"

"No, I don't think so, but they were all gang members. Two of them Dos Hermanos and one was Valdez."

"War?"

She looked down, watching the men gather up the bodies. "I'm afraid it's just the beginning."

"This is bad," I said.

She looked at me.

"Bad for Gabriela," I said. "If Roland doesn't have her, who does?"

"Or she's dead," Boyce said. "But," she added almost to herself, "we have no body."

"I'm not going to think about that until there is absolutely no reason not to."

She shrugged.

"Thanks for calling me."

"Thank Mendoza. He told me to." She cocked her head. "One of these days you are going to explain why he would do that."

"Did you ask Mendoza?"

She smiled. "Yeah, right."

Chapter Fifty-One

Since it was the three of us, we took Nacho's Jeep downtown to the parking garage. We walked the three blocks to Escalona's building. As we moved up the front steps, Emil joined us. Of the four of us, only Nacho looked surprised. Blackhawk was smiling. As Emil came up the stairs, I held the door for him. He nodded as he moved past me.

We rode the elevator up in silence. Nacho was looking at Emil, then stealing glances at Blackhawk and me.

The same girl was behind the desk. She looked up and started to rise, then saw Emil and sat back down. Emil indicated the chairs for us, then moved around the desk and down the corridor.

Nacho and I sat down. Blackhawk leaned against the wall. He never seemed to have any tension. He might as well been at the park watching the ducks. The girl stole a glance at him every once in a while.

It was a scant minute later when Emil reappeared. He motioned to us and we followed him back. He wasn't nearly as much fun to follow as the girl.

Escalona was behind his desk, and he rose and moved around it to shake our hands. Now he indicated the chairs and again Nacho and I sat while Blackhawk leaned against the wall next to the office door.

"Tell me you have found Gabriela?" he said moving back to his chair.

I smiled at him, "No, I'm afraid not. If I had I'm sure Emil would have told you by now."

Now it was his turn to smile, "Then I have to ask, why the visit?"

"I did find Roland."

"Roland? The Playboy Diablo you thought had her?"

I nodded.

"But he doesn't have her?"

"No. I'm afraid he's lost his head over all this."

He looked at me thoughtfully, then smiled. "Ah, you joke."

"Not very well," I admitted. "He and Henry Cisneros were found in the river bottom. At least their bodies were. The heads haven't been found."

"Do I know this Mr. Cisneros?"

"I don't think so. He was the guy that we thought would lead us to Roland. The one that led us to Roland's sister's old place. Where our friend here," I indicated Emil," bailed us out of a situation. The next time I saw what was left of him was this morning in the river bottom."

Escalona leaned forward with his elbows on his desk and pressed his fingertips together, bringing them to his lips. He was silent.

Finally he said, "What do your friends in the police department say?"

"It's a war," I said. "Dos Hermanos and Valdez. Two Dos Hermanos and one Valdez were shot to death in a firefight in Tolleson late last night."

Escalona leaned back in his chair and looked at Emil. I could tell by the look that this was information they already knew.

"Senseless and stupid," he finally said, seemingly talking to Emil. "There are six million people in the Phoenix area, a million of them buy drugs of some kind. There is enough to share. This is just greed. So, Mr. Jackson," he said looking at me. "Where is Gabriela?"

"There are no ransom demands?" I asked.

He shook his head, "Not even false ones, and there are a lot of people looking. But most would know that a false demand would be met with harsh retribution."

"Detective Boyce says there has been no body found."

"No, no body. I think we would have heard." Again he looked at Emil. Emil shook his head.

There was a rustling in the hallway and Blackhawk stepped away from the door, his hand going to his hip.

The ambassador stepped into the doorway. We all stood.

"Good morning," he said pleasantly. "Please sit."

Escalona moved around the desk, "Please, sir, sit here."

The ambassador waved his hand, "That's not necessary, Santiago."

"When you are in this office, it is yours. I insist," Escalona said.

"Most gracious," the old man said, moving around the desk and setting down.

He looked at us, one at a time, ending with me, "I couldn't help overhearing the last of your conversation. So Mr. Jackson, you think Gabriela's alive?"

"Not to be crass, sir, but there is no evidence otherwise."

"At least not yet."

"No sir. I believe she is alive. The mystery is who has her. She wouldn't be out there on her own. The girl I met would need someone to care for her."

He nodded, "Yes, that would be Gabriela."

"So the question is who benefits from having her."

"The obvious answer is Dos Hermanos," Escalona said.

"Dos Hermanos doesn't have her," I said.

"You know this how?" Escalona asked.

"Mr. Bavaro came to Blackhawk's place, El Patron, to see me."

The ambassador's eyebrows went up.

"Mr. Bavaro? What did he want?" he said.

"He was offering me a reward to find the girl."

The ambassador looked at Escalona, "They are becoming desperate."

He looked back to me. "Because of your connections with the police?"

"That's what he said."

"How much did Mr. Bavaro offer?"

"Fifty thousand dollars."

He studied me. His eyes were brown, flecked with gold. His eyebrows hung over them like white brush over a craggy slope.

"That is a large sum of money, Mr. Jackson. A sum such as that would tempt any man."

"Your Excellency," I said, "you don't know who I am. You'll just have to trust me when I say I just want the girl back safely."

He studied me some more.

"What this says," I continued, "is that Dos Hermanos doesn't have Gabriela either. So someone else must."

He stood. He shook his head. "This is a mystery, Mr. Jackson."

He reached out and he took my hand. He held it firmly. He looked deeply into my eyes.

"I am going to trust you, Mr. Jackson. Every old man eventually has to trust someone." He released my hand and moved to the door.

He turned back to look at me again.

"You need to know something, Mr. Jackson."

"What would that be, sir?"

"As of this morning, Valdez has put a $100,000 bounty on the head of Mr. Bavaro."

"That's a lot of money."

"Not to Valdez."

He turned and looked at Escalona. "Anything he needs," he said.

Chapter Fifty-Two

I left El Patron in mid-afternoon and drove back to the boat. My little light was blinking green, green, green. I took a Dos Equis from the refrigerator and popped it open and sat on the couch.

There was something I was missing and it was really bugging me. Maybe Gabriela had found another gangbanger to hang with and they were holed up in another hovel somewhere. That could be, but Mendoza had the whole force looking for her. She would have to surface somewhere. Logic told me that Dos Hermanos had to have her, but why would Bavaro offer me money to find her?

I finished the beer and got a sudden case of the domestics. I started dusting and wiping and vacuuming. I cleaned out the refrigerator. I had two weeks' supply of leftovers. I bagged it and took it up the dock to the dumpster. I hosed the decks down. I cleaned the heads using lots of disinfectant. When I was finished the boat reeked of clean. I was restless. I went out on the bow and looked at the other boats and marveled at how much money was floating on the water. The Moneypenny was still buttoned up and gathering dust.

I stepped out on the dock and went around to the stern and stepped back aboard. I tossed the garden hose up top and went up. I stacked the chairs and moved them around. I hosed down the deck. The water ran down the sides, so now I had to clean the windows.

I took the bedding off the bed and put it through the wash. I followed that by washing what dirty clothes I had in the hamper. I hung everything up nice and neat. Now I had killed enough time that I could fix a drink without feeling like a lush. I took the drink to the stern, moved a chair out of the sunlight and sat and watched the water. I told myself to just sip it and make it last, but when I wasn't watching, it disappeared. I went into the galley and fixed another. This one seemed to go faster than the first. After the third one, I quit counting.

The sun had set and there was a faint glow left in the western sky when I stood up, said "fuck it" out loud, and went to bed. I lay down, closed my eyes and watched Hayden's little blue face for an hour. Finally, I gave up. I got up and dressed. I went up the hill to the Mustang. I took the cover off and stuffed it into the trunk. I dropped the canvas top and drove out of there. I didn't know where I was going. After a while the Mustang seemed to know where I wanted to go.

Chapter Fifty-Three

It was late the next afternoon, and I pulled into the El Patron parking lot just as the downtown offices were letting out and the parking lot was filling. It had been windy all day and the wind had kicked up the dry top soil of the Valley of the Sun and the dust covered the downtown area like a blanket. Driving in, it had looked like tired, brown cotton candy, hovering just above the downtown skyscrapers. As I parked I thought about covering the Mustang but didn't, knowing full well that when I came back out, the cover would have been stolen. I put the Rugar in my back pocket. I was wearing a black tee shirt and another short sleeved shirt over it. I unbuttoned the outer shirt and pulled it loose to hang down and hide pistol bulge.

Inside, there were a handful of customers in each of the side bars and a couple dozen in the main bar. Most were still wearing their office uniforms. The men were in button down shirts and power ties and the shop girls in crisp blouses and trim short skirts or business suits with matching pants and jackets. They had collected for happy hour. The serious customers would be in later.

I slid up on the stool and thought about whether I had the guts to order my cure for a hangover. I had not gotten back to the boat until after sunrise and I had immediately started drinking and continued all morning because there wasn't anyone to tell me what a fool I was being. Finally, I had fallen on the bed and drooled for a few hours, then was awakened by someone hitting my temples with two simultaneous five-pound sledges. I decided I needed to seek out someone who would tell me what a complete ass I was, so I showered, shaved, dressed and drove down to the El Patron.

Jimmy came down the bar to me and peered at me, then laughed, "Man, you look like shit."

"You should see it from in here," I said. "Gimme a red Stella with a splash of hot sauce." It was a compromise.

A moment later he placed a glass, a bottle of Stella Artois, a small can of tomato juice and a small bottle of Louisiana hot sauce in front of me. I mixed them up and drank it down. He brought me another. This time, after mixing, I drank half of it, then left the rest on the bar while my body and mind settled. In a few minutes I began to feel better.

Across the bar from me, a gaggle of shop girls were drinking white wine and cosmopolitans. Every time I looked their way one of them was watching me. She was one of the pantsuit girls with brassy blonde hair and a little too much make-up. The third time I caught her looking I smiled and nodded my head. She leaned in and said something to the other girls and they giggled and looked at me. She picked up her wine and came across the floor. She looked to be a little older than me but had a very good body. She wasn't shy. She slid up on the stool next to me.

"Hey, I know you, don't I?" she said.

I hadn't seen her before in my life.

"How could I ever forget you?"

"No, no shit. I'm sure I've seen you somewhere. Do you work at the paper?"

"No, I'm afraid not. Wish I did. Is that where you work?"

"Yeah, I work in advertising."

"That sounds interesting."

"Boring as hell, but it's a job. A lot of people don't have one, right?"

"Don't I know it."

"Where do you work?"

"I don't," I said.

"Well, that's a bummer. Why don't you apply at the paper? They are always hiring. May not be the job you want but it's something until you get what you want, right?" She drained her glass.

"Absolutely. I think I will. Can I buy you a drink?"

"Sure," she said, then, "Uuh-", she was looking over my shoulder.

I turned to look and there was Boyce walking straight for me. Her badge was on her belt and the pistol on her hip was obvious.

She slid up on the barstool beside me, "Hi, sweetheart," she said wrapping an arm around my neck and kissing me on the mouth. Without releasing my neck, she leaned forward and looked across me. "Who's your friend?"

The girl picked up her wine glass and slid off her stool.

"Uuh, well I gotta get back to my friends. Nice running into you. Nice meeting you," she said to Boyce. She hurried away so quickly she almost tripped.

Boyce was laughing.

"That was just plain mean," I said.

"Oh, come on," she laughed. "Don't tell me you go for the big blond obvious ones?"

I looked at her. "No, I go for the ones that tease you and leave you."

"You talking about the other night?" she said. "I think we both were saved from something we would have regretted later."

"Speak for yourself."

She looked at my drink, "What the hell is that?"

I explained what a red Stella was. She grimaced. "Sounds awful."

"It's a lifesaver," I said. "Are you on duty?"

"Ever vigilant," she said.

"Are you on duty?" I asked again patiently.

"No, I signed out a half hour ago."

"Can I buy you a drink?"

"You have any money?"

I laughed, "Yes, I have money. Why would you ask?"

"You don't work. Did you inherit money?"

I shook my head, smiling.

"Then where does your money come from?"

"Odd jobs," I said.

She looked at me with cool appraisal, then turned and waved at Jimmy.

Chapter Fifty-Four

We were still at the bar when the band took the stage. Elena came through the upstairs door and down the stairs like the queen she was. She spotted Boyce and me and came over to us.

Almost every eye was on her as she came to me and gave me a hug and a kiss on the cheek. She turned to Boyce.

"You must introduce me to your friend," she said to me, looking at Boyce.

"Elena, this is Detective Boyce, Detective Boyce, Elena," I complied.

"Pleased to meet you," Elena said, sticking out her hand. Boyce took it.

"Likewise."

Elena turned to me, "Is your friend going to stay to hear the band?"

I looked at Boyce.

"Love to," she said.

"Good," Elena said. She looked at me. "Blackhawk will be down later, and maybe we can all have a drink together?"

"Great."

She turned and as she moved away she turned with mischievous look, "Oh, by the way, Anita says hi."

Boyce grinned at me, "Anita?"

I shook my head, "Women just like to stir the pot."

"Women don't like anyone else sampling their pot."

"Am I someone's pot?"

The band began to play. She grinned at me again, "We'll see." She took my hand, "Come on, let's dance."

"I don't dance well," I said. "I have a bad foot."

"You have no foot," she said. She tugged on me, "And when it comes to dancing, all men have a bad foot."

I let her lead me onto the dance floor. Elena gave me an *ooh la la* look.

Boyce put her hands around the back of my neck and I put my hands on her waist and tried my best to follow her around the floor.

Elena kept the songs slow and long for a while. Boyce eventually moved into me and laid her head on my chest. I wrapped my arms around her. Elena did her best for us but finally had to please the growing crowd and lead the band into something loud and rowdy.

Jimmy had saved our places at the bar and had two fresh drinks waiting for us. He had made mine a tall scotch and soda and I waved my thanks. Boyce and I sipped our drinks and watched the dancers rip around the dance floor. I don't know if I could learn to do that.

Nacho had joined Jimmy behind the bar, hustling up and down, mixing drinks. Blackhawk still hadn't shown.

We finished our drinks and two more appeared. I noticed Duane, the main door bouncer, come in and go to the bar and signal Nacho. Nacho moved over to him and leaned over the bar and Duane leaned into him talking. Duane had something in his hand. A piece of paper. He handed the paper to Nacho and Nacho read what was on it. He turned and looked at me.

They both moved down the bar to where we sat. Nacho leaned into me so I could hear. Duane leaned into listen.

"Duane says there's a guy out in the parking lot that asked him to give you this," Nacho said, indicating the piece of paper. He handed it to me.

Boyce leaned over to read with me. It said, "*I have the girl.*"

"The guy waved me over," Duane said, "and said give this to Jackson."

"That's all he said?" Boyce said.

Duane nodded. "I wrote the license number on the back."

Jackson turned the slip of paper over. On the back in Duane's scrawl was "YLT 1410."

"This guy still out there?" I asked.

"Still sitting there when I came in here," Duane said.

I looked at Nacho. "Get Blackhawk," I said, and slipped off my stool.

Duane led the way, and Boyce and I went through the double doors and down the crowded hallway. We stepped outside and the sky was dark with the lights around the building illuminating the parking lot. There were a handful of smokers standing around the entrance.

"There," Duane said, pointing at a black Escalade. It was in the back of the north side of the lot. The motor was running and the parking lights were on.

I started forward and Boyce grabbed my arm, "You stay here, I'll handle it."

I shook her hand off and started forward again when the rear window of the SUV rolled down. There was a pale female face in the window, but she was in the shadows so I couldn't tell who it was. The female slowly leaned forward to look at me. The light played across her face.

It was Gabriela.

I started forward and the front window slid down. The barrel of an automatic rifle poked out. I could see the shooter's face. It was Diego.

"Get down!" Boyce shouted, and slammed into me. Diego began firing. I went down on one knee and Boyce had drawn her pistol. I was off balance, but had the Ruger in my hand. She pushed me again.

"Don't shoot, you'll hit the girl," I was shouting, but Boyce was in a firing stance and pulling the trigger. Something was tugging at my shirt. I rolled and the bullets chewed up the asphalt, some whining into the distance, some hitting the building. The lights on the SUV snapped on and the SUV skidded away, tires spinning, throwing gravel and dirt in its wake.

I pointed the Ruger at the SUV but didn't shoot. I didn't want to hit the girl. With squealing tires and a wall of dust the vehicle went over the curb and out into the street and sped away. Then I heard Boyce.

"Shit, shit, shit!"

I looked over and she was rolled into the fetal position. Her back was to me and I could see a widening stain on her blouse.

"Oh, shit," she groaned as I reached her.

I tore my shirt off and wadded it. "Here," I said. "Hold this tight against it."

She looked up at me, "They shot me, Jackson," she said. Her eyes were wide, then they fluttered, then they closed.

I pressed the shirt hard against the wound in her side and screamed, "Call 911. Somebody call 911!"

Duane had it on speed dial.

Chapter Fifty-Five

Blackhawk and Elena were beside me as I held Boyce. Her breathing was ragged but regular. She was losing a lot of blood. I could feel it slipping between my fingers. My shirt, pressing against the wound, was saturated. The parking lot was filling with customers as the word spread. For the first time I noticed that a group had gathered around one of the smokers. He was sitting spread eagled, holding his arm and rocking with pain. Blood was running between his fingers and down his arm.

I looked at Blackhawk and signaled with my head for him to come closer.

He leaned down, his head almost touching mine.

"There will be a million cops here in a second," I said. "Tell Nacho and Duane to keep their mouths shut. It was a drive by with a dark car."

"Yes, of course," he said. "Who was it?"

"Diego."

"Bavaro's Diego?"

"Gabriela was in the back. If he's pushed he'll kill her."

Blackhawk nodded. He looked at me, at Boyce, then back at me; his look wasn't a pleasant one. "And you will want the bastard for yourself."

I pressed the shirt hard against her, "Oh, yeah."

Now the city seemed to be filled with wailing sirens and the squad cars began pouring into the parking lot, followed closely by a fire truck. A screaming ambulance skidded into the lot and the two paramedics ripped open the back doors and pulled the gurney out. The firemen surrounded me. One said, "Are you injured?"

I shook my head and he gently pulled me aside. Another one knelt beside Boyce; he had a large package in his hand and was ripping it open. He pulled out a pure white gauze pad and pressed it against Boyce's side. Another took her wrist, checking her pulse, while another thumbed back her eyelids and shined a light, checking her pupils. Now they swarmed her and I was pushed aside by their urgency.

I moved back and began to shake, and I had been there before. It was the adrenaline. Nacho was beside me now and when I gripped myself, trying to control the spasms, Nacho stripped off his shirt and gave it to me. I slipped it on. Nacho stood with the flashing red, blue and yellow lights bouncing across his bare torso, highlighting the crisscrossing tattoos and scars.

Quickly and professionally, the paramedic team lifted Boyce onto the gurney and loaded her into the ambulance. Her arm was hanging out and flopping as they moved her. Blackhawk led me away to the Mustang and as I looked back I could see one of them had gathered in her arm and was slapping the inside of it trying to draw a vein. They started an IV.

Elena jammed herself into the Mustang's tiny backseat. Blackhawk took the keys from my hand and I didn't argue.

Blackhawk expertly followed the screaming ambulance through the deserted downtown streets, and when the ambulance pulled into the emergency room circular drive, he parked in a no parking zone.

The hospital had been warned, and a half dozen doctors and nurses in their blue and green scrubs were at the back of the ambulance before it stopped.

This hospital probably sees a half dozen shootings a week, but when it is a police officer it is different. As we walked across the parking lot to the entrance a dozen patrol cars came pulling into the lot. When we went through the automatic sliding doors a dozen patrolmen followed on our heels. They were moving Boyce through another set of automatic doors. We started to follow when a young nurse intercepted us.

"I'm afraid you can't go back there," she said with an authoritative voice.

"She's my friend," I said.

"Yes sir, she's in good hands. They are taking her to surgery." She indicated a room behind glass wall. "Why don't you all wait in there? I'll let you know what I can find out." She looked at me, "Are you hurt, sir?"

I shook my head.

"There is a restroom across the lobby, you can clean up." She looked at me closer, "You are sure you aren't hurt?"

I shook my head again, "This is her blood."

"Nothing to do now," Blackhawk said to me. "You need to wash up."

Elena took my arm, "Come on, Jackson. We'll stay too."

I went a across to the restroom. It was as sterile as you would expect. I was a mess. It took several minutes for me to look somewhat normal. I was still wearing Nacho's shirt.

Blackhawk and Elena were in the waiting room. The lobby was filled with patrolmen.

A half hour later Mendoza came through the outside doors. He started past the admitting desk when he caught sight of me. He stopped and looked at me for a long moment. He turned and came into the waiting room.

"Why am I not surprised to see you?"

I shrugged.

"What the hell are you doing here? Were you with Detective Boyce?"

I nodded. "Yeah."

He studied me, then turned and signaled to one of the patrolmen through the glass. The patrolman came into the waiting room.

"Yes sir?"

Mendoza jabbed a finger at me, "Make sure he doesn't go anywhere until I talk to him."

"Yes sir," the cop said, eyeing me.

Mendoza looked at Elena and Blackhawk.

"You two witnesses?"

They both shook their heads. "We were inside the club during the shooting," Blackhawk said. "Didn't see a thing more than the cops and firemen did."

Mendoza studied us another moment, then abruptly turned and left the room. He went through the lobby, then through the inside automatic doors and the nurse didn't stop him. The cop went back out into the lobby, but positioned himself so he could watch me.

Blackhawk put his elbows on his knees and leaned forward, his voice was low, "So the brothers have the girl after all."

"Apparently. Still can't figure why Bavaro offered me money to find her."

"We know where, now?"

"Pretty sure."

"Kamex?"

"Makes sense."

"Diego works for Kamex?"

"Diego works for Bavaro. Bavaro works for Kamex. They all work for Dos Hermanos."

"We going after her?"

I looked at him, "Does the Pope shit in the woods?"

Elena said, "I think you mean the bear. Does the bear shit in the woods?"

I smiled, still looking at Blackhawk, "Think you can get the blueprints to those buildings?"

"It's the middle of the night. Where would I get them?"

"The colonel," I said.

"It's two hours ahead where he is," he said. "He won't like being woke up."

"Wait a couple more hours, then call. Martha will make him coffee."

"What are you talking about?" Elena said. "Who's the colonel?"

"The colonel," Blackhawk said.

"What colonel?"

Blackhawk stood and taking Elena's arm, pulled her up. "I'll explain on the way back."

"We should stay here with Jackson."

"I'm okay," I said as the young nurse came through the automatic doors and into the waiting room.

"She's in surgery," she said without preliminaries. "She was shot once in her left side. The bullet exited cleanly, but they're afraid it may have nicked her intestines."

"Peritonitis?"

"That's what they are afraid of. But they are in there now and they are very good at what they do."

"How long will she be in there?" Elena asked.

"As long as it takes, hon," she said. She looked at me. "I'll let you know when she's out."

"Thank you," I said.

She turned and went back out and through the doors.

Blackhawk said, "You have your phone?"

I nodded.

"Call me when you hear."

"Of course."

They left, and I stretched out on two chairs and thought about the fact that I had just done that very same thing way too recently. I closed my eyes.

I was dozing when Lieutenant Mendoza came in the room. I swung my feet down and he sat beside me.

"They're closing her up now. She's going to be okay."

I closed my eyes, feeling the relief wash over me.

"I am told that you applied a compress to staunch the bleeding."

I didn't say anything.

"They say that may have saved her life."

I still didn't say anything. Wasn't anything to say.

He studied me a long moment, then finally he said "Thank you. When she comes around I'll let her know."

I shook my head, "No need."

He studied me some more.

"You know that I'll need you to come to the station."

I nodded again.

"You need to sleep first?"

I shook my head.

"You need a ride?"

I shook my head again.

"I'll meet you there," he said standing. "I'll need a deposition on what happened tonight, and I need to talk to you about another little matter."

"Another little matter?"

"Oh, just a little thing. I need to know if you know anything about the fact that last night a patrolman saw a car with its door open outside a bar called Tilly's on the west side."

I shrugged.

"Beside the car he found the body of a guy name of Darryl Maupin. It looked like someone had shaken Maupin so hard his neck snapped."

Chapter Fifty-Six

Blackhawk laughed when I told him.

"Jesus, that's rich," he said. "That is no mean feat. That was a big boy."

We were in his loft above El Patron. I had done my duty downtown, and then I had been at the hospital until Boyce's brother had flown in from Seattle. The boat was too far away, so I came to Blackhawk's.

Blackhawk was fixing two drinks. I had my foot off and was stretched out on one of his comfortable chairs with my foot and my stub on an ottoman. I was barely awake.

The television was on but muted. As he handed me the drink, Boyce's picture came on.

"Turn the sound on," I said.

He picked up the remote and pointed it at the TV.

"… appears," the voice said, "that Detective Boyce was off duty at the time and the police say that while she is a member of the gangs division of Phoenix PD they have no reason to believe she was the target."

A female spokesperson for the police came on. She was

standing in the street surrounded by reporters.

"At this point we have no evidence that points to anything but a random shooting. Witnesses put a dark SUV styled vehicle at the scene. The other wounded man has been identified as Edward Tomes. The police say that Mr. Tomes is employed as a landscaper and has no criminal record. He was treated and released. The investigation is continuing, so anyone with any information about the senseless shooting of an officer of the law should call Silent Witness."

She looked at a piece of paper and read the Silent Witness number off.

The television cut back to the news anchor, "Meanwhile, Detective Boyce remains in critical condition. And now to the weather. The unusually hot temperatures....,"

Blackhawk muted it.

There was a dinging noise. Blackhawk dug out his phone and looked at it. "The colonel," he said, looking up at me.

"Fax?" I asked.

"Faxes are gone," he said. "The colonel is texting."

"Was the colonel pissed?"

"I don't know," he said. "I talked with Martha and she's never pissed."

"You told her what we wanted?"

He grinned, "Yeah, she said he was in the bathroom and might be a while." He laughed out loud. "She said that when you get to their age a good bowel movement can't be rushed."

I laughed. "She actually said that?"

"Old people will tell you anything. He's downloading

something. Let's go in the office so I can print it."

"Like on old fashioned paper?"

"I've given up my papyrus."

I followed him.

His office was down the hall from the apartment. There was a foyer, then a door that opened into his office. It was as finely furnished as the apartment. A desk and chair, and filing cabinets, and another work desk, with a computer and printer on it. He took his phone and attached it with a cord to the computer and started fiddling with it.

I heard the outer door open and a moment later Nacho stuck his head into the room.

Blackhawk looked up, "Goddammit, can't you knock?"

Nacho looked bewildered, "Elena's not here," he said.

"What the hell has that got to do with anything?"

"It's not like you guys are in here doing something."

Blackhawk just shook his head.

"That bald guy's downstairs," Nacho said.

I went down. Emil was sitting at the bar, right hip on the stool, left foot on the floor.

I moved up to him, "How you doin'?"

"I followed them to Kamex," he said.

I nodded, "I know."

"You know I followed them?"

"No, but I figured it was Kamex."

"How's the cop?"

"They say she'll make it okay. Gonna be a while before she's back on duty."

"You been to see her?"

"When I'm not here, I'm there."
He nodded.
"What are you going to do?"
"About Gabriela?"
"Yeah, about Gabriela."
"Go in and get her."
"You know that place is like Fort Knox."
I nodded.
"But you are still going?"
I nodded.
"I'm in," he said.

Chapter Fifty-Seven

Blackhawk had printed out the blueprints to the Kamex buildings and had them spread across his dining table. When Emil and I came in, he was highlighting some points on them. He looked up and nodded to Emil.

"Emil will be joining us," I said.

"Good, it will probably take more than two."

He indicated the blueprint he was marking on. "These things I've marked are the surveillance cameras. The north side of the compound is the most vulnerable. Only two cameras. We can take the cameras out and go over the fence but –", he picked up two other blueprints, "these are the two new buildings. They are identical. So, we don't know which the girl will be in. And worse, the outside doors are metal and double bolted."

"So we blow them," Emil said.

"Yes, but we don't know how many men are on the other side and we don't know how many are armed." Blackhawk looked at me. "Last thing we want is a firefight in a closed-in space."

I shook my head, "We can't jeopardize the girl, but I don't want to have to mount a two-week surveillance before we can go in."

Blackhawk smiled at me. "Neither did the colonel, so he had whatever computer pooter that works for him hack Kamex's own surveillance tapes. He has downloaded the last three full weeks of whatever activity took place there."

"24/7?"

He nodded.

"So we have to sit and watch three weeks."

Blackhawk shrugged, "You can fast forward."

"I can fast forward? What about you? What about Nacho, or even Emil here?"

"I wouldn't know what to look for," Emil said.

"Nacho has a saloon to run."

"And you?"

"I'll be waiting to jump into action when I hear you yell *Eureka!*"

"That's really funny." I looked at his computer. "You want to show me how this works?"

It turned out to be easier than I would have thought. Nothing much showed on the screen as I sped through the first day of the feed, which was a Sunday. The next day, just as the screen display showed 11:52 am, I watched a black Escalade pull up to the west building and I watched Frank Bavaro step out and go inside. It made sense he would have the girl in the same building as him, so that narrowed it down. Now we knew where, the question was how? The Eureka moment came as the display on the screen read Wednesday, 10:32 pm. A large van came through the front gates and pulled around to the same building that Bavaro had come and gone from. Two dozen men, women and children poured out of it carrying bundles of belongings, and three armed men herded them through the raised utility door. Two hours later, a stream of black SUVs came out, each packed with people. I fast forwarded to the next week at the same time and watched it again. Then the third week, just like clockwork

Blackhawk, Emil, Nacho and Elena were in the room when I played it back.

"That must be how my cousin got in," Elena said.

"We knew about it," Emil said. "Knew Dos Hermanos was doing it somewhere, we just didn't figure Kamex would be that foolish."

"With power comes arrogance," Blackhawk said. He looked at me, "Got it figured out?"

I took a pencil as a pointer, ".22 long rifle with silencer takes out the surveillance cameras here and here. Exact same time the van rolls up." I looked at Emil. "That would be you." He nodded.

I looked at Blackhawk, "You and me dressed like the illegals go over the fifteen-foot barbed wire fence with a twenty-foot ladder. We go over as the illegals come piling out of the van. As they come out of the van, they move to the building, so everyone is on the building side of the van leaving them blind to our side. We have less than twenty yards to the van, coming in behind it as they are herding everyone. We have about ten seconds. We carry our bundles just like the rest."

"With weapons?"

"With pistols and flashbangs."

"That all?"

"Should be enough."

"What are flashbangs?" Elena said.

"Stun grenades," Nacho said. "Like SWAT uses. You seen it on TV. Someone throws it in through the window and Bam! Big flash, big noise, all smoke and confusion. Then they go piling in and get the bad guys."

"Oh, yeah, like that show I like, LAPD Confidential," Elena said.

"Yeah, like that." Nacho looked at Blackhawk, "What about me?"

"And me," Elena said.

"You two are here making yourselves very noticeable to the customers," I said. "So when you testify on a stack of bibles that Blackhawk and I were upstairs here watching TV, you will be believed."

Nacho frowned, "That's no fun."

I pointed again at the blueprint of the building, "Because of the shipment coming in, whoever is watching the camera monitors will probably hesitate before they go out to investigate the dead cameras. I don't know what they will be thinking, but I'm pretty sure they won't be thinking about us." I pointed at the interior doors. "Once inside," I said to Blackhawk, "if necessary, we detonate a flashbang, disable the guards and get through these interior doors. There is a set of stairs that leads," I pointed at the upper rooms, "to where I think we will find the girl."

"What if there are guards with the girl? What if they hear the flashbangs?"

"They won't be expecting us. We will just be two idiot illegals trying to escape the chaos. My guess is they'll keep her doped till they're ready to sell her."

"What if there are more guards inside at first?" Emil asked.

"Surprise is on our side. We set off two more flashbangs and use the diversion to go through the doors. These interior doors are easy. If there is trouble outside, you'll take care of it."

"What if the girl isn't there?" Elena asked.

"She's there," Emil said.

I looked at Emil, "Do I need to get you the rifle or silencer?"

"Got it covered."

"When do we do this?" Nacho asked.

"Next shipment should be Wednesday night at 10:30."

Chapter Fifty-Eight

Blackhawk's Rolex read 10:37 before the van rolled in. We had spent seven anxious minutes wondering if this was the night the pattern would be broken. It rolled around the corner and I heard two muffled coughing sounds, and simultaneously the surveillance cameras exploded into pieces.

We moved. Blackhawk and I lifted the twenty foot ladder and laid it against the upper barbed wire. Behind us was an asphalt parking lot stretching back to a large metal industrial building. The building and the lot were vacant. There was a wide retention area from the parking lot to the fence and it was completely full of waist-high mallow and tumbleweed. At the back of the lot was a large Penske rental truck. Emil was on top, prone. From this distance you couldn't tell what he was.

I went up first, and without hesitation I went over the top. I hit the ground and rolled, and despite the foot it was just like paratrooper training. In a second I was behind the van and Blackhawk was beside me. We were both wearing ratty old jeans and a short sleeved shirts over the typical ribbed sleeveless wife-beater tee shirts.

I had a short barreled .38 in a holster off my right hip, under the unbuttoned shirt and a seventeen round 9mm Glock and three grenades in the middle of my bundle of old clothes in case I needed to fight a war. Both pistols were unregistered throwaways. I had a Ka-bar knife strapped to my right leg, above the prosthetic. I had split the pant leg to just below my knee for easier access. Except for the Ka-bar Blackhawk was armed similarly and just as anonymously.

Without hesitation, we stepped out and around the van. The last of the illegals were unloading and we joined them seamlessly. One looked over his shoulder at us, but they were hustling everyone into the building so he just kept moving. There was a guard on either side of the door. They looked just like the men that had come off the van, except they held automatic pistols. With our heads down, Blackhawk and I walked right by them.

Once inside, the bay was large and filled with trucks and SUV's. The door the blueprints had told us we needed was to our back right. We mingled in with the others, slowly angling toward it. If the door was locked, the plan was to throw grenades and then use the Ka-bar to jimmy it. These interior doors were cheap, like any interior door in any house. I could pop the lock in seconds.

We reached the door and I tried the knob. It turned and the door opened. Blackhawk grinned at me and I went through with him right behind. It was a locking door handle and I locked it. We stood and waited for cries of protest but there were none. They hadn't even noticed.

We were in the hallway just as the blueprint had shown, and the door to the stairs was a dozen feet down. Now we both took the pistols from the bundles, put the grenades in our pockets, and tossed the clothes aside. There was no one in the hallway. Holding the pistols at our sides, we moved quickly to the stairway door and went through it and up the stairs two at a time. At the top the door had a window in it. It revealed a long empty hallway with a dozen doors along it. Most of them were open. The hallway was wide and carpeted. There were mirrors and paintings on the walls. It looked like a hotel corridor.

We went through the door.

Blackhawk took one side and I took the other. We walked purposely down the corridor, looking in each open door. They were mostly large rooms with desks and cubicles and electronic equipment with clerical types working away. Not one looked up or noticed us. If they did, they didn't care. They were in their safe little world doing their safe little jobs. Up here no one had automatic pistols.

We paused to gently test the doorknobs on the shut doors. They were locked. We made it to the end of the hallway, and on the back wall there was a door facing back at us. It was unlocked.

Blackhawk went in first. It was furnished like an apartment. The living room had a couch and chairs and lamps and a TV, but no people. Blackhawk moved to one side, I took the other. We stood, silent and listening, pistols extended, each of us locked on the front site, lingering on the doors that led off the room.

There were two doors, one to our left which was closed and one in front which was open. We could hear someone in that room talking.

We looked at each other and Blackhawk nodded at me. I moved to the open door and went swiftly through it and angled right, my back against the wall. Blackhawk slid in on the other side.

Frank Bavaro sat at a desk, his back to us. Diego sat in a chair against a side wall reading a newspaper. He looked up and froze. Bavaro was on a landline phone. He sensed Diego's alarm and turned.

"Hang up," I said.

He looked at me, then to Blackhawk, then back. "I'll call you back," he said. He cradled the phone.

He stood up. Facing us, he leaned forward, placing his hands on the desktop. He did not seem afraid. "I won't ask how you got in here," he said. "I'm finding that you are a very resourceful young man. Did you bring me the girl?"

"He doesn't have her," Diego said and I looked at him and he was looking at the doorway. I turned my head and Romy and Gabriela stood in the doorway. Romy's arm was firmly around Gabriela's waist and was the only thing holding her up. Gabriela was stoned.

"Lucienda?" Bavaro said. He was very surprised.

"Gabriela," I said.

Romy laughed, "Jackson, you are such a Boy Scout. He's talking to me. My name is Lucienda. Lucienda Anabell Tachiquin Alvarado. You misunderstood me on the boat and thought I called the girl Lucinda. I thought it was funny.

You also assumed I was his wife." She looked at Bavaro, "But this bastard will not marry me. He thinks the church will condemn him if he divorces his cow of a wife. With all the blood on his hands, he worries about a divorce."

"Lucienda, now is not the time," Bavaro said.

Diego stood and Blackhawk said, "Don't move."

"Don't anybody move," Lucienda said, moving her free hand from behind her. She held an ugly little pocket pistol and put it against Gabriela's head. We didn't move.

"What do you think you are doing?" Diego said. "She is worthless to us dead!"

"I don't want to kill her," Lucienda said. "But I will if I have to." She nodded at me, "You and Tonto throw your guns aside."

"Cochise, goddammit," Blackhawk muttered under his breath as he tossed his pistol. I let mine drop.

I felt like Wile E. Coyote with a big fat light bulb above my head.

"I have a Boy Scout question," I said.

Lucienda smiled, "I'm sure you do."

"Why was she at your boat?"

"It's Frank's boat. I'd been there enough to know who the neighbors were," she said. "Roland was impatient, he brought the girl to meet me and Diego to sell her. But there was a bad accident that closed the Carefree Highway and Diego and I had to go all the way around. When we didn't show on time, the stupid shit panicked, thought it was an ambush, and had his assholes dump her. You pulled her out and I got there just as you did."

She was looking at Frank, then she glanced at me. "Good luck for her, but none of that matters now."

"You've had her all along," I said.

"Right next door."

"Right under my nose," Bavaro said.

"The safest place for the fly is on the flyswatter," I said.

She looked at Diego, "Now we trade the girl for the Valdez money."

"So Roland got nothing and lost his head for it," I said to stall her.

Bravaro said, "That was his Excellency the Ambassador, we had nothing to do with that. That was Valdez. Sometimes harsh methods are used when seeking information." He looked at Lucienda. "Why do you do this? You know we will pay much more for the girl."

"So the girl went back to Roland?" I continued. I looked at Diego, and he was looking at Blackhawk. "And Diego shot four of the Diablos and got her back, and let me guess, he wanted to shoot five to clean things up, but somehow Roland escaped."

"I got what I went for," Diego said.

"The girl," I said. "And you showed me the girl outside the club to draw me out and get a shot at me."

"You were in the way."

"That, and I took your gun away from you and hurt your pride."

"You were very lucky. The little girl cop saved your ass."

"The little girl cop would kick yours."

Bavaro was looking at Diego, "This has been your plan

all along? I have treated you like a son."

"Et tu, Diego?" Blackhawk said.

Diego shrugged, "You would not pay me for the girl. You would expect me to be a good soldier and just give her to you. It is a lot of money."

I laughed, looking at Bavaro. "So Lucienda has been banging Diego and she's been banging me and that makes you a three time loser. It would have been easier if you had married her."

"That's two, what's the third time?" Blackhawk asked.

"Oh, yeah he probably hasn't heard," I said. "Valdez has $100,000 bounty on his head, dead or alive."

"He knows. You should have married me, Frank," Lucienda said. "Shoot them, Diego," she said and shot Bavaro.

The bullet sliced through his chest. He looked down in surprise at the widening stain on his shirt. He fell backwards. She pointed the gun at me.

I am very fast, but Blackhawk is faster and I hesitated. Never sleep with someone you may end up having to shoot. He barely seemed to move as he shot Lucienda center chest and she went backwards, pulling the girl with her. Diego had his pistol out of his jacket and I shot him once, then twice more as he went down. The explosions rang in our ears. Gabriela was on the floor, half on top of Lucienda, moaning.

"That's for Boyce," I said.

I stood looking at Romy or Lucienda, or whoever the hell she was. I don't know what I felt. Blackhawk knelt and checked for a pulse. He went to Diego, then to Bavaro.

He looked at me, "Dead, dead and dead."

I went to Bavaro's body and put my pistol in his hand, and closing his fingers around it I fired into the wall where Diego had been standing. Blackhawk took Diego's pistol and put his pistol in Diego's hand.

"These love triangles are tragic, wouldn't you say," Blackhawk said.

"Tragic," I said.

We each took one of Gabriela's arms and lifted her and took her out of there.

Chapter Fifty-Nine

Emil thumped the top of the boat twice with the butt of his rifle. Blackhawk was on the stern with one of the shotguns and Emil still had the .22 rifle with the silencer. They both had 10 x 50 binoculars.

The signal meant someone was coming down the dock. I glanced down the hall to the closed door of the middle stateroom where the girl was sleeping. I parted the black-out curtains and stepped out on the bow with the Kahr in my hand. It was Escalona. He was alone.

I stepped back inside and Blackhawk was watching me from the stern doorway. I signed *Escalona* and he nodded and turned back to watching the water.

I heard Escalona say something to Emil, then the boat moved slightly as he stepped aboard. It was bright outside. He stepped in and waited as his eyes adjusted.

"Emil called to say you have the girl," he said.

"Yes."

"How is she?"

"Strung out, they kept her doped up. She's sleeping."

Escalona looked around the room. I knew down the hallway he could see Blackhawk sitting on the stern watching the water.

"His Excellency is at the top waiting. Do you think she could go home?"

Before I could answer, the door to the stateroom opened and Gabriela came out. She was rubbing her eyes. Her hair was mussed but clean. Elena had wrestled her into the oversized shower and scrubbed her to within an inch of her life. She wore one of my white tee shirts and it hung on her like a tent. The bones on her shoulders were two sharp points poking against the fabric. Her thighs were concave and there were dark smudges under her eyes.

"Who's here?" she said. She peered at Escalona, then said, "Oh, it's you."

"Someone would have to be with her around the clock," I said.

"Yes," Escalona said softly. "That has been arranged. And, we are bringing her mother back from Bogota."

He turned to Gabriela. "Are you ready to come home? Your grandfather is at the top of the hill waiting for you."

"I ain't staying here," she said glaring at me. "That bastard won't let me smoke."

Escalona looked at me and smiled, "Such cruelty." He took a phone from his pocket and dialed a number.

I could hear someone speak on the other end.

"She's here," he said. He listened, then, "Yes, yes she appears to be fine. Should I bring her up?" The voice said something. "Yes, fine. We will wait here." He hung up. "His

Excellency will come down."

"Do you have a cigarette?" Gabriela demanded, looking at Escalona.

"I'm afraid not, my dear," he said.

She glared at him. "Bastards," she said under her breath. She turned and went into the stateroom, slamming the door.

"Does she have anything else to wear?" Escalona said, smiling.

"We had to burn everything," I said. "But we bought some things."

He moved to the sliding doors and moved the curtains to look down the walkway. "Of course," he said.

He stood there waiting till finally he said, "Here he comes."

I moved beside him. The Ambassador was slowly making his way down the dock. There were two men with him. These were men that looked very capable. They walked easily, their eyes roaming, missing nothing. They wore their shirts outside their pants to cover the pistols on their belts. One of them carried a leather valise with brass buckles that looked very expensive. When they reached us, Escalona and I stepped out on the bow.

The Ambassador looked up at me. "Mr. Jackson, It is so good to see you again. I hear you have something for me?"

"Yes, sir," I said.

"And I have something for you." He turned and the man handed him the valise. He handed it up to me.

"I am very grateful for the life of my granddaughter," he said, his eyes beginning to moisten.

I didn't know what to say to that, so I said, "I'll get the girl."

Chapter Sixty

It was dusk when Blackhawk and I walked into Safehouse. We had lucked into a parking spot, snagging it as a peculiar looking square vehicle pulled away from the curb. We were in Blackhawk's Jaguar, and on this street it stuck out like a super model at a monastery.

The hallway was empty, but Father Correa's office was occupied. She was a big woman. Not big as in fat, but big as in broad of shoulder and strong muscle tone. She had skin of ebony and a cascade of hair pulled back and fastened into a chaotic riot that somehow looked good on her. She could have been the direct descendant of Shaka Zulu. She was at Father Correa's computer working on something. She looked up and studied us coolly.

"Can I help you gentlemen?"

"Looking for Father Correa."

She leaned back, making the spring in the chair creak.

"The good Father is busy right now. Can I help you?"

"Is he here?"

She looked at Blackhawk, then back to me.

"He is here, but he is busy" she said spacing the words.

"We'll just take a minute of his time."

"He doesn't have a minute. It's bath and bed time and he is cleaning the kitchen. That is, if he has finished mopping the community room and fixing the toilet that one of the girls flushed a diaper down. She kept flushing. She thought that if she flushed enough times the ten-pound sack of poop would miraculously go down the five-pound hole. Why don't we see if I can help you?"

"Is it okay if we go back and find him?"

"Only if you are handy with a mop. What is it you want?" She eyed us both. "You realize this is a female facility. If you need a place to sleep tonight you can go to the flophouse on Madison. Just a few short blocks away."

Blackhawk stepped back and looked at me, "She's obviously talking to you," he said.

"My underwear is clean," I said. I looked at her. She wasn't smiling. I lifted the valise I had in my hand, "We have something for him."

"What is it?"

"It is personal."

"You can leave it with me."

"Will it be safe?"

She looked at me.

We left it with her.

Chapter Sixty-One

It was in the late spring and I had moored the Tiger Lily off an island in Scorpion Bay. We had topped off the freshwater tanks and the gasoline, and loaded the oversized refrigerator with delectable tidbits and red prime beef and stocked the bar with fine things. There were two very large white Igloo coolers filled with ice and cold, cold beer. It was our second week out, and I was sitting in the shade up top in the captain's chairs with a fresh Dos Equis by my side. I was repairing the tip on my fly rod where I had shut the door on it, snapping it right off.

I also was watching with great amusement as Blackhawk and Elena were fifty yards off the port side on Swoop, and Blackhawk was attempting to teach Elena to handle a fly rod. Surprisingly, her natural rhythm came through and she soon got the hang of ten to two. Letting the line out a little at a time, whipping it back and forth, longer and longer. Then release and she hit her target and let out a whoop and pumped her fist, waving at us. I lifted my bottle in salute. Another fly fisherperson was born.

Boyce laughed out loud. "I knew she could do it," she said.

Boyce was sitting in the sun, crosslegged in a yellow, faded, sun-bleached bikini working on a book of crossword puzzles. Her dark hair was down and streaked by the sun. Her skin was glistening with sunblock and was becoming a deepening brown except for the puckered white dimple on her side where the bullet had entered. The sun had brought out a dusting of freckles across her nose and cheeks. Her muscle tone was coming back. We had started with just getting in the water and paddling around. Eventually, we graduated into longer and longer swims, and now she could keep pace with me in the sprints. She said I cheated by using my swimming foot.

She put her book aside and stretched languidly. She came to her feet.

"I'm going to get a beer, would you like another one?"

I lifted my bottle, "Still working on this one."

She leaned over and kissed me, and as she turned and walked to the stairs I noticed that her ribs weren't as prominent, and the bottoms to her suit weren't as baggy.

Elena let out a shriek and she had a fish on the hook.

"Fish on!" Blackhawk yelled.

Blackhawk started to reach for the fly rod and Elena barked something at him that I couldn't make out, but whatever she said, he jerked his hand back and looked at me with a grin. She worked the fish, the rod bending almost in two. She finally got it to the boat and swung it aboard. It was a small catfish.

"Oh, my God," she shrieked. "That is so ugly!"

Blackhawk was laughing. He looked over at me and put his hands out and made a shrugging motion like, "what do you do?"

A moment later Boyce came up the stairway with a beer in one hand and my phone in the other. She had a puzzled look.

She handed me the phone. "There's a woman on the line that says a colonel wants to talk with you."

I took the phone, "Hello, Martha."

"Hello Jackson," Martha said. "Hold on, he wants to talk with you."

I could hear the phone being passed.

"Jackson?" the colonel said in that gruff voice of his.

"Yes sir?"

"What are you and number two doing just now?"

Following is an excerpt of
number two in the acclaimed Jackson Blackhawk series.

THE LIBRARIAN, HER DAUGHTER, AND THE MAN WHO LOST HIS HEAD

by Sam Lee Jackson

It was full-on dark and the parking lot, which by now was half empty, was illuminated by lights attached to the roof line of the bar. She had parked her city-issued boat of a vehicle next to where the Mustang had been. The streets were empty. I think they rolled them up at ten. As we reached her car she moved to the driver's side, then stopped, and turned to look at me. I had my hand on the passenger's door. I stopped.

"You know, things don't have to be much different," she said.

"True," I agreed.

"I am very fond of you," she said.

"And me of you," I said.

She leaned on the roof of the car and stared across at me.

"You know, one thing I have been thinking about for some time." She hesitated.

"What have you been thinking about for some time?"

The dim light softened her features. She was quite lovely. This made her even more so.

"All the time we were together we never used the word love."

"Really?" I said.

"Really," she said.

"Commitment issues?"

"Probably."

She turned her gaze across the parking lot, I turned to follow it. The dipshit that had been staring at Dahlia had come out of the bar and was staring across the lot at us. Two of his buddies joined him.

She looked back to me.

"You know I'm a cop through and through."

I smiled. "I know that. I understand that. And I guess I am whatever I am."

"Bon vivant, raconteur, man of the world."

"Unemployed boat bum."

"Speaking of that, you never did tell me where you get your money." Again, her gaze moved to behind me. I turned and the three men were making their way toward us. Boyce moved around the car and came up beside me.

"Friends of yours?"

"Not hardly. Saw them for the first time tonight. The short one is named Calvin. He's a cousin to the guy that lost his head. I think they have been drinking a long time."

"I'll handle it," she said.

I laughed. "The last time you said that you got shot."

"I'll duck this time."

The three men spread out a little as they came up to us. We waited. When they got close, Boyce said, "Calvin, you don't want to bite off more than you can chew."

He peered at her. "Do I know you?"

"Not yet," she said. "But if you have more in mind than just getting in your cars and going home, you will."

"What the fuck does that mean?"

"It means you really need to turn around and go away," I said.

He glared at me.

"We don't need you Phoenix pukes coming up here and getting in our business."

"Calvin, go home now," Boyce said.

He turned his head and spit on the ground. "Shut up, bitch!"

When his head came back around, Boyce slammed him in the nose with the heel of her hand. She stepped into it, the punch traveling about fourteen inches. In a punch like that, the thing is to try to punch through the target. His head snapped back, and he went backward, and sat down hard. Blood was gushing from his nose. The other two were so stunned they didn't move. When they did, they looked back at Boyce and she had moved her jacket aside to show the badge on her belt and the pistol on her hip.

"Get him up," she said.

They stood stunned, looking at her.

"Now!"

They each took an arm and pulled the dazed Calvin to his feet. His eyes were glassy, and he was very unsteady.

"If you boys don't want to spend the night in jail, I suggest you take good old Calvin and yourselves out of here."

The two wouldn't look at her. They started the stumbling Calvin across the lot. She looked at me, and I was grinning.

"That's all it takes to amuse you?" she said. "Give a guy a shot in the beezer and you're a happy camper?"

"Maybe I do love you."

"Shut up."

Did you enjoy
The Girl at the Deep End of the Lake?

If you enjoyed this book, and you bought it online, please go back to where you bought it and let us know what you think. After you get there just click on the book you read then click on the reviews. Thanks for reading.

You can go online to leave a review at the address below, or for more Jackson Blackhawk reading adventures.

www.samleejackson.com

Ever wonder how Jackson lost his foot? Join the El Patron Club and learn this and more behind the scenes information about Jackson and Blackhawk. Also, be included in upcoming notifications for new novels and new behind the scenes content. Have questions about Jackson, Blackhawk and the gang? Leave an email at sam@samleejackson.com and we'll put the answer up on the El Patron Club.

Go to the following url.
Samleejackson.com/elpatronclub

Made in the USA
Columbia, SC
06 November 2023